Take My Hand

Copyright © 2019
J.S. Wood Books LLC

Copyright © 2019 J.S. Wood

Take My Hand

All rights reserved. No part of this publication may be reproduced, distributed, or transmitted in any form or by any means, including photocopying, recording, or other electronic or mechanical methods, without the prior written permission of the publisher, except in the case of brief quotations embodied in critical reviews and certain other noncommercial uses permitted by copyright law.

This is a work of fiction. Names, characters, places, and incidents either are the products of the author's imagination or are used fictitiously. Any resemblance to actual persons, living or dead, businesses, companies, events, or locales is entirely coincidental.

authorjswood@gmail.com

Editing: Editing by C. Marie

Cover by: J.S. Wood Books LLC

WARNING: This book contains subject matter that may be sensitive to some readers. For mature audiences only (18 and older).

To my readers; you guys make it possible.

-J.S.

PROLOGUE

EVERY LITTLE GIRL dreams of the perfect wedding day: the white dress, the sweet smell of the fresh flowers put together in a flawless bouquet, the bridesmaids doing your bidding like slaves…okay, that might be an exaggeration. Anyway, everyone is there to see you marry your Prince Charming, the one man who managed to snatch you up and make you a Mrs.

So today, I think of what I wanted in that perfect wedding with Mr. Charming himself. My father would be dabbing at his eyes, tears of happiness spilling from down his cheeks, sad to give me up but thrilled I found the perfect guy. I think of how the bridesmaids would stare on with joy for me, jealousy hidden behind their carefully placed smiles. I think of the dress—God, the dress.

I have Pinterest boards dedicated to just the dress.

I look around at the current setting, taking in every feature: the faux church pews, some not even in line with others, the tacky red velvet under my heels almost making me fall on my face as I make my way down the aisle.

But I don't pay much attention to that when I see him. When he catches and holds my eyes until I'm standing in front of him, he looks like a damn GQ model. He's the perfect knight in shining armor, someone I definitely would have envisioned as the man I'd tie myself to for the rest of my life.

Never would I have thought things would take such a drastic turn in the past few weeks. Never would I have thought signing up for a dating app wouldn't just help me socialize more, but would completely turn my life upside down.

As the Elvis impersonator starts the ceremony, my reality shifts slightly and I focus on what's going on around me. My new friend stands stiffly behind me, and I see a wink sent my way over Mr. Charming's shoulder. Right. Focus. Breathe.

I stare deeply into my dream guy's eyes for a solid minute, not hearing a word anyone is saying, not caring much either when I have the most gorgeous man committing his life to mine in front of me. He speaks to me, and I tune back in as much as I can force myself to.

"With this ring, I thee wed."

My eyes widen as he slips it on my finger, and I stare in

shock, mouth gaping. We're already at that part? Shouldn't we have been stopped by now? I glance around and see everyone still in place, no one moving, the air still and silent as the officiant continues his ramblings.

Our friend hands me another ring, and I take it automatically. When did they have time to get these?

I repeat after Elvis, going along with it, knowing in the back of my mind not to take it too seriously. Not real, not real, not real. I chant it in my head while on the outside I say, "With this ring, I thee wed."

Elvis tells us we're man and wife, and my heart pounds so loudly I'm sure everyone is aware of it at this point.

Mr. Charming leans in, and I close my eyes. We haven't done this in a while, and I prepare myself to savor the moment. His lips touch mine. I feel my body melt beneath his touch, allowing myself to fall for this moment and believe it's real. I let myself pretend, just for a moment, that I got everything I wanted.

We slowly release each other, our heads still close, and he stares at me with a stony resolve. He's bracing himself—I can feel it in his hold—and when he nods, I know the shit is about to hit the fan.

I open my mouth to speak, but then, as if in slow motion, my eye catches something in my periphery. Several men file into the room, our friends moving fast. Elvis follows suit, as does the man I just married.

Forcing myself into the moment, I reach into my jacket,

grasping what I need, and throw myself behind one of the pews as shots ring out over my head. I steady myself, catch my new husband's eye, and nod, ready for the fight.

Confused? I bet.
I suppose we should start at the beginning.

1

MARGARET

A SIGH ESCAPES my mouth as another disgruntled customer purses her lips, angry at me for a policy I did not make up. Alas, I'm the one she has to deal with, so the upset individual is very intent on letting me know who's really to blame. This day will never end.

"What does that even mean?" Her red lipstick is garish under the lights of the store, her perfectly straightened blonde hair flowing over her shoulders like she just walked off some runway, and the thought I can't help but think is wondering what she could possibly be so dressed up for on a Thursday afternoon. If she's here, what kind of job does she have?

"It's policy, ma'am, that you must present a receipt with the purchased item to return it. The other reason I can't accept this is because of the large hole in the side here." I show her the spot I'm talking about, as if she already didn't know it was there, which is actually what she's claiming. My voice is placating even though I'm trying not to sound condescending, but it's hard when she seems to think anything I'm saying couldn't possibly be important.

"Well, that's absolutely ridiculous." She talks like she's a trophy wife straight out of the nineties when she can't be more than five years older than me. Her suit is ill-fitting, a stark contrast to her red lips and perfect hair. I wonder why she's not returning that outfit. "I want to speak to a manager."

I paste on a patient smile, even when my insides tell me to scream or cry or something, and reply, "Unfortunately our manager is currently unavailable." As I've already said.

She scoffs in my face, flinging a smattering of spit toward my chest, and I have the fleeting, sad realization that I'm just grateful it isn't on my face. "Well, you can let that manager know I won't be shopping here ever again, and you've made a big mistake messing with me."

I scrunch my eyebrows as she stomps away in her heels. Did she just paraphrase Pretty Woman?

Another deep-heaved sigh leaves me as I continue to help with returns. I get lucky with a couple of customers who have their receipts and don't give me any trouble, but my day doesn't pass in a blur like I hoped it would. Instead, I stand like a robot doing restocks and returns until my feet can't handle it anymore.

This is my life. Welcome.

———————

Turning the key, I try to shove open the door to my tiny studio apartment. It still sticks like crazy, even after numerous complaints to the super. It turns out he really just does not care and leaves it up to the people who pay to be there to take care of the things he's supposed to be doing. He's a world-class gentleman, I tell you.

I lean my shoulder into the difficult door and it lets out a groan, but thankfully, it opens. I walk in, putting up an opposite fight on the other side.

The quiet greets me and I frown, hating that I'm the only single person I know in this city. Any friends I have are so busy with their boyfriends or husbands or girlfriends that hanging out with other people is low on their list of priorities these days.

It's selfish of me, I know, to wish they were single and lonely again so I'd have someone to share the quiet with. It used to not bother me so much, being alone, but after I finished college and couldn't find a job to save my life, everything else just started to change. I didn't have a boyfriend or a nice apartment, or even a job I liked. Nothing turned out how I wanted it to.

Kicking my shoes off by the door, I head to my kitchen area

and rummage through the pantry for dinner. I note the amount of pasta I have, look for anything else I might have in the fridge, and ultimately decide I'll be having…pasta for dinner.

Pathetic.

Why am I like this? My mind has been stuck on this negative journey of thought today. It started with Ms. Uppity and just continued from there. No matter how much I try, I can't seem to dig myself out of this slump.

Waiting for the noodles to boil, I think of something my friend Anne said about how online dating would be a great way to find someone, to connect with someone in the real world. Maybe it's time to give it a try.

Thumbing through my phone, I find the app I installed but didn't have the courage to actually launch yet, hesitant to give in to the urge to try it out. I suppose I could try to actually go out to a bar and get picked up, or hell, maybe I'd find my soul mate.

I bite my lip and think it over. Can I do it? Can I try out the app and really put myself out there?

Who knows, the one guy I meet on the app could be the one. I know what my friends would say if I told them that—they'd say I was absolutely crazy for thinking I could meet my soul mate on a hookup app, but hey, stranger things have happened. Look at Pretty Woman, right? I mean, someone thought a prostitute could fall in love with a rich guy and he'd fall for her and bam! Happy ending.

I click the side of my phone, shutting off the screen, and stir my pot of pasta. The only harm that could come from signing up would be...what? A guy gets his kicks and I don't?

I mean, that would be pretty shitty, but not the worst thing that's ever happened to me.

There's always the other side of this, the positive that outweighs the negative, the pros over the cons. Even though I could end up with a jerk, I could also end up meeting someone I really hit it off with. I could finally have someone to fill the quiet in my life, someone to tell about my nasty day, someone who would listen when I was stressed or tired or just unsure of what to do with my life.

A giddy bubble of happiness fills me, and I smile at the thought of having my own person. Mind made up, I grab for my phone and tap the app open then enter my information. I wait for it to load and start swiping.

This is actually kind of fun, I think as I swipe on a guy who's easy on the eyes. Why did I think I wouldn't like this? It's like a virtual version of The Bachelorette: Hey, Baseball1228, will you accept this rose?

I snort to myself and continue swiping. The smirk I have on my face stays in place and I snuggle deeper into the comforter on my bed, my bowl of pasta beside me, loving that I can do this and still stay in pajamas, hair on its third day of dry shampoo and my face free of makeup.

Who needs bars?

I continue my tirade of swiping then I suddenly stop.

Chocolatey eyes peer at me and my breath catches. He's absolutely gorgeous—completely out of my league, but…damn.

I could swipe and he'd get notified, but what if he doesn't like what he sees on my profile? Despite what I look like at present, my profile picture is one of my better ones, full pouty lips covered in red lipstick, hair shiny and done in soft waves…

I sigh, giving this more thought than is really necessary. I stare at his picture then shrug. What is life without a little risk, right?

Swipe.

2

LIAM

THE SUN IS getting lower in the sky and so far, there's been absolutely no movement on this street. People have come and gone, but there's been nothing that sets tonight apart from any other night. My cap is pulled low and the car I'm in is nondescript. I do my best to keep a low profile when I'm around these parts so they don't know I'm watching.

This has been my life for the last three years, and I have a serious love/hate relationship with it—because that's what this has become: my only relationship. Of course, it will be worth it in the end. I have no doubts about that, but sometimes, I just miss that extra touch having someone in my life would provide.

I need to get laid.

I know, I know, what thirty-year-old guy doesn't, right? Except maybe some of the married ones who were lucky enough to find a woman they can have that with. My job doesn't allow for someone like that in my life, which is why I'm sitting in my dark-tinted sedan throwing a pity party. Number of attendees: one.

I'm not great at picking up women in bars. I don't quite have the finesse my looks suggest. I'm not stupid—I know I'm good-looking, know I could have just about any woman I want, but I don't know how to actually make that happen.

I never know what to say to women when confronted. What do they want me to say? How do I say I just want a quick lay without sounding like a douchebag? I'm aware that I have douchebag tendencies, but I don't love advertising it.

And yes, I realize it's ridiculous. What grown-ass man doesn't know how to talk to a woman? What have I been doing with my time?

Well, let's just say my work keeps me plenty occupied. A woman would only complicate matters more, make my life harder. Not only that, it would probably put her life in danger, and I definitely don't have time for that shit.

A sigh leaves me and I rub the side of my face, the side that has seat belt marks on it from falling asleep in my car. I hate doing that, but I often don't get a choice in the matter. I desperately need a night in a bed, preferably after I've had my fill of someone, but I'm not a picky bastard—just a bed would do.

I debate whether or not I want to pull up the app I hate getting on, but when it comes down to it, with my terrible pick-up lines and awkward silences, I need the app to do the hard part for me. All I have to do is match with someone and they know the drill.

Tilting my head from one side to the other, I weigh my options. One, I get a hotel room, look over all the work I've done today on my laptop, order room service, and binge on some sort of TV before passing out. Two, I find a date, have some food, and spend the night in her bed.

Either option sounds pretty good right now, to be honest. I could definitely get on board with option A.

On the other hand, since I'll be off the grid for a few weeks in a couple of days, I should probably meet up with someone while I can. I reluctantly pull up the app and start browsing. I'm not picky; I just want a woman I can have minimal conversation with, one who is maybe funny and—if I'm lucky—a good lay.

That's not too much to ask for, is it?

Swiping, I find a few who might work and put them on my 'maybe' list. There are a few I immediately pass up—like the ones with cats in the picture with them...yeah, no, thank you—then I stop. The brunette whose picture just filled my screen is definitely someone I wouldn't mind spending the night devouring.

I hesitate over her photo. She looks...normal, in a great way, like not crazy kind of normal, the kind of normal you'd take home to Mom, someone who has 'serious girlfriend material' written all over her face.

That's not what I'm looking for. It's actually the opposite of what I'm looking for.

However, I can't help but tap the heart button under her photo. Maybe if it's meant to be, she'll tap it too.

Not even a minute after liking her photo, I get a notification from the app.

Congrats! You've been Super-Liked by Margaret!

"Shit." She's definitely girlfriend material.

3

MARGARET

OH SHIT! OH shit. Shit shit shit. What is Super-Liked? How do I take that back? What is happening? My panic is overriding my ability to function. The hottest guy on this app just heart-ed me and I Super-Liked him back, though I'm still not sure what the hell that means.

Why is that even a thing? I can't find a button that says 'undo' or anything like that, and the guy at the other end of this connection is probably chucking his phone across the room. I mean, Super-Liked is serious, at least it sounds serious to me.

I throw my head back on my pillow and groan. The first decent guy on here and I screwed it up within a second of seeing him. Of course I did. I shouldn't be so damn surprised, yet here we are.

I throw my phone on the floor, determined to leave the app alone. I can't imagine what that guy is thinking—probably that I'm crazy. I am certainly feeling that right now, thumbing through profile after profile of prospective dinner companions.

It's not that there's anything wrong with it. There are hundreds of people who meet online. In fact, 19% of brides met their spouses online (Yes, I looked it up), so obviously it's not totally bad. Maybe it's not that online dating is bad; maybe it's that I'm bad at online dating…or dating in general. Sometimes I'm even difficult to talk to if you don't want to date me.

I mean, seriously, ONE guy hit like and I acted like he was asking me to be his wife. Oh honey, you want shrimp cocktails for an appetizer at the wedding? (Insert giggle here.)

Damn you, Super-Like button.

A ping from my phone alerts me, and I grudgingly heave my head off of the pillow, rolling out of bed to retrieve my thrown phone. It's probably my mom sending me another cat video. You show your mom YouTube one time…

My eyebrows rise when I see a notification from the dating app, more specifically, from Dan, the Super-Liked guy—the hot, hot, hot guy.

I quickly, carefully open the app and navigate to the message.
Dan: Hey there.
Hey there, yourself. Trying to be casual, as the app suggests,

I type a quick Hi and leave it at that. I can't have him thinking I'm actually crazy. Wait, was responding so quickly a good idea? Maybe he should think I actually have a real life.

Oh, who am I kidding.

Dan: You free tonight?

I quickly think of the night ahead: it's four o' clock on a Friday and I'm already in my pajamas. The real question is: how fast can I shave all the bits?

Margaret: I am. What did you have in mind?

Damn, that sounded suggestive. I'm suspecting this guy won't mind that, but it's definitely not the way to meet the man of my dreams.

Dan: How about some dinner? O'Callahan's Pub at eight?

O'Callahan's is only a few blocks from me—perks of living in the city. It's also the hangout of many of my miserable coworkers, but it might not be a bad idea to prove I have a life if someone happens to witness it.

Do I do it? Do I let this guy into my life? Jeez, Margaret, I didn't propose.

But then there's the other thing—can I do a one-night Can I give myself over and say goodbye at the end of the

Knowing how I'll answer those questions without re needing to ask them, I send a quick reply agreeing to his suggestion and rush off to start the process of shaving. going to be one night, I'm going to make it count.

———

choking, and I finally reach out to grab his hand.

"You okay?"

"H-Hi." I clear my throat and—very, very carefully—take a drink to wash down what spit was left. "Um, yes, I'm fine. Thank you."

"No problem. So, cosmo, huh?" He snags the chair beside me and gives the bartender his order: a Guinness, of course. Why does that fit him so perfectly?

"Well, yes. I like cosmos…is that bad?" I raise a sarcastic eyebrow, trying to get him to argue with me.

"No, no, not bad per se, but not a real drink, either." He takes a long swallow of his beer and stares me down.

"Not a real drink? It's vodka." I quirk an eyebrow to challenge what he's saying.

"Sure, sure. I mean, it's juice with a splash of vodka."

I scoff but laugh. His sense of humor is a good sign. "Okay, whatever you say, but I'm not one to change my drink of choice just because some guy didn't like it."

He raises an eyebrow, and I can't tell if he's offended or impressed, but I try to keep an impassive face so he can't tell I was bluffing. "I like that. Good for you." He smirks and looks around the restaurant, which is continually getting fuller. "I was imagining dinner a bit differently, like actually getting a table." He laughs a little, and it almost sounds nervous.

Is the hottest guy alive nervous to be on a date?

"We serve the full menu right here if you want to order

something," the hipster bartender informs us.

I look at Dan, give him a smile, and shrug. "I don't mind eating here."

Looking skeptical, he replies, "Are you sure? It's not exactly what I had in mind."

"No, it's totally fine." I sound overeager and silently chastise myself.

"Okay then, garçon, two menus please." Dan uses a goofy voice, and I can see he regrets it the second he does it by the flinch on his face.

And here I thought I was the odd one.

"So, what do you do, Margaret?" Dan asks after we've given our orders to the bartender. We were silent while we browsed the menu, and I couldn't stop watching him out of the corner of my eye. The tick in his jaw, his sleeve up pushed over his forearm, the clearing of his throat—all of it made me squirm.

It either means I am insanely attracted to him, or it's just been a long time.

How about both? my inner voice tells me, but I shoot that bitch down with a swallow of my drink then I clear my throat to answer him. "Uh, I work in retail." I hate my answer. I hate it when anyone asks what I do for a living because it's not the answer I ever want to give.

I want to say something different like, Oh, I'm just a

lawyer. Then I'd laugh lightly like I'm bashful about having this wonderful career, waving my hand at their gushing compliments. A lawyer?! But you're so young!

Alas, when I tell people I'm in retail, I get the sympathetic nod, the Oh, well…you still have time.

It grates on my last nerve, mostly because I absolutely hate my job.

"Yeah? You like that?" Liam asks. He's so intense when he's talking to me, maintaining eye contact, not paying any mind to anyone around us, and it makes me feel like the most important person in the world.

"Uh…" I hesitate, trying to find something positive to say, and then I relax my tense shoulders and give him a bland look. "No." I laugh a little like it's funny and am rewarded with a sexy grin from him. "Not at all." As I shake my head, my fingers play with the napkin under my drink, and I wait for him to change the subject to something easier to talk about.

"Why not?"

I look at him again. "Well, frankly, it's terrible." I frown when I think of all the things I hate about it; the list is too long to recite completely, but I pick a few. "People are rude. They always go through the clothes like it's a never-to-happen-again sale only to throw them back on the table and walk away. They're all so entitled, too, like I'm somehow less than them because I work in retail—which I guess I am."

"You're not, though," he replies. "People suck. That's the sad truth, and most people don't even realize when they are talking to someone extraordinary."

I blush a little and look back at my drink, unable to hold his intense stare, crinkling my eyebrows. Does he think I'm extraordinary?

"Let me ask you a question," he starts, and I look back over at him. "If you could do anything in the world, no matter how crazy, what would you do?"

I open my mouth to answer but stop, thinking about my answer seriously. Anything in the world? I've never been asked that before, maybe in high school when career day would come around, but back then I was naïve and didn't have a clue what the real world is like. I probably said something along the lines of becoming an actress or a singer, maybe a writer, dreamy goals that seemed so attainable at that age but are now way too far-fetched.

When I really think about what I want to do, what I would want to be remembered for when I'm gone, that's actually simple. "I would want to help people." My voice is quiet, and he doesn't respond right away.

His eyes soften and he nods. "I knew it."

"What?" I ask, my eyebrows pulled together again.

"I knew you were one of the good ones."

Blushing furiously, I look away and am barely saved by our dinner being delivered, but I can't stop thinking about what he said. It gets me thinking about what I said, and now I just gotta figure out how to make that happen.

After devouring dinner, Dan and I don't move from our bar stools the entire night. It's like two old friends catching up. We both laugh and tell stories, a lot of his about his travels all over the world. It's like listening to the adventures of a book character, and it's fascinating to hear about all the places he's been as a travel agent.

We have more in common than I would have thought. He grew up much the same way as me in a smaller town with small schools, and when he graduated, he left that town and never looked back, which is how I felt about my own town. It was how I ended up in Denver, wanting to live in a bigger city with new experiences.

His stories are just another added bonus on the attraction scale, and he's quickly becoming the most amazing man I've ever met. He's kind but direct, shy but confident, gorgeous but humble. I even mention it once.

"I never thought I'd get a date with someone like you."

"What do you mean?"

I shrug and gesture toward him. "You know…"

His eyebrows scrunch, and there are little laugh lines beside his eyes, which I catch myself staring at more than I should. "I don't have any idea what you're talking about."

"Come on. You know how handsome you are."

"What does that have to do with you?"

"Well, I mean, I'm no model." I gesture back toward myself now, stopping at the massive hips I try to pull off as 'curves' but are really just a nod to the fact that I love carbs.

"Margaret, first of all, looks have nothing to do with connection." Oof, is this what swooning feels like? "And second, you are absolutely beautiful."

He orders two more drinks and acts as if nothing happened, but I'm looking around at the strangers surrounding us wondering if anyone else heard him say I was beautiful like it was a known fact to the universe.

I'm pretty certain I've fallen in love already.

Just kidding.

But seriously…

4

LIAM

MARGARET IS SO far away from what I was expecting going into this date. I was ready for a giggling airhead, maybe a crazy cat lady who was desperate for a little attention. I thought the picture on her profile might be a catfishing scenario, but when I walked in and saw her sitting at the bar, talking with the bartender and looking around nervously, I was struck for a moment, just watching her.

And fuck, she's perfect. From her gorgeous curves to her incredible laugh, she's any guy's dream girl, and I find it incredibly hard to believe she hasn't been snatched up already. She's not someone who tries too hard, her awkwardness even adding to her character, and I find myself completely charmed.

The nerves I felt earlier are set at ease around her, and it makes the night that will inevitably come to a close have a different result than I wanted. As much as I would love to take her home tonight or even extend this to a second or third date, I can't drag Margaret through that. She's the type who would get hurt, and I can't do that with the profession I'm in. I can't put an innocent at high risk.

If I had any other job, I wouldn't hesitate to lock her down.

"So, what's it like seeing the world?" Her pouty lips wrap around the rim of her cosmo, and I realize it's at least her fifth one. We've been ordering drinks left and right, neither of us wanting to end the night just yet.

"Well, a little different than you'd think. It's not like I go to the touristy areas," I reply.

"What do you mean? Don't you take clients to the popular destinations?"

I pause. Shit. I just shoved my foot in my mouth. "Uh…well, I try to make their visits more…authentic."

She gives me a look like she just met a superhero. "Wow. That's amazing. Is that normal or just your type of work?"

"Just me." I chuckle awkwardly, knowing I barely saved myself and grateful Margaret didn't catch me in my lie.

We carry on until last call, and when I glance up at the bartender in surprise, he points to the clock, which reads two in the morning. Holy shit. I didn't even think we'd been sitting here for more than a couple of hours; it felt way too quick.

"Wow. I've got to get going." Margaret reaches for her purse where it hangs on the back of her chair, and I take the opportunity to quickly pay our bill.

"Are you sure?" she asks, eyeing it.

"Of course. This is a date, Margaret," I reply with a smile. "Can I drive you home?"

"Oh, I can walk. It's not far."

Not wanting to separate yet, even though I know that's what I should do, I ask, "Can I walk you home?"

Her face morphs into a blinding smile and she nods her head. Her excitement makes my gut tighten; she probably thinks this night is far from over. I breathe in a deep breath and let it out slowly, trying to control myself, weighing what I'd like to do and what I'm sure I shouldn't do in my mind.

We walk out of the bar and onto the sidewalk. What's normally a very busy street is only occupied by a few random stragglers. Walking closely to Margaret, I take in my last few minutes with her. Knowing I'll never see her again makes a pit form in my stomach. Very briefly, I think about what it would be like to be able to take her to bed tonight, and somehow I already know it'd be the best night of my life.

She's not a random hookup. She's a special person who deserves better than that. As a matter of fact, she deserves better than the app we met on—she's a solid Match.com type of chick. I just can't believe I was matched with her. It's like a tease from the universe that she was put in my path and I have to shove her out of it.

"What made you want to sign up for the app?" I ask before I can think better of it.

"What do you mean? Why does anyone sign up for a dating app?" she replies.

"Well, that question can have a couple of different answers. The obvious is hookups, another is love."

She pauses and thinks about her answer. "I don't know if it's that black and white, is it? Who says you can't start with the intention of having sex and ending up finding more?"

See? I knew it, a total commitment girl, and I'm about to shatter the pretty little image she's painted.

"Ha. That's not what most people are looking for on there."

"How could you possibly know that?"

"Because I've met a lot of people through the app."

"How many is a lot, exactly?"

Yikes. I didn't think that through very well. I think about lying to her but decide the truth may be the best way to start pushing her away and have this night end without her being totally crushed.

"Uh, a few dozen." I shrug my shoulders, trying to seem nonchalant about it.

"A few dozen? As in twelve times…"

"Yeah," I reply, a bit embarrassed. I've never been ashamed of how I've behaved when I give myself the time to act on it, but for a reason I can't or won't put into words, I want her to think better of me.

Margaret goes silent, and I can only imagine what she's thinking. I bet she's wondering if I have any diseases. "Huh," is all she says. What I wouldn't give to break into her brain right now. I'm good at reading people, but I expected her to go a little crazy on me, not just act as if that is an interesting but inconsequential factoid.

"That's all?" I burrow my hands in my jean pockets then turn slightly her way so I can see her face as we walk.

"I really don't have a reply to that."

"Okay." I search for something else to talk about. "I guess I should've kept that little bit to myself."

"No, it's okay. I mean, who knows how many guys have just lied about it, ya know? Your honesty is refreshing."

I blink. Study her face. Then blink again.

"This is me." I didn't even realize she'd stopped and have to backtrack a few steps to get back to where she's standing. I look up at the apartment building and am surprised by how rundown it seems. It looks like it should be condemned.

"This is you? For real?"

"Yes."

"This isn't safe."

"Isn't safe? I mean, it's not the Ritz, but it's not bad."

I apparently can't help myself when it comes to putting my damn foot in my mouth tonight, but there you go. Foot, inserted into mouth. "I'm sorry. You're right."

She shuffles her feet and grabs the strap of her bag, reaching in and pulling out a set of keys. "Did you want to come up?"

I sigh and realize we're at the end of the shortest relationship in history, one I would give up nearly anything to explore. I've never felt this way about someone so quickly—so attracted, so intrigued—but inevitably, we wouldn't work, and us sleeping together would only hurt her more. "Look, you're amazing."

She drops her head and has a small smirk on her face. "Ah, I see."

"No, wait. It's just…I'm not looking for a relationship, and I can see that you are. I don't have the time for a girlfriend, or the patience, if I'm being honest."

"Okay. Well then, Dan…" She pauses, and I realize how much I wish she knew my real name. That's not the deal, though. "It's been…fun."

We stare at each other for another minute and she turns toward the steps, slowly ascending them, jingling her keys in her hand. We both hesitate, the tension between us palpable even from this distance, neither of us ready to walk away. I start to turn away and bite my lip, my hands resting in my pants pockets, but I can't make myself walk away.

"Ah, fuck it."

Running up the stairs two at a time, I reach for her waist and twist her toward me. I don't give her a chance to protest before I slam my lips down onto hers, pushing her up against the door

and claiming her for myself.
 Just tonight. Just once.

5

MARGARET

HIS HANDS ON my hips are burning my skin, his mouth on mine a war; a battle of who wants it more. I think I win when I tug on his bottom lip and a groan leaves his mouth. I can't seem to catch my breath when he breaks away from me and starts down my neck. I feel like my entire body is on fire.

We barely make it into my apartment before he slams the door shut and lets me drag him to my bedroom. I'm glad I took two seconds to make the bed before leaving the house; it's a small miracle.

He lays me back and I reach for his belt, undoing it before he can change his mind and leave. He wastes no time undoing the buttons on the front of my dress and before we know it, we're both nearly naked.

We're panting hard, me more than him, but that's more than likely due to the adrenaline coursing through my veins and the lack of cardio in my life.

"I never do this," my mouth says before my brain can stop it. Did I really just say that?

Dan pauses and looks down at me, his eyebrows creased in confusion and his mouth tipped to the side in thought. "Do you not want to do this?"

"No! I mean, yes! I mean, no, I do want to do this. I do want this." My blabbering makes my breathing even more rapid and I plead with my eyes, trying to convince him.

He tilts his head. "Are you sure?"

"Positive." He nods at my affirmation and goes back to what he was doing before my stupidity nearly stopped him.

I watch him lean over me, his strong forearms flexing, the veins popping out, and why is that so damn sexy? My eyes trail up his arms to his shoulders, and when they land on his face, I see him already peering down at me. He's breathing quietly while my pants echo throughout the room. His gaze, though—his gaze is trained on mine, and he doesn't break eye contact when he lifts me farther up onto the bed and lies over me gently.

I grab his shoulders, holding him to me and kissing him like I've never kissed before. God knows I've never kissed someone like him before. His mouth is pure magic, his lock on my hips possessive, and yet I'm more comfortable than I've ever been.

He slips my bra straps off my shoulders and reaches behind me. Using expert fingers, he unclasps it and throws it over my head, out of sight.

"You're gorgeous." His voice is raspy. His lips latch onto my shoulder and make their way across my collarbone, down between my breasts. The attention I'm receiving is something I've never experienced before and I close my eyes, savoring it.

"I can't believe this is happening." I don't even recognize my voice.

"I can't wait," he says quickly before he reaches for his pants and whips something out. When I see what it is, I sigh in relief. I didn't even think about a condom. I'm out of practice—and by that I mean I was second string on the team and never even had to worry about drinking water during the game.

He hurries through the task and is back over me after quickly removing my panties. When he's nearly lying on me, he locks eyes with me again and asks, "Are you sure?"

I nod my head quickly. "More than."

With my approval, he lightly pushes into me, slowly at first, letting me adjust. I pause my breathing, watching him move above me. He's straining, trying not to hurt me, but I pull on his shoulders to give him the go-ahead.

He pushes all the way in and rocks his hips back and forth. His grunts match my moans, and it's a feeling I've never felt before. It's not the obvious connection; it's something more than that. It's a new experience for me altogether. That's not to say I'm a virgin, but I've certainly never been comfortable enough with someone to have sex with them after one date.

It's not just comfort—there's something about Dan that I trust. Maybe that's naïve, but I feel like if it came down to it, he wouldn't break that trust.

The sensations of having him inside me make goose bumps rise on my skin, and I tremble when my orgasm hits me suddenly. Out of nowhere, he adjusts his angle, and I look up to him to see him already watching my face. He looks like he's in shock, like he too is experiencing something new.

He leans down onto his forearms and slips them under my shoulders, encouraging me to grab his, and he cradles my body against him, moving his mouth down to mine and kissing me slowly, tenderly, like if he presses too hard, I'll shatter like glass. In this position, he's hitting me deeper than ever before, and with a moan of surprise, it happens again, making me let out his name on a whisper. It's only a couple more minutes before Dan follows me and, with a last grunt, he stills, a tremor running through us both.

With a happy sigh, he collapses to the side. We don't say anything at first, me wondering how on earth I could already be feeling something about this man I met only hours ago, wondering if it's the alcohol or the comradery of feeling like I know him better than I've ever known someone, wondering if it's possible that he could possibly be feeling the same way.

"That was amazing," he whispers.

I agree with a hum and watch him slowly close his eyes. With a smile on my face, I let sleep take me, feeling a hope I've never had before.

Except, when I wake up, that hope deflates as I take in the empty bed, the empty room, and nothing to show for the night before.

The fabric twists roughly in my hands as I fold it with a certain vigor it doesn't require. It's the only way I can release my pent-up tension at the moment. My time with Dan is on constant replay in my mind, and when I get to the morning after, all I can do is shake my head in disbelief.

I know he said he didn't want to hurt me, said he wasn't looking for anything real, but to leave without a word? I didn't really peg him that way. Despite his premature departure, the night was still the kind I've always dreamed of. It was basically straight out of a modern-day rom-com, and I loved every second of it.

It's been a couple of pathetic weeks since my date with him, and it seems he was a needle in a haystack. I've been on four dates—yes, four—since then, and every one of them ended with the line, "So, you wanna go back to my place?" No, I really don't, Brad.

I realize that may sound hypocritical, but they weren't even subtle about it, which turned me off immediately.

Dan was right, though—I'm not going to find the love I want on the stupid little app. So, finally, I deleted it and decided I would wait for fate to make something happen for me.

A silly part of me was hopeful that I would hear from Dan again, but he kept his word and has probably slept with another dozen women already. That should warn me away. It should, yet here I am weeks later still dreaming of him and our night together.

Dan was the ultimate package—gorgeous, funny, and smart—and something about his shyness made me want to wrap him in a hug and not let go. There's something seriously attractive about a man who's good-looking and not a showboat about it. He never once acted like he was better than me or anyone else. When he paid our tab, he tipped the bartender generously and waved it off like it was no big deal, but I could tell it made that guy's night. It was something tiny, simple, yet huge to me all at the same time.

I continue to fold the shelf of clothes in front of me, cleaning up the kind of mess that can only result from a customer who is in a hurry and, frankly, a jackass who thinks they are too good to put the clothes back properly. I move from station to station, doing my job, and I'm just glad to not have to deal with returns today, even if folding laundry is something I barely even do for my own clothes.

When the time comes for me to leave, I walk out of the department store and onto the busy city streets. It's a welcome hum compared to the quiet lull of the Celine Dion songs they play in the store. I mean, I love Celine as much as the next person, but even she's got to get tired of her own voice eventually, right?

I'm passing my favorite coffee shop when I suddenly feel like someone is watching me, an eerie sensation that crawls up the back of my neck. I glance over my shoulder and see a man in black walking behind me, a hand to his ear, but from what I can see, he's not holding a phone.

Strange…

I continue on my way home and wait a couple blocks to see if he's still following me. When I look, I don't see him again, and I release the pent-up breath I was holding. Then, I get yanked into an alley that smells of rotten fish.

Before I can scream, a hand is pressed over my mouth, and I bite down on it. I kick my offender and then finally get a good scream in.

"Margaret, quiet!" The offender pulls me farther into the alley then bends down behind a dumpster.

"Let me go!" I yell. I'm not about to let this dude tell me what to do. If I'm going to get raped, I'm going to do it on my own terms!

Wait, that's not right…

"Get off me, you crazy psycho! I know kung fu!" Do they teach that anymore? Not that it matters—I'll just play it up until this person believes me.

"Margaret, it's me, Dan," the man whispers in my ear. We're still crouching behind the dumpster, his hold on me not so tight that I can't move, so I take a chance and glance back. Huh, look at that. It is Dan.

"What the hell is wrong with you? I thought you were a crazy rapist!" I shove out of his arms and take a step back.

"I'm sorry, but I couldn't let anyone see me." His eyes are peering into mine, his skin is pale, and he's panting like he can't catch his breath. He looks awful.

"What? Why? Are you on the run?" I gasp and cover my mouth. "Are you a rapist?"

"No! Look, it's complicated." I stand up and walk backward, but he follows me and pulls me back down. "You can't be seen."

"What? Why not?" I crane my neck to look down the alley, suddenly sure a mob of men in black will walk over and steal me away. I've got to get ahold of my imagination.

"Because the man who got to me may be after you as well."

I think I've lost the ability to comprehend what he's saying because I just sit there and stare at him.

"Look, can we go to your place? I need your help." He grimaces, and I crinkle my brow.

"Why? What is going on? Who's after me? What do they want?" The questions spill out of me without pause, and I think I'm about to go into shock.

"I'll tell you everything eventually, I swear." He gasps and clenches his side; I noticed he's been holding it. "I just need some help." His eyes show his desperation, and I feel myself start to soften. "Please, Margaret."

I know this is a bad idea. I realize this—I have seen Dateline. I know the risks, and yet here I am, about to aid a hot guy because…why? I don't even know.

"Okay."

He closes his eyes and sighs in relief. "Thank you." He reaches to the ground where a hat is lying. I'm guessing I knocked it off his head in my haste.

I walk toward him, and he clutches his side again. "Are you hurt, Dan?" I may be terrified, but I'm still human.

"Yes," he replies, and he hisses when he moves wrong. I walk to his other side and sling his arm over my shoulder. It's not that I think I could actually carry him, but I'm hoping he can lean on me a little. "We need to be discreet. Don't walk too fast, and keep your head turned toward me like we're a couple."

That won't be hard to do since I've thought of little else since our date. I give him a thumbs-up and keep my smile to myself. Pretend to be your girlfriend? Don't mind if I do.

"What…what is that?" I ask, feeling something warm on my hand.

"I was hit. It's not too bad, but I need it cleaned and sewn up." He says it so matter-of-factly, like this is a common occurrence for him.

"Hit? Hit by what?" He doesn't answer, so I look at his face, which he's hiding under his baseball cap.

"Margaret, let's just get back to your place."

I decide to not argue and just hold him tighter. This was so not how I pictured us getting closer again, but a weaker part of me I refuse to say aloud loves every second of his body pressed tight to mine.

We stay side by side, his weight getting heavier with each passing second, and he seems to be struggling with his breathing. My anxiety kicks in at that moment, but I try to push it aside and focus on getting to my apartment.

Opening the door to my building proves to be a challenge, but I finally manage to do it. I help guide him toward the elevator and pray it's working today. "Shit," I say when the button doesn't light up. Come on!

I grunt and reposition Dan then look over to see he's almost passed out. Double shit. This is going to very difficult.

Hefting him as high as I can, I half drag, half beg him to walk to the door to the stairs and start making the trek up the six floors to my apartment. I hate, hate stairs. I hate cardio. I hate…I don't know, because I'm running out of things to hate as the oxygen leaves my brain at a fast pace.

I'm up one flight when I trip over Dan's feet, and he rolls over onto his back on the landing. I nearly land on him as I stumble, and I try to hold myself up.

Not exactly how I pictured us getting horizontal again.

I let out a small whimper at the thought of the passed-out,

model-like guy under me. How am I going to get this man up the stairs? I stand and assess my situation.

"This is so not how I thought my day was going to go," I say to him, even though I know he's not going to be replying any time soon. I now have an unconscious man lying at my feet, waiting for me to take action. Again, not how I envisioned this going.

I walk around to his shoulders and decide pulling is the only way this is going to happen. There's no way I can fireman-heave him up these stairs. Grasping below his armpits, I start to pull, using all my might to get him up the steps. About halfway up the second flight, I realize how bad this would look if someone suddenly showed up. It would be horrific to see someone lugging a giant, unaware man up some stairs.

I somehow manage to get up to the next small landing. It's about three square feet, so his feet and calves are still hanging down the stairs, and he's twisted at an odd angle because I was trying to turn and pull. As I readjust, something slimy touches my left hand, making me pull it away in fear. I look to my fingers and see they're dripping crimson.

Oh God, that's the metallic smell. I turn away from hovering over his face as best I can in the small space. Oh God, I'm going to puke. I'm gonna puke right here on this landing.

Pull yourself together, Margaret!

Dan is in need, and if I can force myself to focus on that, maybe, just maybe I can heave him up the rest of the way. I keep pulling, blocking out any thoughts of what caused the wound—stop thinking about it!—and get him up another flight.

I think I've nearly gotten him there when I lose my grip, which results in him sliding down a flight of stairs. I chase after him and wince every time his head hits one of the steps. If he wasn't knocked out before… When I finally get to him, I check his pulse and breathe a sigh of relief when I find it. I close my eyes for a moment then eye the stairs I have to drag him up again.

God send me some strength, and please don't let me puke on the unconscious hot dude.

6

LIAM

GROANING, I COME to in a place I vaguely recognize. I've never felt so sore in my life, and that's definitely saying something considering the things I've done.

Shit.

I reach up to grab my head but feel a pull in my side. Right, I got shot. That's what that is.

Looking around at my surroundings, I see an old TV and a couch above me where I lie on the floor. It's dark outside, there's a soft-as-hell blanket covering me, and my shirt is ripped where the bullet went through. I look at the wound, wondering why I'm not dead from bleeding out, and see silver strips of duct tape patching me up.

Duct tape. Covering a gunshot wound.

Catching movement out of the side of my eye, I see Margaret sitting on some kind of ottoman, staring at me with wide eyes. I sit up and catch a whiff of something horrible.

"What's that smell?"

Her eyes widen at me and she twists her hands nervously, looking like she's about to bolt. "I'm not good with blood, I'm sorry." Her words come out quickly.

"What do you mean? Looks like you kept me from bleeding out." I gesture toward the makeshift bandage.

"The second I saw it, I puked." She whimpers a little and looks like she's about to cry. "I'm sorry," she whispers, looking nervous.

"So…" I clear my throat and look down at my stained shirt. "You're saying I'm covered in your puke?" She nods her head in affirmation. Well this is a first. I lean against the couch and decide my next move. "Are you okay?" I ask her.

She looks like she's stricken with fear, and I wonder if it would have been best to keep my distance, but when I thought they might have found out I went out with her, I couldn't stop myself from coming to her rescue, making sure she was safe. I've gone out with plenty of women, plenty I've had fun with, but Margaret was different. Being around her and with her was different, important. It isn't something I can explain.

She nods at my question and gestures toward me. "Yeah, I

was just, uh, surprised is all." Swallowing, she finally looks me in the eyes. "Who did this to you?" Her question is a whisper, and her expression has morphed from scared to concerned, maybe even angry—on my behalf. Huh. That's new, and I have a hard time admitting to myself that I kind of like it.

"Some not-so-good people," I answer, thinking about what I need to do before I lay out exactly what I've gotten her into. I have to help her while keeping myself in check around her. Despite our amazing night together, treating her like I did won't help this situation. I clear my throat and refocus. "Okay, I need a little help." I look at her and she nods, though it's a bit hesitant. "Can you get me some alcohol, a small knife, and some tweezers? I'm also gonna need a sewing kit. Do you have one of those?"

She nods again and scampers off to get the items I requested. I figure I'll wait until she's back before breaking the news that I can't really see my own injury. I can reach it for stitching, but getting the bullet out without being able to look would be much harder a feat. I groan again and feel my head; I feel like I fell down a flight of stairs.

"Here." She comes back and hands me the items I need, and I lay them out beside me.

"Duct tape?"

Margaret shrugs and gives me a shy look. "I'm not a doctor. It was all I could reach in a hurry, and once it was on, I didn't want to pull it off."

"But…duct tape? On a gunshot wound?" I don't know if she

can tell I'm giving her shit, but she starts fanning herself and pales.

"A gunshot—" She expels some air and I worry she's going to pass out, but I can't even get up right now to catch her. "Is that what it is?"

"Margaret," I say firmly, "sit. You're going to faint."

"I'm not," she insists, but she complies anyway. I watch her for a minute and assess our situation. I guess it was too much to ask to have fallen for a nurse or something, or hell, anyone who isn't afraid of blood.

"Mo, do you think you could help me out?"

"Mo?"

I shrug; it just came to me. "It's short and sweet." A mix of her name and her favorite drink.

"What do you need help with?" She looks worried about the answer, and maybe she should be, because there's still a bullet lodged in there and I need it out.

"You gotta help me here." Standing, she heads over in my direction. I lie on my uninjured side and hand her the alcohol first. She reluctantly takes it from me. "As gently as possible, pull the duct tape off. Then pour the alcohol over the wound."

"Oh God." Her words are barely audible. With her bending over me like she is, I can see straight down her shirt, and for a second I let myself pull up the memory of them. A flush makes its way onto my face but before she can see it, I turn away from the gorgeous view and focus on the situation at hand.

I can tell this isn't going to be easy, being around her for however long it takes me to find her a safe place. Since we're in a bit of a predicament, I haven't been able to gauge how pissed she is that I left before she woke up, but I have a feeling it's coming.

I feel the tug of the tape and suck in a breath. Holy SHIT that is not a good feeling. I hold as still as possible because, from her heavy breathing, I know Margaret is doing her best not to freak out—or puke—on me.

When the tape is all off, she pours the alcohol over the wound like I asked, and I keep it together as best as possible, trying not to scream out. "Shit," I let out through gritted teeth.

"Okay, now what?" She sounds calm, and I look up to see her face devoid of any emotion. I'd guess she's in shock.

"Now"—I blow out a breath—"take the knife and sterilize it with alcohol. Then, very carefully, run the knife straight across the wound, but only about an inch."

"What? Cut you more? I can't do that!" Finally, some color has returned to her face. Even though she's protesting what I'm saying, she's following my directions by dousing the knife with the alcohol.

"You can. You have to. We have to get the bullet out."

"Oh. Okay. Okay, I can totally do this." She gives herself a little pep talk, and I turn from her as she takes the knife to the spot. My entire body tenses as I feel the light slice of the knife. Before I can express any sort of reaction, she's already done, and I couldn't be more grateful that she was quick about it.

"Take the tweezers and sterilize them too." Margaret does so then looks me in the eyes and waits. I take a second, knowing this will be a bitch to feel. "Okay. Take them and very carefully—wait. You need a towel," I say, remembering another piece to this. "It's gonna get bloody.

When she returns, I tell her to have it close by then explain how to get the bullet out. She takes a deep calming breath and dives in, literally. Margaret must feel me tense because she rests her left hand on my arm and uses her other hand to extract the bullet from the wound.

I sigh in relief that it's almost over then suddenly see Margaret land on the carpet beside me.

Well shit.

She passed out.

I look down at my wound and see a serious amount of blood coming out. It's not life-threatening, but it is enough to give anyone a good scare. I quickly grab the towel and press it to the wound. Looking at Margaret, I see she didn't seem to hit her head too hard, and at least she landed on carpet.

I gather the rest of the supplies, hoping the bleeding will stop long enough for me to be able to sew it up. It's nothing I haven't had to do before, and I just hope I can manage to get it done before she wakes up.

"Hey, Mo," I say when I finally see Sleeping Beauty come to. I managed to lift her up onto the couch so she didn't wake up sore as hell like I did.

"Hi." She rubs her head then sees what I'm wearing. "Is that mine?"

"Yeah. Sorry, I had to change." She examines the shirt I threw on; it was the only one big enough for me.

"Girl Power? That's all I had for you?" There's a bit of humor in her tone, and I chuckle.

"Hey, power to the woman is what I always say."

"So, did you get everything all put…back to where it goes?"

I lift the edge of the shirt and gesture to the wound I found some bandages for, giving her a thumbs-up. She stands up slowly and walks into her kitchen. Grabbing a glass from the cabinet, she fills it with water and chugs the entire thing.

"You okay?"

She lets out a huff of laughter. "Dude." Scoffing, she sets the glass on the counter and turns toward me, throws her hands up, and gives me crazy eyes. (I'd never say that out loud to a woman because, damn, I like to keep all my parts.) She shakes her head at me. "No! I'm not okay!" She enunciates the last word then starts stuttering. "I-I just pulled an unconscious, gorgeous man up six flights of stairs! I duct-taped a gunshot wound! Someone crazy is supposedly after you—maybe even me! None of this is okay."

I open my mouth to assure her but then pause. "You hauled me up six flights of stairs?" I turn my head to look out a window—damn, we are up a little high. I didn't really note what floor we were on last time I was here; the elevator worked then and I was occupied with other thoughts.

"I dropped you, too." My eyebrows shoot up and I shake my head. Of all the people in the world to be in peril with. "But that's not even the crazy part. Who are these guys? Why are they after you? Wait—first question: who are you?"

I sigh and realize I've never actually told her my real name. Maybe I'll hold off; there's no telling what she'd do with that now. "I'm not exactly what I told you I was." I lean against the counter. "I'm not a travel agent."

She gives me a look that's almost disappointment. "You mean you don't travel to all those wonderful places like you said? That was all bullshit?"

Slightly choking on a laugh, I reply, "No, I've been to those places, just not for the reasons I said. I'm…" I pause and think about how to explain this to her. My job isn't something that's normal. Most people have no idea what I actually do for a living, and that's the way I've always liked it. "I'm a…spy."

There's a brief silence, a staring contest between the two of us to see who will crack first. It won't be me—I've been extensively trained to not give in to pressurized situations. The last thing I expect is for her to keel over in laughter. She can't seem to catch her breath and has tears running down her face.

"A sp-spy?" She loses it all over again, and I close my eyes, trying not to lose my shit. "That's the funniest thing I've ever heard."

"I'm being serious. I'm undercover. I've been trailing an entire organization for three years."

"Right, and I'm Lady Gaga—p-p-p-poker face." Her obnoxious singing doesn't stop for another minute, and I wait until it's all out of her system.

"You done now?"

"Uh-huh. Don't worry, little spy man, your secret is safe with me." She raises an eyebrow. "So, tell me, what bank did you clear out? Or did you rob a gas station?"

I walk back over to the couch where the bullet that was in my side is lying and hand it to her. She stares at it rolling around in the palm of her hand. "I work for the FBI, or at least I try to. You took this out of my body today. I was made today by someone I get into contact with, and guess what, you were too, because they've been tailing me—since before our date, I'm guessing. So, now you're compromised. I took care of the man who gave me this"—I point to my wound—"but that doesn't mean more won't come."

Her face blanches, and a sick satisfaction that she's finally taking this seriously fills me for a second before I give her an ultimatum.

"Either you stay here, enjoy your brief freedom before they find you and kill you, possibly kidnap and torture you to get to me—which, by the way, won't work—or you come with me now and your chances of survival go up about, oh, I don't know, one hundred percent."

Between you and me, I wouldn't let her die, not purposefully—I still like her—but sometimes fear does half the job for you.

"Oh God! I don't want to die! I've never even held a gun! I need to know how to shoot a gun!" Her hysteria takes over and I rush her to her room, guiding her to grab a backpack and stuff it full of whatever she can fit before we take off. "Money!" she suddenly shouts then reaches underneath her bed and grabs a gold box. It looks like it was spray-painted years ago, and she pulls out a wad of bills—a big wad.

"The hell? Who keeps that kind of cash lying around?" I scold her.

She looks at me, and for the first time, she looks angry. She hasn't shown me that look before now. "I don't trust banks."

Of course she doesn't.

We start to make our way out of the apartment, and she stops suddenly at the doorway. "Wait." I turn and impatiently wait for her to explain whatever it is she needs, but she just looks at me. "Will I never come back here?"

Pinching the bridge of my nose, I say, "Say goodbye to it or your life. It's your choice, but I've gotta go."

"Right. Perspective. Sorry." She hustles past me and starts darting down the stairs. I shake my head and quickly get ahead of her, looking her in the eyes.

"Let me lead so you don't get yourself killed. They could have followed us."

"Oh." Thankfully she doesn't argue and lets me walk ahead. Some weird visions of being bumped around on these stairs assault me, but I just shake my head, clearing my mind and listening for any signs of a threat.

A door opens just as I'm walking past it and I whip around quickly, utilizing skills I've developed over the years to catch the assailant off guard. Before he knows what's happening, I've clocked him in the Adam's apple.

Unfortunately, it's not who I thought it would be.

"Oh my God! Mr. Samson!" Margaret bends down to the old man who's on his knees, gasping for air. She turns worried, accusing eyes my way and says, "Why did you do that?"

He starts coughing rather violently and shouts, "You'll pay for that, young man!" At least that's what I think he says, but it's really hard to understand him. I grimace, feeling horrible.

"Are you okay?" Margaret asks as she helps the old man to his feet. Before he can get a look at my face, I grab Margaret's hand and pull her down the next flight.

"I'm sorry, sir!" I call out.

It's the best I can do for now. Even if I feel horrible, it's too risky to hang out in the middle of a stairwell.

"Dan! You could have killed him! He's old!" Margaret's brown hair is flying behind her because we're running so damn fast.

"He'll be fine. I wasn't intending to kill anyone. If I had been, he'd be dead."

Her horrified look almost makes me feel bad. Almost. "You're horrible!"

I look at her then and disregard her comment, noticing the way her hair shines and remembering running my hands through the silky strands. She snaps her fingers in front of my face.

"Your hair is too distracting. We need to fix that."

"What the hell? Where did that come from?" She pats her head as if that will help.

"I'm trying to not let the bad guys who want to kill you find you too easily. We need a disguise." I say it slowly, explaining it like I'm talking to a four-year-old.

She pinches my arm—hard.

"Damn, Mo. What?"

"I'm not a little kid! Be nicer."

I scoff. Being nice is the last thing I'm worried about right now. Right now, we need a car.

And a gun.

7

MARGARET

DAN IS QUITE literally dragging me through the city streets, and I have a strong urge to dig my heels in and not let him move me another inch. This guy is certifiable. This whole thing is absurd, and I can't even begin to comprehend who could possibly be after me. There aren't even that many people who know who I am.

I can't believe I slept with him!

Yeah, we all know that's a lie.

We come to a stop at the corner of a busy intersection, and Dan dips into a CVS, immediately going to the hair care aisle.

"Uh, no. That's not happening," I protest the second his hand comes into contact with a box of hair dye, the color named Bronze Blonde.

Maybe it's a weird thing to be proud of, but I've never, ever dyed my hair. My chocolate locks are all natural, and I intend on keeping them that way.

"Yes, it is. Also, I need…" He looks around until he finds what he's looking for. "Aha, there we are." He hands me the scissors and I look to him, waiting for some kind of punch line.

"Are you crazy?"

He gives me a look, and I already know what it means: Your hair or your life?

Tough decision… I bite my lip and weigh it out.

"You've got to be kidding," he scoffs, acting like I'm the one being unreasonable.

"Don't be so self-righteous. A woman's hair is half her identity." I just made that up on the spot, but it sounds pretty good, right?

"Mo, this is important."

I shrug my shoulders and decide he's not going to understand why I'm being stubborn about this. Carrying the blonde dye and scissors, I follow him around as he grabs other items including water bottles and protein shakes. As I pass the processed food section, which is basically half the store, I snag a few bags of mini chocolate donuts.

Dan shakes his head at my selection. "That's not nutritious."

"Dude, if I'm going to die soon, I'm going to eat whatever I want."

We begin another staring contest, and it seems we both have strong wills. Given that we are in a bit of a perilous situation and have bigger things to worry about, we both drop it and move over to the counter to pay.

To my surprise, he pulls out his wallet, and I notice his own little wad of bills in there. He hands over some cash to the cashier, and I eagerly grab my mini donuts before he can stop me. We walk out, bags in hand, on to an adventure I'm not prepared for.

A pay-by-the-hour hotel is our next destination a couple miles away from my apartment, and this will be another first for me. I haven't had a ton of experience with hotels to begin with, but I've definitely never wanted to go to one you don't have to have a deposit for. Ugh.

We enter the room Dan got for us and dump our bags on the small bed. The bedding looks worn out and I cringe, trying to stay brave and thanking the good Lord we don't have to sleep in it. He informed me we weren't staying any longer than however long changing my hair takes.

"What about your hair?" I ask, hands on my hips and eyebrow raised.

"I can wear a hat. Guys have it easy. You're the only pain in the ass here."

"What kind of FBI agent goes on an app for dates, huh? I wouldn't even be here if it weren't for you."

A flash of guilt crosses his face. "You're right." He sighs, stepping forward, invading my senses with that man musk all hot guys seem to just always have. "I'm sorry for getting you into this."

I lift my chin, having been unprepared for his apology. "Fine. Help me with my hair."

"Yes ma'am."

I enter the dingy bathroom, where the light flickers for a moment before deciding to work. I sit on the toilet lid while he starts setting up his supplies and reading directions. It's almost cute. Almost.

He's got a nice scruff going on his jaw, and I wonder if it would be rough or soft under my hand. He's also really tall, a feature I loved the minute I met him. There was so much amazing chemistry between the two of us on our date, and there's a reason I couldn't stop thinking about him.

As he mixes the nasty-smelling chemicals, I watch carefully. "Are you sure you're doing that right?"

He looks about ready to snap, but I can't find it in me to care. I'm the one getting that crap put on my head. "Yes."

"But like, you read the directions correctly? Followed them to a T?" I pester. "Because this shit has never touched my head before. What if I go bald?"

"You won't. I watched my sister do this a million times when she was a teenager."

"You have a sister?" I'm temporarily distracted by this bit of personal information about him, and I close my eyes tightly as he slathers the concoction on my head.

"Yes."

"What's her name?" I breathe through my mouth.

"Layla."

I look up and see his eyes are watering. Dammit. Now mine are too because I opened them. "Is she…" I let a breath out of my mouth again. Damn, this is rank. "Is she older or younger?"

"Older. Has a family and all that."

"Really? Do you see her often?"

"Nah, my job doesn't allow for that. I haven't seen her in years."

"What? You haven't seen your own sister in years?"

He continues to wipe the bleachy crap on my head as he answers. "That's just how it works. I can't exactly be undercover and have real relationships."

"Is that why you were on that app?"

"Mm-hmm. Can't have a girlfriend—not that I want one. It's just easier."

I sit silently for a bit, not because I don't have a million questions but because this is quite possibly the most uncomfortable thing my head has ever felt. "So, do they know what you do?"

"Kind of. They know I work for the government, but they're not exactly privy to the particulars of my job."

"Wow. I can't imagine that." I'm not exactly proud to tell my parents dealing with disgruntled customers day in and day out is the hardest part of my job, but at least they know what I do.

"Eh, you get used to it." He stops, rips off the gloves he was wearing, and throws them away. "Okay, wait like fifteen minutes."

"Fifteen minutes?" I squeak. It's starting to burn, and I don't know if that's normal, but it can't be, can it?

"Let's keep talking, keep your mind off of it."

"Okay."

We enter a silence that is the opposite of what we were supposed to be doing, and I giggle a little at the thought that that's what happens when anyone tries to fill a silence. "Oh, I know."

"Okay, shoot."

"It's actually something I've been meaning to ask but I keep getting distracted." He waves his hand like, Carry on. "Why can't you just go to the FBI to get help with this? I mean, won't they help you? Isn't that their job?"

He sighs and looks away, as if weighing his answer. "It's complicated."

"Complicated how? Like you're actually a bad guy and not good and they figured that out and now you're running from two sides?"

Dan looks at me like I just figured it out, and I feel like crying. Is it the chemicals or the fact that a bad guy is in this bathroom with me that's bothering me? Did I just stick my foot in my mouth?

"You are suspiciously close. However…" I hold out for what comes next. Please God don't let him be a murderer. "I'm not a bad guy. I just had to step back from the FBI a little once I got in deeper with the crew I'm trying to track down."

"What does that mean?"

"It means getting caught talking to the FBI while trying to pretend I'm a buyer would look pretty bad."

"Huh. I guess I can see where that would screw you over."

"Yup."

I resist the urge to scratch my head. The burning has intensified tenfold, and I started sitting on my hands about three minutes ago. I look to the sink and then the ceiling, the tub, the door, the floor, trying hard to distract myself.

A few more minutes go by and I look to Dan again. He looks at his watch. "I think that's good."

I rush off the toilet and shove my head under the faucet. He turns it on, and the burning finally starts to fade. He rubs out whatever is on fire, and I can't even enjoy having his hands on me because I'm concerned my hair is going to fall out.

After a minute of him shampooing out the mess, using the three little bottles the motel supplied, he wraps a towel around my head, and I stand for a minute, letting the blood flow normally through my body again.

"Whew," I say, giving a little chuckle, embarrassed that I was so impatient. I start rubbing my hair with the towel, drying it as much as possible, then I flip back over and face Dan. His eyes go to my hair, and his small smile fades. "What? Is it bad?"

I turn to the mirror and gasp in horror. My hand goes to my mouth, and tears spring to my eyes. I move my head side to side, looking at the new hair Dan has bestowed upon me, touching it like it'll set me on fire. I mean, it looks like fire.

"Oh my God," I whisper at the same time I hear Dan mumble, "Shit," under his breath. "My hair is orange!" Turning, I point my finger in his face and scream, "Why is it orange?!"

8

LIAM

WE'VE WALKED A few blocks away from the motel where I turned Margaret's hair into something a clown would envy, and she hasn't spoken to me since she cursed me out in the bathroom. I tried to assure her we could turn it back, but even she knew I was full of shit.

Maybe it was possible, but I was no hairstylist.

I was on the lookout for a car when she hmphed again and shoved another chocolate donut in her mouth. Somehow those little donuts seemed to calm her down, and I stored away that nugget of information.

Even though we've already royally fucked up her hair,

unfortunately I am going to have to do something else to it. The orange is very…obvious, and now, instead of blending in, we stand out even more.

Out of the corner of my eye, I see what I'm looking for and jog across the street to where it sits. I look around for people watching and see most anyone in the vicinity is either on their phone or doesn't care. Using a tool I keep handy for situations such as these, I thrust it into the car's lock and jiggle it until I feel it break free and the door unlocks.

I watch Margaret go around the other side and silently wait for me to unlock the other door, her silence making me more nervous than the constant rambling she normally gives me. At least when she's yelling at me, I know why she's angry. The silent treatment makes me uneasy.

Jumping into the car, I reach underneath the steering wheel and pull the cover off revealing a plethora of wiring. Ripping down the wires underneath and finding the ones I need, I cut them with the knife I always carry and twist them together, effectively starting the car.

I look over at her with a smirk on my face, prepared for her to be completely impressed by my skills only to find her staring out the window.

I sigh and pull the car out onto the street then try to engage her in conversation. "I'm sorry about your hair. I'll pay to have it fixed as soon as we can."

She swallows her snack and looks at me, seeming to

contemplate what she wants to say. "It's fine. I'm just not happy with how my day has been going."

"Well, it's a new day now," I say, looking at the clock, which reads two in the morning. We've accomplished a lot in the last few hours. "We just have to get to someone I know who can help. I can leave you there with him."

"What?" She whips her head toward me. "I'm not staying with some stranger. I barely trust you."

I push down the unfamiliar sting I feel when she says that. "I can't take you where I need to go. It's too dangerous."

"Are you serious? I pulled a bullet out of you. I dragged you up six flights of stairs. I changed my hair for you. Now you're just leaving me?"

"I'm just trying to keep you safe!" I take a breath, trying to control my rising temper. "You want to end up on the nightly news as a sad story, you can stick with me. Otherwise, you stay with Mike."

"Mike?" She shakes her head. "No. No way. I'm not leaving your side. You said you'd keep me safe, and that's what you're going to do."

I release a sigh and give her a sideways glance; she looks like she's ready to throw down, and I stifle a chuckle. I'll play her game for now, but there's no way I'll let her come with me.

"So...are you going to tell me what all of this is really about?" she asks, biting into another of her precious donuts.

"They call themselves G3, though I have no idea what it

stands for. It's an operation based out of Russia that's infiltrating America. They have a few setups, but I've been trailing Anton Sokolov. He's a notorious drug lord in Russia and has decided he wants more for his little business. I've been following him and the organization for three years."

"Three years? All alone?" She looks sad when I glance at her.

I nod. "Yeah, that's the job. It's hard work, lonely, but the outcome always outweighs all that other bullshit."

"What bullshit? Having a family or a girlfriend? Real friends?"

"Exactly that shit." Margaret looks like I kicked her puppy, and I keep my eyes trained on the road. "I'm not saying that stuff is bad, but in my life, in my line of work, the two just don't mix. If by some chance anyone got ahold of who I was, not my undercover alias but my real name and family, they would use it against me to get whatever they wanted. It's not worth the risk."

She seems to think that over, probably wondering the same thing I've been contemplating since she came crashing into my life: But what if? What if I wasn't a spy for the FBI? What if I had a normal job and could actually be someone?

I'm too chickenshit to admit that if I were normal, if my job were even close to normal, she'd be who I would go for. No doubt.

"Okay, well, tell me everything else then." Her change of subject is a good idea, and I appreciate her not digging deep on this one even when I can tell it's exactly what she wants to do.

"G3 has been a big name in the drug industry from Denver to Nevada, and while that may not seem like a lot of space, it's way too much. They've even been trying to get Mexico in on it, but thankfully—if you want to look at it that way—Mexico already has their own shit and they don't want to play nice with the Russians."

"But what happened with the FBI? Why won't they help you?"

"The FBI thinks I'm a traitor," I say, and her eyes widen a bit. "But I'm not. I swear I'm not," I rush out, hoping to reassure her. An unrelenting need for her to trust me churns in my gut. If this is going to work, she has to believe me. "I was just questioned by some of the handlers there and because of that, I had to cut off contact. I had every intention of getting back in touch with them, but I haven't had a good way of doing that just yet."

"Oh. But are they like, after you now?" Her question seems uncertain, and she waits patiently for me to give her a good answer.

The thing is…I don't have one. I don't have one because they are after me. They're treating me like an enemy of the state, and that puts her in just as much danger as G3 being after us does.

I just can't tell her that. Not yet.

Driving the highway in the middle of the night is the best

way to travel, and there's no way they've been able to track me. They could have only gotten as far as Margaret's apartment, and even then, they may not have found it yet.

I look over to see she is passed out, and it gives me a minute to breathe for the first time since I grabbed her off the street. Finding out she was being tracked, knowing they'd seen me with her and maybe even going into her place had induced a rising anxiety I'd never experienced before.

It was a natural instinct, I think, to feel protective over women, but ever since our night together, it wasn't just that. It was more. She was more—more than I was expecting, more than I was ready for, more than I wanted.

I grew up with an older sister in a small town. There were only a handful of guys she liked over the years, and even then, it was scarce. There was one time in high school that started me on a path like the one I'm on now, the one that has me trying to protect and serve the innocent of the world, to stop harm from coming to their front doors.

I was a sophomore and she was a senior, so we didn't run into each other much during the day. I was trying out for the football team when I saw it. I was listening intently to what the coach was saying; we'd just finished with the tryouts, and I heard a grunt. It was so faint that if you weren't aware of your surroundings like I had always been, you wouldn't have thought anything of it.

But I heard it, and when I saw what I saw, it was like a whole new side of me was unleashed.

One minute, Layla was pinned underneath the biggest linebacker I'd ever met, and the next, I had him pinned under me as I reeled back and punched him again and again until his face was unrecognizable and the coaches had to pull me off.

Thankfully, Layla was fine, but I wasn't. I was pissed. I was adamant he get kicked off the team, expelled from school, arrested—whatever it took.

Unfortunately, his father was a powerful man in town, and all he got was a two-week suspension.

The damage was done. I'd already proven that no one messed with my sister, and according to her, no one ever tried to after that. Everyone seemed slightly terrified of me for the rest of my high school career.

I didn't give a shit about that, though. I wasn't there for long and had never planned on sticking around. I signed up for the Army the minute I graduated and was gone a month later. I only ever went back to see my sister, and these days, that didn't happen very often.

Layla is the only person in the world besides my buddy Mike who I am protective over—until Margaret came along and that feeling arose again in full force. I don't know what to do about it, but I do know it is a dangerous feeling in this situation.

When we reach the town I know Mike retired to, I start to relax for the first time.

Mike and I served in the Army together, and I consider him a brother. He didn't join the FBI after the Army like I did, but he's just as loyal to the cause as I am and the only person in the world I trust with this kind of work.

Plus, I know he'd keep Margaret safe if something were to go down with me.

I pull into the neighborhood, and Margaret starts to stir. As she yawns and stretches her arms over her head, her shirt rides up a little, and a sliver of her skin peeks through. A memory of our night together flashes through my mind before I refocus and clear my throat.

"We're here," I say, unbuckling my seat belt and turning off the car. I'll need to steal another one when I leave here.

"Wow. Nice neighborhood for a bachelor," she replies, eyeing the house in front of us.

"He's married, actually." I met Jen after Mike and I got out together. She was Mike's high school sweetheart, and they reconciled over the years when he was in the service. When he was discharged, he snatched her up right away, and I was the best man in his wedding.

"Oh. I assumed he was like you, I guess." She looks to me, and I shake my head.

"Nope, he doesn't work for the government anymore."

We don't say anything else as we climb out of the car. She grabs her bag and slings it over her shoulder then I lead her up to the door. I notice the sun beginning to rise and hope I'm not about to wake anyone up.

We wait for someone to answer the door, and I see Margaret nervously shuffle beside me. "Don't be nervous. It's gonna be okay." I grab her hand, and she lets me.

"I'm not nervous." She bites her lip but continues to fidget. Rolling her eyes, she looks at me and says, "I'm about to pee myself if I don't find a bathroom in like one minute."

A chuckle escapes me when I realize she's serious. I should have known nothing would faze her at this point and her biggest concern would be making it to the bathroom in time.

The door opens then and Mike is there, looking worn out and tired, and he gives me a shocked look. "Holy shit!" His grin widens as he pulls me into the house, and I drag Margaret behind me. He wraps me in a hug and I groan, my wound stretching with his intense hug. "What the fuck are you doing here?" He gives me a look and helps himself, lifting my shirt and eyeing the haphazard bandage I've got on it. "Dude, you get into some shit?"

"Yeah, it's a…long story." I pull Margaret forward. "This is Margaret. You got a bathroom she can use?"

She pinches me. "Hi, it's nice to meet you." She takes Mike's hand and gives him a smile. "Excuse Mr. Rude over here—he's not house-trained, I guess."

Mike laughs and points her toward the hall bathroom. She rushes off and he ushers me into the kitchen, starting a pot of coffee as I take a seat at the breakfast bar. Mike's house is seriously nice. He's worked hard to get where he is, and his job in construction keeps him busy and well compensated. I've kept tabs on him even when I couldn't communicate with him, and though I was initially bummed he didn't want to stick with me and go into the FBI, I was happy he'd found his place.

"Man, it's been some time."

"It has, and I'm sorry about that. Work has kept me away," I say, following his movements with my gaze. He knows I can't tell him everything, which is why he's my only friend. He understands.

"Ah, that's all right. So, got yourself a girl there?"

I hesitate, wishing I were here under different circumstances. For the first time, I wish I could say I did have myself a girl and was just here to visit, though I can't decide if that's because of the girl or just my subconscious working its way in.

"Uh, no. Not exactly." I take my time telling Mike as much as I can. At some point Margaret enters and takes the stool next to mine. Mike pours her some coffee, and I get distracted by the grateful smile she gives him. My admiration gets cut short when Mike's wife, Jen, enters the kitchen with a baby propped on her hip.

I hop up and give her a hug around the baby. "Holy sh—oops. Uh, I mean, when did this happen?"

Jen laughs. "This is Benny. He happened about five months ago." Mike comes around and takes his son, gives Jen a kiss, and then holds Benny's little hand out to me. I grab it and can't help the smile that takes over.

"He's adorable," Margaret says. "I'm Margaret, by the way.

I'm sorry to be intruding like this."

"Oh, don't even worry about it! It's about time Liam found a good one!" Jen laughs, and I look up to see the smile slide from Margaret's face and a look of realization cross her features, followed by a short scoff that only I can hear. It's in that time that I remember I never bothered to tell her my real name, which wouldn't be a big deal except for her serious trust issues.

Margaret just shakes her head at Jen. "Oh, we're not together. Definitely not." She shyly reaches over for her coffee and sips. Jen apologizes and offers to make everyone some breakfast, then Margaret excuses herself and walks back through the front door.

"Dude," Mike says, getting my attention. "You didn't tell her your real name, did you?" Being that he's my only friend, he also knows the techniques—or lack thereof—I use when getting a date, including my alias. "Damn man. Go out there and make that better."

I reluctantly make my way outside. She's sitting on one of the chairs on the porch, staring off into the distance.

"Hey, you probably shouldn't sit out here," I tell her.

She turns to give me a frosty look, and I rock back on my heels. "When were you going to tell me your name isn't Dan? I feel like an idiot."

Sighing, I try to find a way to phrase what I want to say. "I'm not sure... I've been a little more concerned with keeping us alive."

"Oh my God! You couldn't take two seconds to say, 'Oh

by the way, I've been lying the entire time and my real name is actually Liam'? How hard is that?" She shakes her head. "I slept with you, for crying out loud! Didn't that mean anything?" She looks like she regrets saying that, and I raise my hands and search for a defense, but she continues talking before I come up with one. "If you think I'm staying here with them, with this family, and putting them in danger, you're crazy."

I open my mouth to reply, to tell her Mike is more capable than anyone I know, but she doesn't let me get in a word edgewise.

"And if you won't take me with you"—she stands and puts her chest right up to mine, trying to intimidate me—"I'll go somewhere myself. I'll take a bus, and I'll leave."

I don't say anything. I stare into her eyes and see the fire burning there, see the conviction that tells me she's dead serious. It's hot. I want nothing more than to crush my mouth to hers and say Screw it to the reasoning in my head about why that would not help our situation.

But I don't. Getting more emotionally attached to her would be a train wreck on top of an already difficult predicament. Instead, I say, "You can't go somewhere alone. You'll end up dead."

"Then I'm going with you."

Rubbing my jaw, I look out over the field beside Mike and Jen's house; they don't have neighbors on that side, just open space. "Fine. You can come, but you're going to learn how to shoot a gun. I'm not having you out there unprotected."

For the first time since we left the motel, I see the vulnerability she carries shining in her eyes, but then she straightens up and it's gone. "Deal."

She reaches for my hand and I set mine in hers, smirking at her false confidence, both impressed and terrified this chick is gonna get me killed. I didn't exactly care about her qualifications for shooting when I thought the only reason I would interact with her was to fulfill a need.

Here's to hoping she's a natural sharpshooter.

9

MARGARET

"IT'S HEAVIER THAN I thought."

"That's what she said."

I look up to see a smirk across Dan—er, Liam's lips and roll my eyes at his joke. "That's immature."

The smirk stays in place. "Then why are you smiling?"

"Now's not the time for Michael Scott humor." I let the lie pass through my lips—it's always time for a Michael Scott joke.

"Come on, that show is a classic." I quirk an eyebrow at his remark. "What? There's a surprising amount of downtime in my line of work." He gives me one of his killer grins, and I try to rein in the tingling that shoots down my spine at the sight.

I clear my throat and straighten up, pointing the gun at the wall. Mike has a man cave in the basement of their house, and it's also where he keeps his guns, along with a large TV and a setup that looks like it belongs in the office of S.T.A.R. Labs. It's seriously geeky down here.

We head outside, where I get the chance to fire the gun a few times. Before I do that, though, Liam makes me put on his sunglasses. I highly doubt I'll have time for eye protection if I get in a situation where I have to actually use this thing, but I don't say a word to try to stave off another argument.

I aim at the pop can he set far off into the field. The neighborhood they live in is small, and according to Mike, no one cares if you use this field for anything.

"Okay, just breathe out a long breath, keep your eye on your target, and pull." Liam's voice is hushed and he stands behind my right shoulder. I try not to feel intimidated that he's watching me shoot for the first time.

I pull the trigger and the gun rocks me back a step. I look at the can, and it hasn't moved an inch. Groaning, I turn my head to Liam, keeping the gun facing forward. "I missed." My voice is pouty, and he smirks before he nods at the can again.

"Yeah, well, it was only your first try. Give it another go."

I follow his instructions and keep shooting until the magazine is empty. I thought that'd be the hardest part, but then he makes me reload it, and pushing the bullets into it is more difficult than anything I've done yet. It takes me an embarrassingly long time.

"You'll get better with practice," Liam says, and he shows me two more magazines he pulled out of the backpack we've been carrying. "But that's why I keep several guns loaded at the same time, and you will too. There's no time to load in the middle of a situation. Just push the release like I taught you and reload. I want you to do it now."

I follow his previous instructions, releasing the mag, letting it fall to the ground, and shoving another one in, quickly aiming at the can and letting off another few rounds. It's such a weird sensation, and my adrenaline is definitely coursing through my veins.

I'm surprised by how much I love shooting the gun. It's actually kind of fun.

"I think you've got the basics down. In the event you ever have to fire it, just remember not to hesitate. Even if you think you might not be in danger, consider that, in this situation, you're always in danger." He's so close to me now, and his voice is rough.

"That doesn't sound healthy."

"Healthy or not, it might just save your life someday."

I nod at his serious look. He's taking this training thing seriously, and I have a need to impress him coursing through me. It's climbing as steadily as the urge to do something else with him, but I have a feeling our time for that is long past, no matter how much I wish that weren't true.

Our eyes hold steady and his hand reaches for me, coming in contact with the gun and brushing his finger over the back of my thumb. That small, seemingly insignificant touch leaves me reeling, wanting more, and I can't help the goose bumps that scatter across my arms.

"Hey, Mo!" Jen's voice breaks through our tension and we both blink, the moment over. Liam turns away from me and starts reloading the magazine on the gun. I should do it, but I'm almost afraid to get too close to him. Instead, I turn my attention to Jen coming over to where we're standing in the field.

It's best I don't let my emotions get involved with the hot FBI agent. Too late, says the little voice in my head. I tell it to go suck a lemon.

"I got the stuff for your hair," she says when she reaches us. The saint that she is, she offered to help me make the fire on my head look more human, and I immediately took her up on it. "We should get started before dinner."

"Are we good, you think?" I look to Liam and feel like I'm seeking his approval. For what, I'm not sure yet.

"Yeah, go," he says, dismissing me with a wave of his hand.

I nod and follow after her, leaving Liam to his surly thoughts. He's been standoffish ever since we got to Mike's this morning, but I don't know if it's just having to have real human interactions or something else completely.

I sit in the chair Jen has set up just off the kitchen. As it turns out, she's a great person who doesn't care that we're in some sort of trouble; she immediately just wanted to help us out. That's not something you come across very often, and it's a wonderful change of pace.

She was a hairstylist before she decided she wanted to be a full-time mom, and now she's about to become my savior if she can fix the mess on my head.

"Are you sure you can get it to a normal color?" I ask, nerves creeping into my voice.

"I'm sure we can get it close. I can't promise perfection, but it'll be better, I swear." She holds out her pinky, and I link mine with it as I laugh.

Jen fills me in on her and Mike's relationship, and it sounds like a perfect romance. They always knew they loved another and wanted to make it work. A bout of envy hits me, and I scold myself for being so petty. Here they are putting their lives on the line to help us, and I'm jealous that she found a guy who loves her without condition.

"It sounds amazing. I hope I find that someday."

"Oh, you will. Just give Liam some time," she whispers, a conspiratorial smile on her face. "He's just stubborn."

"Oh, no. He won't be a boyfriend for me." I pause, my mind wandering to our first date and the somewhat magical night we shared—a night that feels like it was ages ago. "He's already made sure of that," I say, not meaning to come off sounding bitchy, but he's told me he doesn't do girlfriends. He's an FBI agent, one in some serious trouble—what kind of relationship could we ever have?

"Because he's in the FBI? You don't do that?" I'm losing her. One look at her face shows me she's ready to fight for Liam.

"No, no. Well, I mean, I would, but he doesn't want that."

"Did he say that?"

"Yes."

"He specifically said, 'Margaret, I will never be your boyfriend.'?" She gives me a pointed look.

"Uh, well not in that way, but yeah, kind of." I almost blurt out, We slept together and then when I woke up, he was gone. Not exactly boyfriend material, am I right? I keep my mouth shut, though, not because I think she'd argue, but because I feel a small sliver of shame for having fallen for a man after one date only to have him sneak out the next morning.

Jen gives me a secret smile then nods her head. "Okay. We'll see." Her voice holds a lilt of song, but before I can say anything more, Mike walks in with Benny.

"Someone wants Mama." He hands her over to Jen, who is still fixing the orange on my head, and gives her a kiss. Jen asks him to get a bottle, and I stare at the adorable chubby baby in her arms. My staring is noticed, and Jen asks if I want to hold him.

"Oh, that's all right. I've never held a baby before." I wave my hand at her and smile.

"Nonsense. It's easy, here." I don't get to protest before she places him in my arms, and he looks at me with a toothless grin then giggles. I smile instinctively and grab the hand he holds out.

"Boy, you are cute, aren't you?" I say, laughing when he garbles back at me.

"Here, you mind giving him this? I'll finish up here." Jen hands me his bottle and watches as I get him adjusted, and he immediately starts sucking it down.

I don't take my eyes off him for a second while Jen finishes my hair and teaches me the art of burping a baby. Benny doesn't even fuss once in my arms, and I can't help but feel a sense of calm settle over me as I stare at him.

"Hey, guys." I look up as Liam enters the room, and we lock eyes. He sees me holding Benny and smiles at us. "Getting baby fever over there, Mo?"

I laugh and shake my head. "Who wouldn't with this cutie?"

"Okay, time to rinse. Boys, take the little one and let me work my magic."

"Yes ma'am." Mike takes Benny from me and I release a sigh. I didn't even worry about my hair that entire time, the baby a nice distraction from my concern that I'd be stuck with only one career choice after this little adventure is over. Who doesn't want to join the circus though, right?

When I'm thoroughly rinsed, I tell Jen how I'd like her to style it, and she gives me a serious look. "Are you sure?"

"Yes. Liam went through the trouble, so I don't want all the effort to go to waste."

"Okay, you're the boss."

I stare into the bathroom mirror and sigh. It's short, like above my shoulders short, barely grazing the tops of them, and the light color makes me look like a completely different person. The panic in my chest seizes me and I wait for it to take control, but then I tell myself to get over it. If I want to stick with Liam, I need to have something to disguise me from what these guys following us know, and they know a long-haired brunette.

A knock at the door startles me for a moment. "Mo, dinner's ready." Liam's voice comes through softly, and I wonder what he's going to think.

No time like the present.

I open the door and stare at him, not saying anything, just letting him take it in.

"Wow." His eyebrows rise and he gives me a soft smile. "You cut it all off."

"I did."

He reaches forward and touches it with his fingers. "It looks nice. I liked it long, but this is just as good."

"Thanks," I say, feeling shy. An uneasy feeling niggles at me, and I wish we could go back to cracking jokes at each other like the first night, wish we could go back to the easy and comforting feeling I felt on our date, and after our date, and every minute in between—but we can't. No matter how I feel, he's made it pretty clear that I shouldn't expect anything from him.

"Hopefully when I get back to my life, guys won't find the new hair too manly." I chuckle then move past him out into the hallway to head to the dining room. "You comin'?"

He hesitates for a minute then smiles, following my lead, and I try to convince myself that I can date other guys after this whole damn thing. Maybe next time he won't be a secret spy with bad guys in hot pursuit.

My smile falls at the thought. That would make my life easier, safer, and yet I feel like I would be losing something important.

10

LIAM

WE LEFT MIKE and Jen's place around eleven last night and started driving. After an hour, we found another car and continued on the way to the headquarters of G3. One of the only two handlers I have ever been in communication with, Rafael, was the one to shoot me, and even though I made sure he didn't make it back to his boss with my identity in hand, there is always a chance they still know who I am. As such, I'll have to play it extra safe.

We'll camp out nearby until I can find solid evidence to send to the FBI. They don't trust me anymore, and granted, I haven't spoken to them in quite a while, so it's a valid concern on their part. It wouldn't be the first time someone got too deep into the crimes and just switched sides, deciding this life was better than being the spy who took them out. The money was better, the work easier, and I could understand the reasoning, but I wasn't a bad guy. I was a good one, and no matter how it happened, I was going make sure these bad guys never got a chance to sell, smell, or touch a drug ever again.

Margaret fell asleep after a couple hours, and the silence fills the car. It's almost strange after being around her for so long. She can't stand the silence, I've noticed, likes to fill it with her chatter. I take the time to think, to figure out where I slipped up and got her caught up in this mess.

I was tracking G3 through the city when I realized they were stalking a particular person, not meeting with buyers like they normally did. They were too focused, too anxious, and I knew I was caught when I discovered the person they were following was Margaret.

They knew who I was, or were at the very least suspicious of me, but what tipped them off? I can't pinpoint a time where I could have given myself away, but now I am a bad guy on both sides of the fence. While I don't really care what that means for me, it does put Margaret in danger, which was the only reason I went to her and took her with me. She couldn't be left alone because if they got her, they'd use that against me.

As hard as my exterior seems, I knew I wouldn't be able to let her go with them, because they would kill her without hesitating.

I feel like I am barely keeping a grasp on myself, shoved into this new territory of having to watch over someone else while trying to stay on top of my mission, of ending this tortuous job I've been stuck in for years. One date was all it took for me to develop feelings for her, something I never, ever do, and if I think back to that night where I decided to let go of all my control and let myself be with her, despite all it's led to, I can't say I wouldn't do exactly the same thing again. The only difference might be the morning after, if I allowed myself to do that, if I could allow myself to be with her in some real sense, which I couldn't.

I still can't.

I need to sort through a plan, one that makes Margaret feel like she's a part of it. She puts us at even more risk, but she is stubborn, which is both infuriating and fascinating. Not wanting to be bossed around and pushing back makes her interesting.

Her telling me she was going to set off on her own without me was the tipping point for me. My protectiveness kicked in, and I wanted—no, I needed to protect her. This is my fault, and I have to fix it.

I just need to plot out exactly how this has to play out. I have to figure out what G3 is planning, who they are using to angle against me and what they know about me. Ricardo is the only other man I ever saw or spoke with whenever I purchased product. It's how they operate to keep from being infiltrated: every person who buys has only one or two specific handlers. Ricardo had quite a few clients, and there are dozens like him doing the same job.

I don't know how deep Ricardo is in, or if he is even alive. I also don't know if Rafael has been talking to him about what he thinks, about who I am.

He never knew who I was or that I was reporting to the FBI about them, but I did think he was getting suspicious, acting nervous around me whenever we'd meet up for a deal, so I slowed communication with the FBI because I didn't want to give myself away.

It wasn't easy. For the last year, I have been completely on my own, using burner phones for everything, even that stupid app, and not having any contact with my family. Admittedly, that was the hardest part of the whole thing.

Now, as I drive us into another dangerous situation, I look over at Margaret peacefully sleeping and wonder how I'm going to get us out of this alive.

"This is it?" Margaret asks, leaning in to look over me. A waft of her scent infiltrates my nose, and I keep my hands down at my sides. We've finally made it back into the city, and we're a few blocks away from where G3 sets up, watching and waiting.

Truthfully, I'm not sure what they know, and I'm also not sure what I'm going to do with them when I can finally take them all the way out.

My priorities have shifted slightly due to the woman who is currently leaning over my lap to get a look at the building. My hands twitch, wanting to touch her again the way I did before, but I refrain, knowing that's the fastest way to get us both in trouble.

"This is it. I've got to make a move, but I wanted to be sure they hadn't changed locations yet." I finally decided the only way to make this happen was to send Ricardo a message and set up a meeting. That way I can find out, one, if he is alive, and two, what they're after.

"What move are we making?" Margaret asks without looking away.

"We aren't making a move. I am," I say pointedly. She turns to glare at me, but I don't back down. "You are going to stay somewhere far away and safe."

She huffs out a breath. "How many times do I have to tell you I'm not going anywhere without you?"

"You don't seem to understand how dangerous this is," I say, looking at her face. She's not someone who hides her emotions; they all play out across her face plain as day. She looks pissed right now, but there's a vulnerability there as well. "I promise what I'm doing will be quick. You won't be alone for long. Plus, you're my backup. If I don't return, you call the only number in that phone." I nod to the one in the cup holder that I gave her for emergencies.

"I'm not afraid," she says, puffing out her chest. My eyes are immediately drawn to that spot, and I can't even help myself. Margaret smacks me in the arm and I look up, giving her a small smirk. "Fine. I'll stay away, but this is the only time I'm allowing it."

I smile at her 'allowing' me to do my job. "Trust me, Margaret."

She doesn't look reassured, but I don't let it bother me. Margaret doesn't know the half of what I've done in this life. She was thrust into it without warning, yanked out of her average life working in retail.

I knew what she did before I met up with her—I never meet up with anyone without finding out who they know, where they work, and what they are after.

She doesn't reply to what I say, just folds her arms across her chest and sighs, turning away. I can tell she's still upset, but she's not going to tell me she is. She's a woman who knows exactly how to manipulate the situation to make it harder than it needs to be.

I should have left her back at Mike's. Would've been easier.

We drive out of town a little ways, looking for a place to crash. I send Margaret into a motel office to get us a room, knowing we'll have to switch things up so we won't be as easy to track.

Each grabbing a bag, we haul them into the drab room. I take stock of everything and immediately get to setting myself up for the night. Once I send a message to Ricardo, it will go down rather quickly. He's never made me wait long before meeting up.

"I'm going to freshen up," Margaret says. Her tone is flat, but I don't know, nor do I have the time to know what's bothering her right now. She probably has a pretty long list at this point.

I'm setting up my laptop when I hear a bloodcurdling scream coming from the bathroom. My instincts kick in quickly and, clutching my Glock 19, I run over and bust open the door. Margaret has the water running in the shower and is standing on the edge of the tub.

She's also buck naked.

"What's wrong?" I ask in a huff, not sensing any real danger.

"There's a spider!"

"A spider?" I ask incredulously.

"It was huge, okay!" she shoots back defensively, hopping—yes, hopping—off the edge of the tub and turning toward me. Like she is in a fog, she slowly realizes what's happening, and I don't look away.

We stand there staring at each other for a few minutes, me wondering why I'm restraining myself, and her…well…

"Oh my God! Get out! Get out!" She rushes me and shoves me out the door—naked.

God how I missed those curves. Only one night with her and she's the only one I've been able to think of for the last few weeks.

The door slams in my face and I gather myself. "I'm sorry, Mo, but to be fair," I say through the door, "you did sound like you were being murdered."

She doesn't say anything, but I can still hear the water running. Then I hear the sound of her groan when she comes to her senses.

"I'm sorry. Should have thought about it, I guess."

We don't say anything and I lean against the doorjamb, waiting for something else. All I hear is the shower curtain rustling around, and I know she's done with this conversation.

I resist a sigh and head back to continue getting ready. My mind needs to be on my job, but all I can think about is Margaret's body, her plush curves and her soft, supple skin under my rough hands.

Being a dude is hard—literally.

11

MARGARET

WITH MORTIFICATION FILLING every inch of me, I exit the bathroom and find Liam sitting at the small desk, if that's what you'd consider the foot-wide table that looks like it might fall over if you breathe on it too hard. This motel is not one that would get five stars from me on Yelp, but in a pinch, it works.

The smell alone makes me want to gag, but I don't complain, mostly because I know if I complain, Liam will use it against me in making me stay away from him, which is not what I want. Until this is over, I can't leave his side. Otherwise I'll be looking over my shoulder every second, waiting for the other shoe to drop—at least that's what I tell myself, ignoring any other possibility for why I'd want to stay near him.

"What are you doing?" I ask softly, ignoring what went on thirty minutes ago. I was grateful I remembered to bring my clothes into the bathroom with me. He's already seen enough.

"I'm just looking at the address Ricardo sent me."

"Ricardo?"

He looks at me then, sees I'm fully clothed, and gives me a small nod. "Yeah, he's my contact with G3. He used to work for the Mexicans but switched sides a few years ago, better money for him with the Russians."

"Right. So, when are you guys meeting?"

"Tonight."

My stomach flips and nerves fill me. Worry gnaws at me when I think of him meeting with potentially dangerous people, but I tell myself I shouldn't get attached. Liam is someone who doesn't allow his personal feelings to dictate how he acts or what he does, and I need to do the same…even though it goes against everything I stand for.

"I want to go with you." I try again, setting my chin high, holding a pose I hope looks confident.

He replies immediately. "No." Standing in front of me, he holds himself a few inches away, and his height has him looming over me. I probably look like a toddler compared to him height-wise, but I stand tall, not letting him intimidate me.

"Liam, I can help you."

He sighs and sets his hands on his hips. "I believe you think that"—I scoff my offense—"but this isn't something you can help with. For one, if I suddenly show up with someone else, they'll immediately think I work for someone. Second, this is too dangerous for you to be part of. You staying here is better for both of us—I need to focus."

I relax slightly. I didn't think about being a distraction for him. Considering how dangerous this supposedly is, I decide not to fight him on it for now. I do, however, ask myself why it is that I want to put myself at risk for a man I barely know.

It's not long before Liam leaves to meet his contact, and horrible scenarios shoot through my head as I think of him out there alone, wondering who will show up. If they know he's FBI, there's a good chance they'll kill him.

A slithering sense of panic slides into my thoughts and I pack up the small backpack I brought along with me. It's not much, so it takes no time at all. Liam left me with a gun, and using what I learned when we practiced, I check the chamber, making sure it's loaded, and put it in the back of my pants.

It's not exactly comfortable, but it'll have to do. I have to be able to protect myself, just in case.

A knock at the door startles me, and I look at the clock on the bedside table. Liam left twenty minutes ago, but he wouldn't knock. I stay as quiet as possible, throwing my backpack over my shoulders, and then I grab my gun. A quick glance shows Liam left his bag behind, so I grab it as well.

I search the room and look for an escape.

There's a window near the back of the room and I turn to inspect it. Since it's an older motel, it doesn't locked closed like others do. I open it quickly as another knock comes at the door. My pulse skyrockets as I push the screen out of the window and throw Liam's bag out then quickly fall through it with an oomph.

And by that, I mean I fall on my face.

I shake it off as I hop to my feet and turn around. I take the extra seconds to close the window, hoping it won't be obvious that I was there. Scooping up Liam's bag, I keep my body bent and run the length of the motel to get a look around the other side.

There are two people standing in front of the door to our room, both wearing black, and I can see the distinct shape of a gun in a holster on the hip of the man closest to me. My defenses immediately rise.

Would they help us if they knew the truth? Liam said they didn't trust him because he stopped checking in, but maybe they would if they understood the situation.

I make a decision and step out of the shadows, waiting to see if they notice. They don't, and I instantly change my mind about talking to them. But, before I can slip away, they notice I'm there. I try to walk away as calmly as possible, but they still start after me.

"Hey, you!" I hear one of them yell, and I start running. This town is in the middle of nowhere, and there's basically just the motel, a gas station, and a couple of rundown buildings.

I keep up the pace, grateful for the Converse I chose to wear instead of something that would make it impossible to run in. They yell at me to stop again, and I can feel them gaining on me, especially when a bullet whizzes past my body. Now they're trying to kill me?

I'm still holding my gun, so I risk a look back and aim it behind me. I don't take too great of care as I fire off three shots, hoping they hit someone. I feel a nasty bit of gratification when I hear a yell, and I keep running.

Once I've gone some distance, I give myself a minute, my sides pinching from the running, something my body is not very good at. When I look behind me, I see they haven't followed me this far, and I quickly hop down into a ditch on the side of the road. It's at least four feet deep, and there are tumble weeds all around it. I gather some of them and lie down, covering myself and then staying as still as possible.

The irony of me lying in a ditch doesn't escape me, but desperate times calls for desperate measures.

I briefly think about calling the number Liam gave me but decide against it, knowing he's out there meeting with his contact and not wanting to distract him, and also not wanting to make any noise that would attract attention.

I wonder if I seriously injured that guy, but since he was

trying to kill me, the guilt doesn't linger.

The dark encases me from all sides, and I see how beautiful it is out here without all the city lights taking away from the stars. If I didn't know people were trying to kill me, I would lie back and enjoy the view above me, but the fear of being caught keeps me stiff and alert.

My gun sits on my chest as I listen for any sign of movement. When I hear a car coming, I practically stop breathing. A beam of light shoots across the ditch, and I wait.

"Come out now, we don't want to hurt you." It sounds like the man is talking through a loudspeaker of some sort. Don't want to hurt me? Um, the bullet zipping past my head told a different story, bud.

I don't move. I don't breathe. I practice round breathing like I did in high school band. Never did I think that was going to come in handy.

The light is right on top of me and I clench my eyes shut. It doesn't really help me hide, but I can't stop the instinctive reaction. The light moves again, going past my head and farther down the ditch.

I stay there for a long time. I can't tell you how long it really is, but I wait and wait for them to come back. I hear other cars pass me by, but I don't dare try to get out until it's been enough time for them to be long gone.

I'm sure they're still searching for me, so for my safety, I stay nice and low and creep my way back toward the motel.

I pray Liam is back and doesn't think I left, but with how long I've been gone, it could be possible that he thinks I ditched him. My stomach knots as I hope he didn't leave me behind.

It takes me a long time to get back to the motel. I still practice caution, aware that they could be anywhere still searching for me. Knowing I won't be able to collapse on the bed has me growling in frustration, but I try to put it out of my head. I mean, considering I'm not dead, I should be grateful.

Eyeing the surrounding area, I see that no one seems to be occupying the parking lot. Our door is closed and left alone now, and I wonder if they went in. I walk around the back of the building in case they came back and are waiting for one of us to show our face. Again, I go to the window, and I nearly cry with happiness when I see Liam through it.

When I gently knock on the window, he spins around, gun pointed at me, and I duck. No doubt he would shoot first and ask questions later.

The window creaks open and he peeks his head out.

"What happened?" His voice is a mix of anger and concern, his brows pinched together as he hops out the window. Before I can answer his question, he wraps me in a hug and squeezes me to his strong chest. I can hear his heartbeat thumping against my ear, feel his lips touch my head in a kiss, and it takes me a moment to overcome the surprise from that and answer his question.

"Some people…" I try to swallow down the sudden emotion I'm feeling. I pull away to look into his eyes, and he keeps his hands on my shoulders, like he's reassuring himself that I'm okay. "Two men came. They knocked on the door, but I didn't know who they were, so I hopped out here." He looks livid as I continue the story, hissing a curse when I tell him about shooting one of them. "You're not mad I shot him, right?" I'd never considered that it could be someone he knew if they were FBI.

"Fuck no. I'm happy you did that. I'm pissed that they found you." He pushes his hand through his hair then abruptly grabs mine and starts pulling me toward the parking lot, where he doesn't hesitate to break into a SUV and hotwire it.

I jump into the passenger seat without a second thought. I shot someone today—stealing a car is basically nothing in comparison, right?

I breathe my first real breath in a long time once we're on the road, and I can't decide if it's because I'm with Liam or just because I'm away from the people who were chasing me, though my suspicions are that it's the former.

"Where are we going?"

"Somewhere safer."

I really look at him for the first time since I got back and realize he's got dried blood on his face. I try to stay calm as I ask, "What happened with Ricardo?"

Liam scoffs. "Ricardo wasn't there." He lets out a deep sigh. "Well, his head was. His body, not so much."

I feel the blood drain from my face and I roll down my window. I don't puke this time, but I do breathe in like it's the only remaining fresh air on the planet. The image in my head is grotesque, and I can't imagine what really went down.

"Sorry, Mo." Liam rubs my shoulder, and I try to calm down just to enjoy the affection I'm getting, which probably makes me pathetic.

"It's fine," I whisper, interlacing my fingers with his when he offers. It's nearly instinctive, and I'm grateful for his touch.

"I'm lucky I got out of there."

"Who were the people coming after me? Should I have talked to them?" I look to Liam. He takes a minute to answer, and I wonder if I did the wrong thing by hiding.

"No, you did good." He takes a turn, getting onto a highway. "Where did you hide?"

I tell him my innovative hiding spot, and I think it's the first time I've seen him display admiration when it comes to me, at least since our first date anyway.

"That was smart. I'm glad you thought of it. If they'd gotten to you, I don't know what they would have done. I don't know what I would have done."

I keep my reply to myself. I don't have a good one, not knowing who was chasing me, who Liam was meeting up with, or how the hell any of this could end well for us.

"We're gonna drive for a while. You might need to get some sleep now while you can."

I don't need him to tell me twice. I lean the seat back and finally breathe easy knowing I'm safe—for the time being, that is.

12

LIAM

THE ROAD FEELS long before us, and I have no doubt I'll need to hijack a different car before we make it too far. Finding out we were already located and not knowing who found us puts an uneasy feeling in my stomach. I can't let us be compromised again.

Whoever was there, I'll find them eventually, and they won't be pleased when I do.

Margaret becoming vulnerable like she was when I purposefully left her behind to keep her out of danger scares the shit out of me. Hearing her tell me she had to shoot someone makes me glad we took the time to work on shooting before we got to this point. What if we hadn't?

Don't think about it.

She took care of herself when she had no prior experience. Being able to think on your feet when you're in a situation like that is imperative.

The other issue I'm dealing with is Ricardo, or the lack thereof. When I showed up to the meeting, a man I hadn't met before was there. He introduced himself as Viktor, and I knew of him already because I'd seen him act as the right hand of their top honcho, Anton, who was here on a travel visa, running this entire thing. We had a lot on him, but we wanted enough to put him away for good. That came to an abrupt end when they moved their location at the last minute, which took another six months for me to uncover.

Viktor knew I wasn't who I said I was. He didn't know Liam, but he knew Dan wasn't who I said he was. Fortunately, he still didn't know who I worked for, which gave me a little power, but since he had even an inkling, it meant I was going to have to be stealth about getting them shut down.

I sent a nice little message to Anton in the form of a few of Viktor's missing fingers. All they needed to know was that I was dangerous, that I wasn't afraid to get dirty and do what needed to be done.

That said, the FBI hunting me down wasn't going to help things. According to them, I was a huge risk now, and they don't take risks lightly.

I lost contact when I moved from one location to the next, but the trouble is, G3 is moving again. I recognize the signs this time around. They're skittish, worried, rushing from place to place, and multiple trucks showed up a couple of weeks ago, meaning they need to transport something big. I'm not sure where they're headed yet, but I can get in touch with someone who might know.

Using contacts in Las Vegas, where they are headed, is a risk, but it is necessary. Contacts I had a year ago could have changed positions by now. It's only a matter of time before everyone I know is going to be on a different side of the fight.

That's the nature of this business.

The only thing I know for sure is that no matter how this plays out, my main objective has shifted. It isn't just about taking out a hated drug cartel, but also protecting the feisty woman in the seat next to me.

Because she didn't deserve any of this.

It's still fairly early in the day when I wake Margaret up to move cars. She doesn't say anything as I hotwire another vehicle, and I wonder if there is an imaginary board in her head where she tallies the strikes against me. It isn't in my nature to care what others think, but even as far gone as I must be in her eyes after everything she's heard and seen, I want to be someone she can respect and trust.

I doubt any of that will ever happen, because when it is life or death, these are the things I have to do in order for us to live through this.

We arrive at another cash motel; it's the only type of place we can go without leaving a trace. I walk in ahead of Margaret, telling her to wait outside while I check out the room, clearing all the spots anyone could hide. Can't be too careful when you're on the run.

"Whew, this is an upgrade. Look." I turn to see that Margaret has come in, and I smirk at her sarcasm. "A top and a bottom sheet. This"—she gives me a look full of sass—"is luxury." I can't help the chuckle that escapes me, and she gives me her first smile in a while.

That's one thing that's been unfortunately lacking since everything happened. Our first date was full of her laughter and smiles, and it was the main reason I found her so attractive.

I sit on the bed, the exhaustion washing over me. I've been awake for over forty-eight hours, and it is catching up to me. Some days are like this, but with the added stress over the last couple days, I am pretty spent.

"Uh oh," Margaret mutters. Following her gaze, I see that the patch job we did on my side has started leaking and blood is seeping through onto my white shirt.

"Oh." I pull my shirt over my head. Before I can get up to get my bag that holds extra bandages and a first aid kit, Margaret is back with everything and starts pulling off the old bandage. "You don't have to, Mo. I know it freaks you out."

"It's hard for you. I don't mind." I could stop her. I could make the point that she doesn't handle blood well, that she doesn't need to do this because it's not a big deal, but I don't. I don't because having her help me gives me a strange type of comfort. Feeling her hands on me soothes a burn that hasn't been cooled since the first time I saw her.

I don't say anything as she works. At times when I should be wincing, I don't move. This kind of thing doesn't bother me anymore. I watch as she works diligently around the stitches, cleaning up blood that's stuck to my skin and then carefully placing a new bandage over the wound. I sit and admire her new short hair, which doesn't do a damn thing to hurt her looks. If anything, it makes me want put my hands through it and kiss her.

It's not the first time I've wanted to break the unspoken rule and give her a kiss she'd remember forever, smash my lips to hers and claim her as my own.

She puts the last piece of tape on my skin and sits back on her heels. She's at a good height to bring to life a dream I had after our first date.

Our only date.

She realizes I'm watching her and pauses her movements. Tension fills the air, and I allow my hand to move through her hair. Her eyes flutter closed and I watch as her lips part slightly, all from me putting my hand in her hair. I breathe out a sigh, one of comfort and relief that we've gotten this far, one of worry that I won't be able to protect her. It scares the shit out of me to have her in so much danger.

Using my other hand, I touch her cheek with the tips of my fingers, slowly cupping her jaw, and she rises up until we're eye to eye. I lean forward until I'm nearly touching my lips to hers and wait for her to protest. When she doesn't, I kiss her, savoring the taste I've been dreaming about since the minute I left her lying alone in that bed.

She stands all the way up and I wrap my arms around her waist, lying back on the bed, being careful of my wound. Flipping us so she's underneath me, I hold myself up on one arm and explore with my other hand. I love her body. She's not skinny like some, has something to grab hold of, and I love that about her.

A little moan escapes her and she starts pulling her own shirt up. I waste no time in helping her push it up over her head, reveling in her soft, supple skin under my rough hands.

A voice in the back of my head tells me this is a terrible idea. I know it's a terrible idea, know having a girl like her attached to me is only going to end badly, but ever since Margaret entered my life, something shifted inside me. I suddenly don't want to be alone anymore. I want to know how she is, how her days are. I want that come-home-to-someone life.

Using a quick maneuver, I release her bra, and my breath

literally catches when I get a good look at what I've been missing. I let out a low growl of approval.

She reaches for the button on my jeans, and that's when our bubble is popped by the sound of my burner phone ringing from the depths of my bag.

I pause and look at her. She stares back, waiting for me to make a move. Keep going, or stop and answer the phone.

I groan when I realize there's only one thing I can do, and she covers herself as I hop up to find the ringing device. The only person I gave the number to is Mike, and he wouldn't call if it wasn't serious.

"Yeah," I answer.

"Dude." Mike's voice catches, and I am immediately on high alert.

"What happened, Mike?"

"They took them." His words are full of heartbreak and desperation.

"Took who? What happened?"

"The FBI…they took Jen and Benny."

13

MARGARET

MY GASP CATCHES Liam's attention, and his expression must mirror mine; I can hear Mike's worry through the phone, his voice reflecting his anguish. I can't understand why the FBI would take them. They're supposed to protect families like Mike and Jen.

This is all our fault. We went there and they helped us, and now they're separated.

"Okay, we'll meet you there." Liam turned grave the second he heard what they'd done to his friend.

He and I were so wrapped up in each other, and the feeling of him over my body, touching me like I've been craving

It was something I never thought I'd get to feel again. Getting interrupted made me angry at that phone.

Now I feel horrible for worrying about us when poor Jenny is being held somewhere, isolated, trying not to let her little boy see or feel her fear.

"We're meeting Mike in the morning." He turns from me, and I throw my shirt back on to give myself the semblance of normalcy then walk over to Liam.

"We'll help him," I say, even though I have no idea how we're going to do that. I don't know the first thing about the FBI or how they'll operate in this situation.

"We have to." Liam's voice is low, and I try to think of how to take away his guilt, but I can't. There's nothing I can say that would help him with that.

I decide to change the subject, hoping I can get him to think about taking care of himself just this once. "Let's get some sleep, and we'll see him tomorrow. We'll make a plan." I turn him so I can see his eyes. I level with him, trying to be the strong partner. "We will find them."

Liam nods and allows me to pull him to the bed. I didn't question him getting a room with a single bed, his idea being that it was less suspicious if we shared a bed than if we were separate. He crawls under the sheets and pulls me down with him. A selfish part of me is glad for the comfort I can give him. It's something I've wanted to do all along, and the domestic act of spooning makes me nearly giddy.

When I hear him succumb to sleep, I wonder how long he's had to deal with this stuff alone.

———

The next morning, we hustle through showers and are out the door by five. We're meeting Mike on our way to Nevada, which Liam has finally informed me is our destination. I don't ask how Mike is going to get a flight without leading the FBI directly to us. It's on the tip of my tongue, but I don't want to add stress to the situation.

We arrive at a diner off the highway where Mike is due to meet us. I'm hoping I have time to eat some food before we have to leave and sigh in relief when Liam tells me to order whatever I want. He leaves to go to the bathroom, so I order several things from the menu and sip my coffee as I wait.

Liam chose the corner booth in the restaurant, and I know now that it's because he doesn't like to have his back to the door, which is smart. I'm learning all sorts of self-preservation strategies while being hitched to Liam. I get a feeling I've never had, one of excitement and rightness. This adventure we're on finally makes me feel like there's something I can do in this life, like there's a place I finally belong. I only wish it wasn't currently hurting innocent people. My thoughts turn to Jen and Benny, and I send up a quick prayer that wherever they are, they're safe.

I sit looking around the room, trying not to be obvious

about it. I wonder if I'm doing a good job of that, but it's hard to tell. I note everyone in the café and don't see any suspicious characters. The bell rings above the door and I see a large man enter. I immediately stiffen, my nerves shot from the last few days, and when he turns toward me, I relax only slightly as I realize it's Mike.

He comes toward the booth and I stand, giving him a tight hug before I can think about it being awkward or weird. The man just had his wife and his son taken away, and comfort is the best—and nearly only—thing I can give him right now.

"Sit," I say, gesturing toward the booth. He takes the seat across from me, and I resume my position.

"Where is he?" I wonder if he's purposefully not saying his name. I just nod in the direction he went in, and Liam pops around the corner at that moment and heads our way.

When he sits down, he nods at Mike. I wonder if that's his normal with Mike in public, because it doesn't seem very friendly.

"How you holding up, man?" Liam asks, and I glare at him for his insensitive tone. He's acting like this guy isn't his best friend.

"I'm okay. I've just got to get them back." Mike rubs his hands together, the worry clear in his voice.

The waitress comes and takes his coffee order.

Liam looks Mike over, taking in his appearance. "How'd they know I was there?"

"I don't know, man. I have no idea," Mike says, shaking his head.

"Well, I sure didn't lead them there."

Mike shrugs. "They had to have looked into our past. It's the only way they'd connect you to me."

"Yeah." Liam agrees, but he doesn't sound convinced. "So, where's the wire?" Liam changes his position, and in the span of a second, he looks and sounds dangerous.

"What?" Mike asks, looking at Liam like he's crazy.

"Where is it? You didn't come here for my help. You came here for me. That's why they took Jen. I'm your ticket to getting them back." Liam says it so matter-of-factly that I just sit there stunned.

"Hey, you don't know that," I say to Liam. I want to hit him for accusing his friend of something so horrible.

"You know I'd do anything for you...except give up my family," Mike says, confirming Liam's suspicion.

I gape at Mike. "You gave us up?"

"I had to, Margaret. It's Jen." He looks distraught. "It's my boy...my son."

My expression softens when I see the look on his face. I nod, understanding why he did what he did. Then I look to Liam, wondering how we're going to get out of this. "What do we do?"

"We go." We get up and rush out of the diner. I mourn the food I'm not going to get but try to remember it's my life or my stomach.

Mike chases after us and into the parking lot. "Wait!"

Liam pauses slightly and turns, holding a gun straight at his friend's head.

"Liam!" I scold, my brain taking too long to catch up to what's happening in front of me. I'm worried for myself, but I'm also worried for Jen and her son. "He's helping his family."

Liam looks at me, and we challenge each other for a minute.

"Will you help me?" We both look over at Mike. His eyes are serious as he holds the wire in his hands.

We stare at him; Liam lowers his gun and looks at Mike seriously. He throws the wire to the ground and holds his hands out.

"Get in," Liam replies, and we both follow him to a new truck, our bags over our shoulders as Liam hi-jacks another vehicle.

I'd be annoyed if I wasn't so damn hungry.

I don't know where Liam is taking us, but I don't ask any questions. You can feel the tension pumping through the stolen truck, and I know Mike is losing it over his family. I can't decide if the anger is all directed at Liam, but I don't try to decipher it.

We make our way through Salt Lake City, heading south away from where we were initially headed.

"Aren't we going back?" I ask, my voice the first to break the silence in the few hours we've been in the truck.

"No," Liam answers sharply. I've never had him act short with me, and I stare at his profile, trying to decipher if he's angry or just frustrated at the situation.

I twist in my seat to talk to Mike. Maybe they have an unspoken secret between them, some sort of telepathy that they didn't feel like sharing with me, but I would like to actually know the plan.

"Hey," I say softly, encouraging him to give me his attention. He looks up at me, his eyes haunted, and I immediately want to give him some type of reassurance. The vulnerability on his face slays me, and I think about Jen again, how scared she must be. "Did they say where they're taking them?"

"No," he rasps. "They said they'd contact me once I had Liam." Mike runs a hand over his face and looks out the window. "But I might as well have killed them. They know I threw the wire out."

"You're doing your best, and it will be fine." I'm surprised by how sure I sound. This whole time I've been worried about my own well-being, but when it comes to worrying about someone else, a new sense of confidence settles over me. "We're going to get them back. They'll be okay, Mike."

"We don't even know where they are."

"Yes, we do." Liam speaks up, and we both turn to look at him. His hand is fisting the steering wheel, and he doesn't turn to look at us.

"Where?"

"Moab," he answers, checking a mirror before changing lanes.

"Moab? Why there?"

"There's a safe house, and they wouldn't take them any farther than they needed to. They're using them as leverage."

"Okay, all right." Mike rubs his hands on his jeans and licks his lips, this information seeming to have given him some hope. "But how do you plan on getting them back?"

I look at Liam, wondering the same thing.

"A trade."

"A trade?" I ask, my voice a whisper. My stomach twists, and my gut tells me I'm not going to like what he's hinting at.

"Yeah." He looks at me for the first time since we got into the truck. His eyes tell me all I need to know.

"You're trading me for them?" I ask, my voice rising.

"It's the only way they'll release them. You tell them who you are, what you know, and they'll release Jen for the information."

I feel the tears that threaten to spill down my cheeks as I stare at Liam. He doesn't give me his eyes, but his hands squeeze the steering wheel; it's the only emotion he shows. My heart breaks all over again when I realize he's doing this for his friend. I hate every minute of it, but their bond outweighs the one we've formed, and he's making a choice.

"Dude, there has to be another way," Mike says, his voice tense. He doesn't look at me, and I know he's on the fence about this: his family or me, a stranger.

He should choose his family.

"It's okay, Mike." My answer is automatic. Saving Jen and that little baby will be worth it if I can do it. It's not the fact that I'm putting myself on the line; it's the fact that Liam was so willing to do it for me.

I don't speak the rest of the way; I don't know what I'd say even if I wanted to talk to him. He's betrayed me by not talking to me about it, by not even considering another option.

I shouldn't have trusted him to begin with.

Thinking back to being at Mike and Jen's, I know I should have left then. I shouldn't have even thought for a second that this man would protect me, and I know, I know I shouldn't have opened my heart to him either.

We stop at a gas station in the middle of nowhere. It's much the same as the one by the motel where the FBI—or whoever it was—initially tried to pick me up, where I shot someone.

Should've let them take me then, all the stealth hiding and shooting someone wasted.

I grab my bag, make sure the gun Liam gave me is loaded, and throw open the door to the truck.

Mike and Liam both get out and meet me on my side of the vehicle.

"All you have to do is walk down the road that way." Liam points in the right direction and shrugs as if this doesn't affect me whatsoever. "They'll pick you up once you trigger the warning system. They won't hurt you."

I stare at him and wait, for something, for anything…and I see it. It's brief, but I do see it—the tick of his jaw as his teeth clench. He's holding himself back, hiding behind a wall to keep any emotion he might feel at bay.

I don't answer him, and I'm careful to keep my face blank.

"Thank you, Mo," Mike says. I can tell he's genuinely worried but grateful that I'm willing to do this for his family.

"Make sure to hug your family extra tight when you see 'em," I reply, and he surprises me by giving me a hug.

I toss my bag over my shoulder, keeping the gun in my hand, and start to walk in the direction Liam told me to go.

"Margaret." His hoarse voice sounds from behind me, and I turn to meet his eyes. They look determined, but if I stare long enough, vulnerability comes through.

"What?" I wanted to sound firm, hard, even, but my voice comes out as barely a whisper.

His hand reaches for mine and grasps it tightly in his before I can think to pull away.

I wait for him to answer, to give me some kind of inkling that this hurts him as much as it hurts me. When he opens his mouth, though, there's none of that, and I wish he hadn't said anything at all. "Be safe."

I open my mouth to reply but then realize I don't have any words to offer. Settling on a nod, I turn away so he doesn't see the tears that break free.

The air is slightly humid, and a trickle of sweat falls down my forehead. I don't bother wiping it away, both of my hands gripping the weapon in front of me like a shield. I search the pitch black, looking in every direction for a sign. When I look back at the gas station, I see one standing figure and no truck. Liam already took off, not wanting to get caught himself.

It takes a long time, probably an hour, before I must trigger a system like he told me I would. Headlights come from the darkness, heading in my direction, and I move off to the side, waiting to see what will happen. I keep the gun low, waiting.

The SUV skids to a stop beside me and two men jump out of the truck. "Drop the weapon!" one of them shouts, but I don't flinch. I do as he says, seeing as he has his own drawn on me and I'm guessing he has better aim than I do.

"Are you Margaret Davis?" the driver asks, and I nod. The man, who seems to like yelling at me, comes and grips me by the arm, pulling me toward the back door of the SUV. He doesn't say anything, and I crawl in obediently.

The only good thing that can come from this is if they send me home and Jen gets back to Mike.

"Where are you taking me?" I ask as the car makes a sharp U-turn in the middle of the road.

"Back to the safe house."

"Am I safe?" I can't help the question. My life has been in peril for too long for my liking.

"You are," the driver replies, and then we don't speak the rest of the way. I stay quiet, taking in any details I can about the surrounding areas. There isn't much to go on; it's too dark for me to see anything.

We arrive at a small cabin. It's surrounded by trees, and I find it ironic how homey it appears considering what it is. One of the men, the one who yelled at me and who has a particularly douchey haircut, opens my door and yanks me out. The driver comes around the back to flank my other side, and that's when I recognize him—it's the man I shot.

"Shit," I whisper, and he smirks at me like he finds it funny. "I'm sorry for, uh…" I pause and gesture to him.

"For shooting me?" He smiles at me. He's a good-looking guy with dark hair that's nearly black, eyes a warm chocolate color, and two dimples that frame his grin.

"Yeah." I chuckle when he lets out a soft laugh. "To be fair, you did shoot first."

He tosses a look to Douchey Haircut, and I realize he was probably the one who shot me, which is confirmed when the guy in front of me says, "We didn't intend for that to happen. We're very sorry about that."

I shrug, not sure how to respond. Oh yeah, no hard feelings. Not the first time someone's shot at me without cause! (Insert laugh here.)

I follow them onto the porch and they walk right into the house. I hear a little baby babbling when I cross the threshold and know it has to be Benny. The living room floor has baby items scattered around and Jen is sitting close to him, her hair a mess and her face red from crying.

"Jen," I say, relief apparent in my voice, and her head shoots up, her mouth opening in shock as she jumps off the floor. We both embrace in the middle of the room, and she immediately starts crying on my shoulder. I can't imagine the stress she's been dealing with.

"You're okay. Mike's waiting for you."

"Ah, the elusive Ms. Davis." A woman enters the room, and the two men who picked me up stand straighter.

"Who are you?" I ask, releasing Jen, who goes back to her son.

"I'm Agent James." She's tall and sharp, her suit pristine and her long blonde hair in a perfect ponytail. "I'm the lead on finding out where Agent Stokes is."

"Can I see some sort of identification?" She looks almost amused by my question and holds a badge open. I analyze it like I know what I'm looking for and nod my head, confirming that she is who she says she is. Perhaps she's just an excellent forger, but there's not much I can do about that. She holds her hand out, and I shake it. "Why did you have to take Mike's family?" I ask, anger in my voice.

"Collateral. I needed a way to track him down."

"Fine, but now I'm here, so let them go. I'll tell you anything you want."

Agent James looks over at Jen and Benny and back to me, deciding if she can trust that I'll hold up my end of the bargain.

"I don't want to die. I'll cooperate, I swear."

She nods her head. "Fine. Agent Perk, take them."

"Yes ma'am," Douchey Haircut replies. There's a slight tilt to his voice like he's only appeasing a superior, and when he looks over at me, he smiles a smile that has my skin crawling.

I ignore it and say, "He's at the gas station down the road. He's alone."

They leave quickly after Jen gives me a quick hug and whispers her gratitude to me. Agent James has me take a seat, and Agent Dimples—or whatever his real name is—stands beside her.

"So, tell me everything, starting with"—she sits up pin straight and clasps her hands over her crossed knee—"where Agent Stokes is."

I stare at her and wonder what exactly she'll do with the information I give her. I feel like I'm betraying him by tattling, but isn't that what he told me I should do? Isn't it the whole reason he let me go, or was it just to get me out of the way?

Sighing, I shake my head and say, "He dropped me off at the gas station and told me to walk. There wasn't much information given except that he was using me to get Jen back."

"Where is he headed?"

"He said Nevada."

"Nevada? Why?" She pinches her eyebrows and looks to Agent Dimples.

I shrug. "He said G3 is headed there. He thinks he can get to them there."

She stares at me, probably wondering how accurate the information is. "He's still trying to stop them?"

"Yes. He told me he had a problem communicating with the FBI—with you guys—and he had to go out on his own. That's why I'm here in the first place, because he couldn't ask for help when he was exposed."

Agent James stands and starts pacing, looking at Agent Dimples, whose expression conveys concern. She turns on me and says, "If he goes there, there is a good chance they'll kill him before we can stop it. We think they know who he is."

What she says makes my stomach turn, and panic grips me. "Well, stop him then!"

"I can't. I have no way to reach him."

"Well, there has to be something you can do! You're the FBI, for crying out loud." I practically shout it at her, and then I look at Agent Dimples as he approaches me.

"Calm down. Is there anything else you can tell us?" His eyes watch me, presumably trying to determine if I'm lying or not.

"No. I mean, I don't think so." Tears unexpectedly well in

my eyes when I think of what could happen to Liam. Leaving me behind or not, I don't want him to die.

"What about names? Did he tell you any names?" I think hard, remembering what he told me after Agent Dimples found me the first time. I tell them Ricardo and Rafeal's names and then relay the Russian's names that Liam's mentioned and look at him again as he sucks in a sharp breath. "Are they bad?" I ask helplessly.

Agent James is on the phone with someone, speaking frantically. Agent Dimples takes my arm and has started ushering me out the door when the front door explodes.

I land on my ass, dust and smoke clouding my vision and the ringing in my ears preventing me from hearing anything anyone's saying. I look around and see that a good portion of the house is missing, not just the front door. I look to my left and see Agent James's body on the floor; I don't see her move at all. To my right, his hand still outstretched toward me, is Agent Dimples. His eyes are closed, and he's not moving either.

I start crawling toward him then hands grab under my arms and lift me up. I'm thrown in the air, and the abruptness of it makes my head spin. Before I can question anything, the world slips from my grasp, and the last thing I see is two unconscious agents who didn't stand a chance.

14

LIAM

THE SUN IS just starting to rise behind me and I keep driving. Nothing is going to stop me from finishing this damn mission—not the FBI, not G3 sending thugs after me, and even though it sends a twisting feeling through my gut to think it, not Margaret.

Sending her into the clutches of the FBI was the absolute last thing I wanted to do. I knew there would be no turning back the moment I decided it was what I had to do, knew she wouldn't trust me ever again, but because I've already dragged enough people into my mess, it was my only choice for saving them all.

Her coming with me to Vegas was only going to make life that much fucking harder anyway, having to protect her and myself, at least that's what I tell myself when I start missing the way her hand feels in mine, the way she smiles at the most obnoxious moments, the way she calls me out, no matter the consequences. But, as I think of all the things I miss, I remember why FBI agents don't do relationships. We don't want to deal with the repercussions of having someone too close, someone who could be found and used against you.

I haven't even seen my own sister in years for that exact reason. If anyone caught wind that I had family, they'd use them against me in a heartbeat. I can't have them getting caught up in anything 'Dan' is doing when all they ever knew was Liam.

It's exactly why I did what I did. I didn't hear if Mike was back with his family, but I was pretty confident they didn't give two shits where they got their information from as long as they had something to go on.

I don't wonder about what happened because it would distract me from the primary goal. That goal is too damn important to worry about a woman.

I shake my head at my internal dialogue. Who the hell am I?

I've never let someone come into my life this way. I should've just let her be. They probably would have left her alone, so why did I drag her into this? I don't have an answer except the one thing I don't want to believe: that I care. I care about a woman for maybe the first time in my life, and letting her go—it feels as if a dagger is shoved straight into my chest.

It's too damn dangerous.

Even though this mission is going to come to a close, I won't be done with this job. I will have other missions, other assignments. Once I inform the FBI about what I've been doing, they will send me somewhere else, and Margaret will go back to her simple nine-to-five job.

Hell, now that she is with the FBI, I'll probably never see her again.

A distraction by way of a growling stomach comes and I pause, briefly wondering when I last ate. It's been a while, like maybe a day. It's hard to keep track when you're on the move like I have been.

I take a break from the drive, pulling over at a roadside diner. I empty the truck of everything I have, planning on not using it again once I've grabbed some food.

It's not until after I've eaten that I get a call on my burner phone, the one only Mike and Margaret have a number for.

"Yeah," I say, taking a last gulp of my water and standing, leaving cash on the table.

"Liam, look…" Mike takes a deep breath. Guy always has to make everything dramatic.

"Mike, you don't have to say anything. I'd do anything for you," I say, assuming that's why he's calling—to thank me for helping with Jen and Benny.

"That's not what—no. Liam, I'm still with the FBI."

I stop my stride toward the next car I'll lift and say, "What are you doing?" My voice is borderline violent. Even if it doesn't matter now, Margaret already told them everything she knows, so it wouldn't surprise me if they try to pick me up on my way into Vegas.

"Something bad has gone down. The FBI agent they sent with Jen had only just gotten here when there was an explosion."

My stomach churns, threatening to reject the food I just ate. "An explosion?"

"Yeah, man. Look, the agents were all okay, but…" His hesitation tells me what his voice can't. Margaret is dead.

"Who did it?" I ask. My voice is steel, but my eyes start to burn, a reaction I wasn't expecting.

"I don't know, but they can't find her body."

I pause again, thinking about this. If they can't find her body, that means something completely different. I reach the car, make quick work of opening it, and start driving.

"They took her," I inform him.

"Who?" Mike asks. "G3?"

"It's the only logical explanation."

"Okay, what do we do?"

"You do nothing. Go home. I'll handle it."

"Dude." Mike scoffs. "You may be the hotshot FBI agent, but I'm your friend. We've seen more shit than any normal human should, not to mention the fact that she willingly sacrificed herself to save my family. Let me help."

I hesitate then say, "I can't. I'm sorry." I hang up the phone, tempted to throw it out the window, but I refrain. I don't regret hanging up on him; he's still with the FBI, and I can't have them stopping me from doing what I need to do. G3 just fueled a fire, and now they have someone I care about. It isn't just about shutting down their operation now. If they hurt her, there is going to be a bloodbath they aren't ready for.

When I meet Anton, he'll regret taking her. He'll regret everything, including ever trying to go up against me.

15

MARGARET

GROANING ECHOES ALL around me, but I can't see anything. The black engulfs me from every angle, and I squeeze my eyes closed again against the pounding that fills my head. I can't move my arms or legs, and I just know, without even seeing it, that I'm in some nasty cellar-type room. It's just cliché enough to believe.

I cough and something warm fills my mouth. Ugh. The sharp taste of blood. Whatever happened, something or someone got a good shot at my mouth.

Whoever took me hasn't paid me a visit recently, which is probably a blessing, but I'm kind of hoping I can use my charm to get some water from them. My throat is so parched that I feel like it's been weeks since I was taken.

The only logical explanation is that G3 found us out.

Was someone following us? Maybe. It's hard to say—unless the agents aren't really FBI...but then that doesn't really add up either, because then why would they pretend once they already had me? There would have been no reason to fake it, and how would they know where that safe house was? I may be pissed at Liam for what he did, but I don't believe he would willingly let me go if he thought it was a trap.

I stay still to try to listen for any clues about where I am, but a ringing in my ears prevents me from hearing anything. I twist my head and feel a faint bit of tickling on my face then realize why it's dark—someone put a bag over my head.

Great. "Way to be completely original, kidnappers!" I hope my yelling is heard so I can get that drink.

Honestly, the only good thing to come out of leaving Liam's side is that Jen and Benny were out of danger before whomever it was decided to blow my ass up. I can't imagine what it would have done to Mike if they had been in that explosion. He probably would have lost his mind.

It's genuinely hard to remember what it was like before Liam came into my life, back when I was still using the app to find dates. I'll bet Brad wasn't a secret spy with enemies ready to use me against him, thinking of my last date on the app. Brad was a nice guy who worked for a car dealership, went home at six every night, and watched sports on the weekends.

If only he hadn't gone straight to wanting sex before we'd even started our date, I might have actually gone out with him more than once.

Maybe.

My thoughts are interrupted by metal scraping on metal and the sounds of a door creaking open. I practically hold my breath, not ready for what could possibly be happening right now.

If only Liam hadn't just thrown me to the wolves.

"Well, what a mess you've created." The voice is deep and heavily accented, Russian, I think, and I can't help but smirk at the predicament, like this is some sort of terrible movie.

"I'd like to point out that I wasn't the reason any of this happened, just so it's on record." My sarcasm is clear even through the hoarseness of my voice.

"You're funny. Let's see if we can use that to our advantage." He rips the cover off my head and I blink; I was totally right about being in a weird concrete cellar. It's almost too cheesy to take seriously.

I look to the man who's holding me hostage, and he regards me with amusement. His suit is a nice one that looks like it cost more than my minimum-wage-paid self could afford in a year. I would guess this guy is the boss, and that's confirmed when two men step through the doors, both packing guns and standing behind him intimidatingly. One of them has a bandage on his hand, and it looks like he's missing some fingers. My eyes widen slightly but I quickly try to school my features.

"What do you want from me?" I ask, tilting my head slightly and looking Boss Man in the eyes. The false bravado makes him raise an eyebrow, and I intend to continue making this lunatic think I'm not scared of him, even though I abso-fucking-lutely am.

"Nothing." He shrugs, casually slipping a hand into the pocket of his slacks. When I take a minute to actually look at him, I notice that he's a handsome man, despite, ya know, kidnapping people. I would say if he were on that dating app, I definitely would have swiped right.

Why am I thinking about that right now? Your life is in danger, Margaret—act like it!

"If you want nothing, why am I here?"

"Where's Daniel?" he asks.

I raise an eyebrow at him like he did before. "Who?"

"Daniel." He points over to me. "The man you were with."

It dawns on me then who he's talking about. It seems Liam didn't use 'Dan' just for his dating profile. This man has no idea who he really is, and that's not something I can just give away.

"Right. Daniel." I nod my head seriously, using any acting skills I might have hidden deep down to try to stay on track with Boss Man. I shrug. "I have no idea."

I don't expect it, and that's why it hurts so damn bad when he strikes me in the side of the face. I groan a little but bite my lip. Can't let him get to me. This is about survival. You are a finalist on the show, and now you just need to win the money.

I wish my inner monologue would chill, but I can't seem to help myself.

"You are lying. Tell me now," he says, his accent getting even thicker as his anger grows.

"I don't know." I enunciate every word. Even if it kills me, a protective instinct forms in my gut. I can't let them know where he was going; he has to end this before they continue to ruin lives.

I barely have a clue as to what they do, but if there was cause for the FBI to get involved, it has to be important, right?

"Fine. If you won't tell us, we'll see what young Daniel thinks of us having you." He shrugs again, pulling out a phone, which I realize is the one I had in my pocket, the one I was given by Liam. He fumbles with it at first, and I realize the bravado he's trying to scare me with is fake. He's actually scared because his business is being threatened. "Maybe he'll come to us."

"He won't!" I say. "He doesn't give a damn about me." Looking at Boss Man, I'm trying to think of a way to keep Liam out of this.

Even if it is all his fault.

"If that were true, he wouldn't have brought you into this in the first place," he says, challenging me.

"Come on, I mean—" I stumble, trying to think fast. "He let me go because he doesn't care. Just let me out of here!" The panic builds in my chest, but before I can say another word, a voice fills the room.

"Who is this?"

"Ah, Daniel," Boss Man starts. "I have something I think you'd be interested in."

"I highly doubt that, Anton." I suck in a breath when I realize this is the worst of the worst standing in front of me. This is the man Liam said was the most dangerous.

The thought that I won't see the light of day again strikes me, and I try to push the fear away.

"Oh really?" he says. His face shows he's almost amused at the situation. "Say hello, Margaret."

I won't let him get to me, and I won't make Liam worry about me when there's so much more at stake.

"Fuck you!" I yell, spitting in his face for good measure. Looks like watching all those action movies came in handy.

It hurts even more this time, and I'm pretty sure the liquid I feel on my face is blood from my nose breaking. I growl at him and try to keep the tears at bay, even though it's damn near impossible because, hello, my nose is broken.

"If you hurt her, I'll put you in the fucking ground and not think twice." Liam's anger vibrates through the room, and Anton laughs at him.

"Boy, you only wish you could get to me," he taunts. "Tell you what, you come and try to get her. If you succeed, I'll forget you exist, and we'll go our separate ways."

I don't believe this guy for a second, but the naïve part of me hopes Liam will take him up on it. There's silence for a while, and I lean slightly forward, hoping whatever he says will save me.

"Well, it doesn't seem like you're that important after all," Anton says, his eyes cold and proud before he turns the phone off.

I realize then that Liam has hung up, and my hope deflates.

He starts walking toward the door, and I wait to see what order he'll give his goons. When he doesn't snap his fingers at them and bark out instructions, one of his guys asks, "What are we doing with her?"

Anton looks back and considers me for a minute. "Leave her for now. We'll kill her later. I'm not convinced we can't still use her."

The goon who asked looks at me with a frown, but he follows his boss out of the room and leaves me alone.

I breathe my first breath in minutes and then curse, having completely forgotten that I desperately need water.

It could be hours later when my stomach revolts, but then again, it could be seconds. The lack of food or any nutrition finally shows, and I end up puking everywhere. Thankfully, if you can look at it in a positive light, I didn't have much to expel, so it wasn't as bad as it could have been.

I wonder what they're doing beyond these walls, wonder where the hell I am. I forgot to ask the important questions when they were in here threatening me. It must have been a while since that happened, and it feels like days since I was put down here. I want to scream out for help, but my throat is so raw it comes out as a gasp.

My mind wanders away from my current situation to Liam, wondering where he is, if he's coming, if he's going to let me die down here…

I guess I wasn't nearly as important as I gave myself credit for.

It's the second time he's given me up since I met him, so I can't really put any faith in him at this point. I briefly wonder how Mike and Jen are doing and hope for their sake they got out of town as fast as they could. I don't want them to have to deal with anything involving these crazy Russian bastards.

I look around the room. My body feels sluggish, my eyesight blurry, but my brain—what's left of the functioning parts, anyway—looks for my way out.

If Liam is leaving me to die, I owe it to myself to at least try to get out of here.

I start twisting my wrists. They're tied together, but the rope isn't tight. It's loose enough for me to wiggle, so I move my arms back and forth, guiding my hands to do what's necessary. My right shoulder twinges against a pain as it shoots up my arm, no doubt pulling some muscle while trying to be a damn acrobat.

I feel my right thumb slip out and sigh with relief, easily wiggling the rest of my hand out. I grab the binding with my right hand and let the other hand out then look around the room, looking for any cameras. I don't see anything, so I quickly pull my hands to my front and get to work on my feet. They're tied much tighter, and it takes me several minutes to get them loose. Once I'm free, I stand up, but I didn't consider how that would go and immediately fall to the floor.

My head swims, and it feels like I got punched in the face. Oh wait…I did get punched in the face.

"Ugh," I groan. How could I forget that? I slowly reach up to feel my nose; it's tender to the touch, and I know it's broken. I really don't want to see what it looks like now.

I slowly get myself back on my feet, and I grip the rope, holding it tightly as I stalk toward the door. I try to remember any self-defense moves I've ever seen. The only thing that comes to mind is Sandra Bullock's display in Miss Congeniality, which I'm not sure will help me at this point.

Looking down at the rope, I make a quick decision just as the door opens.

16

MARGARET

THE GOON ENTERS the room, and before he can turn and run out at the sight of me missing, I move the rope over his head and down onto his neck. He grabs at it, but I pull, hard.

It's way harder than they make it seem in movies, and I have to use every muscle in my body to pull against him. He backs me toward the wall and slams me into it, knocking the air out of me. I gasp, but I don't let go—this is life or death, and I can't let him win.

He's grappling for my arms and tries to get a good hold, but I don't let it stop me. He uses his nails to scratch my arms and I growl at the burn of pain when he takes a few chunks of skin.

He falls to his knees and I push forward with my leg, hoping he falls onto his stomach; his arms are still holding mine so he can't catch himself, and his head hits the ground. I wait while his body goes limp, and I stare in amazement at his unconsciousness. When I'm sure he won't be popping up to get me, I release the ropes and jump off of him.

I can't believe I actually pulled that off. I've never so much as smacked someone before—minus shooting Agent Dimples—and I just knocked a man out cold. The smile that pulls at my lips terrifies me for a second before I chastise myself. He did hold you hostage, Margaret. And who knows what else they were planning on doing to me.

Deciding I need to bolt, I quickly search his body, grateful to find a handgun at his side, and I snatch it up. I pull back the slide and smirk when I see it's loaded.

Good. I might need it.

I exit into the hallway and check to find it empty, no guards. Going right, I stay close to the wall, doing my best impression of Tom Cruise in any one of his infamous movies. I'm so glad I've seen them all.

The end of the hallway forks and I make a quick decision, going left and continuing down the hall. There's a door with a small window on the left side, and I risk a glance inside. I see men and women wearing masks; it looks like a lab of some sort, and each person seems to be in charge of their own work station. I look closer and see them packaging a white powder.

Holy shit. This is their operation. This is G3's secret location that Liam was trying to track down, which means I'm more than likely in Nevada.

"Hey!" I turn toward the yell that comes from behind me and see one of the goons who was in the room with me when Anton threatened Liam. I point my gun at him, and he halts slightly at the sight of it. I wait, not sure how I'm going to get out of here. He's a few feet away and I think if I ran, he'd just shoot me in the back anyway. Don't hesitate. Even if you think you might not be in danger, consider that, in this situation, you're always in danger. Liam's voice echoes in my head.

Before I can decide what to do, my body betrays my concentration and I sneeze. On accident, I also pull the trigger. I'm still recovering from the sneeze when his body thumps to the ground. "Oh my God!" I shriek, staring at the hole in the man's head. The blood seeps out and I gag, covering my mouth. I can't puke on the man I killed. I can't. I won't.

I look away, and the nauseous feeling fades slowly.

The shot drew attention, and one of the men from inside the room comes out and sees me. He doesn't seem alarmed until he sees the man on the floor. Before he can get me, I bolt in the direction I was headed before.

It's a never-ending maze of hallways, and after multiple locked doors, I finally find a staircase. Flinging open the door, I start to run up the stairs, only to be stopped by a body. I start carelessly throwing punches and use the gun to hit whomever is in front of me. One more hit and I spin to run in the other direction, but then the person's hand grasps my wrist.

"Stop." The voice halts my movement, and I look up into familiar eyes.

"Liam?"

He doesn't speak, just drags me up the steps and keeps a hold on my arm as we quickly ascend the staircase.

I breathe hard, barely keeping up and tripping every few steps, Liam silent as he keeps going. He holds me tighter when I slip, and he helps me stay upright. When we reach the top of the concrete steps, he keeps me back as he opens the door. I don't pay much attention, relief filling me now that someone else is taking the lead. A pressure I didn't know I felt lifts from my shoulders now that he's here.

When Liam grabs my hand again, we both go through the door, and I see bodies on the floor, most unmoving, some groaning and crying in pain. I look to the man holding my hand; he doesn't pay them any mind, doesn't hesitate as he makes his way out the door and into the bright sunshine. It burns my eyes after so long in the dark, and I hold tight to his hand, letting him continue to pull me down the sidewalk.

I look back one more time as the realization kicks in that he must have done that to them. He killed and hurt all those people. I stare, seeing him in a new light. A weird feeling comes over me as I think about the fact that the man I'm refusing to let go of is a murderer, but it should have hit me sooner. I should have realized this sooner. So, why didn't I? What does that say about my sense of self-preservation?

When I was kicking myself, feeling guilty about killing a man who wanted to hurt me, Liam was killing twenty times that to get to me.

But what makes my frown even bigger is the fact that it doesn't seem to bother me all that much. I'm stuck on the fact that he did all of that just to get to me.

Maybe that makes me stupid or desperate, but it's not in my nature to acknowledge that I'm either.

Liam steals us a random car, which is surprisingly easy considering where we are. It's Vegas, a place I've always wanted to visit because it looks fun and now want to leave because people here want me dead. Anton's business is smack dab in the middle of the Las Vegas Strip, though it's impossible to tell that it's a front for a drug operation, and a major one at that.

People don't care that it's there. Most of the people here are far too focused on their own shit to worry about something illegal going down in Sin City.

"How'd you find me?" A husky voice escapes my mouth, and the sharp sting in my throat makes me cringe.

"The phone," he finally says. "I had a tracker in it."

Huh. Clever.

We don't speak again as we drive through town. I don't ask where we're going, and he doesn't tell me. My head starts feeling fuzzy again, and I rest my head on the window. As I close my eyes, my body shuts down, and I feel the world slip away.

I wake up moaning. My face is burning, but more specifically, my nose. I immediately reach for it, but a hand holds mine down. I open my eyes then and try to get away, my mind not quite caught up with the events of the day yet.

Liam's face becomes clear through the haze and I relax again. He stares at me with sadness in his eyes, and it's then I remember the reason for the burning in my nose and the fact that it probably looks disfigured as fuck right now. I grimace then silently scold myself; that's not allowed with a broken nose.

I sit up in the bed and look at our surroundings. The room is a much nicer version of the motels we've been staying in. Out the window, I can see we're much higher up than most of the city, and I wonder how far away from Anton we are.

The farther the better.

Liam hands me a sports drink with the cap off and I drink greedily, needing the hydration. I finish a few big gulps then force myself to stop; I've puked enough, and the last thing I want to do is vomit in front of Liam. I set it on the nightstand and look at him. He looks tired, worn out, and I'm guessing he hasn't slept for as long as I've been away from him.

"How long was I gone?" I can't even remember what day it could be at this point; time hasn't mattered much, and when you're locked in a cellar with no windows, there's no telling how many days and nights pass. All I know is that my stomach and body need some serious attention. The last time I showered was too long ago, and the basic human need to be clean hits me fast.

He clears his throat. "Two days." He stands and heads to the hotel phone. I hear him ordering some sort of room service and space out. Two days of my life missing…I guess it could be worse.

I could be dead.

I shrug to myself, and when I see Liam glance over, I shrug again. I'm losing my damn mind.

I sigh and lean back against the fancy upholstered headboard. Liam hangs the phone up and walks over, sitting on the edge of the bed, close to where I'm sitting but not close enough to be touching. His expression tells me something is wrong, but I don't speak. I wait for him to process whatever it is he needs to tell me. After the last few days I've had, nothing would surprise me anymore.

"I'm so sorry, Mo." Except that. His voice cracks on my name, and he rubs a hand over his face. I don't reply, even though a defense of him is on the tip of my tongue. I don't know what he wants me to say, but I'm sure it's not that. "None of this should have happened to you."

"How do you know?" I ask, surprising us both. I don't even know why I said it, but then I continue to follow the train of thought that enters my head. "We don't know what my life was supposed to be like. How do you know this isn't exactly where

I'm supposed to be?"

"You really think you were supposed to be chased by mobsters? Kidnapped and beaten by them? Nearly blown up?" His voice escalates by the end of his questioning. "You sure as hell weren't supposed to end up attached to a guy like me." He continues to rub his face, and the stress that lines his skin makes me feel bad, even though I know it shouldn't after everything that's happened.

I'm not sure what exactly he means by 'attached', but I don't answer his questions, not directly. "I wouldn't have said no to the date."

"What do you mean?" He sounds exhausted. His body is hunched over, and he looks defeated.

"If I'd known what was going to happen, I wouldn't have said no."

Liam looks up then. "Are you kidding?"

"No," I answer vehemently. "I'm not kidding. You don't understand." I breathe a deep breath and release it, gathering my thoughts on how to explain what I've been feeling ever since I shot someone for the first—and hopefully—last time. "Before our date, before I met you, my life was in limbo." I raise my eyes and see his curious ones searching my own. "I didn't know what I was doing. I was working a job I hated, I don't have any friends anymore, and I have a shitty apartment. My life had no meaning."

He scoots over and grab ahold of my hand. "Everyone's life

has meaning." I'm surprised by the amount of compassion in his voice.

"Well, that may be and probably is true, but I didn't feel like I was in the right spot." I search his face and see some recognition in his gaze.

Finally, I see a smirk grace his lips. It's the first smile I've seen since the spider-bathtub incident. It's amazing how handsome this man is. "So, you think being chased by bad guys is the 'right spot'?"

I hesitate to answer, not wanting to go overboard. "Maybe, but also, knowing you, I think, is the right spot." I don't know if what I'm saying makes any sense, but I say it anyway, hoping he'll understand my meaning.

"Mo…" He trails off, pulling my hand so I'll move closer to him. "I don't want you to get hurt here."

"I know you won't hurt me," I reply immediately. His eyes brim with a tenderness, a passion burns in them like no man has ever shown me. I've never been on the receiving end of a look like his.

"I can't," he admits, looking away, staring down at where our hands are intertwined as he sighs. "I can't hurt you. Hurting you would hurt me." Liam's head shakes with genuine concern. "I don't know how to do this."

"I don't either, but it's not something you can plan for. Did I think the last week of my life was going to happen the way it did? No, I didn't, but for some insane reason I can't explain, it's been the best week of my life."

Liam looks up at me, a mixture of shock and amusement on his face, and a light chuckle escapes him. "You're absolutely insane."

I bring my finger to my chin and tap. "I'll take that as a compliment." I wait, biting my lip before I ask my next burning question. I take a deep breath. "How did you get us through all those people back there?"

He pauses, his entire body tense as he looks away again. "You don't really want to know the answer to that question, Mo."

"I need to know," I say, pushing him. I don't know why; I know what happened, but for some reason I need him to say it out loud. I need him to say it to my face.

He sits up straight before letting the words out. "I killed some, but I mostly just badly injured them."

There's a silence between us as we both digest this information and wait for the other to reply. Thinking about him killing and hurting those people makes me…sad, not because of him killing them, but because he seems genuinely upset that he had to. I suspected he had done it after seeing the scene before my eyes, but hearing it from him is different.

Would he have told me had I not asked point blank? No, probably not.

"Are you okay?"

His head pops up, and he looks startled by the question. "Am I okay?" He scoffs. "The real question is, are you okay?"

take my hand

I think about my answer before I give it. I am okay. Does that make me a bad person? I'm not sure. "I'm okay."

"How?" he says, looking straight into my eyes, his brimming with worry. Is he worried that I'm crazy? Or is his worry more about me being okay with him being a murderer?

"I guess...it was them or me, right?" I ask the question, but it's one I don't expect an answer to. "If you hadn't come, they would've killed me. They were planning on killing me, Liam. They said it right in front of me. So...I guess I'm selfish because I'm grateful that I'm the one who made it out alive."

"You're an innocent," he replies. "You'd only need to feel guilty if you were guilty of something. You're not selfish, Mo." He looks like he wants to say something more but holds himself back. "Come on, we gotta get you cleaned up."

"Ow." I try my best to not grimace at the pain. "Ow. Ow. Liam, ow."

"I'm sorry," he replies, lightly dabbing the cut on my nose. It seems Mr. Wannabe-Russian-Mafia had a sizeable ring that sliced through a good portion of my nose. So, while I'm lucky he didn't make it crooked, there is still a good chance I'll have a scar there. "That should do it."

He pauses, checking over every inch of my face, and my breath catches in my throat. Maybe I'm a glutton for punishment, but I wish, not for the first time, that we were just normal people, that we could act on the tension that seems to always pulse between the two of us. I pull away first, remembering how we ended up here in the first place.

I thank him and immediately move into the dining area of the hotel room. It's really just a table and chairs, but my entire attention is on the tray of food sitting there. My stomach rumbles with anticipation as I pull off one of the silver covers to reveal a cheeseburger and fries. Yes, please.

"Hold on," Liam says, replacing the cover. I frown immediately and prepare a valid argument as to why I want—no, deserve the cheeseburger and fries. "You need to try something lighter. If you can handle that, then you get the good stuff." He reaches for another cover, revealing a soup that resembles chicken stock, and I sit down with a huff.

I'm sure he's right. I haven't eaten in far too long and my stomach would probably revolt at the intrusion of heavy food, but the fries…

"So, what's the plan now?" I ask, gently spooning broth into my mouth. I drip a little onto the hotel robe and stare at the drop of soup on the fabric like it personally insulted me. My hand-eye coordination really needs work.

"The plan…well, I've got to find Anton again. It seems he has many hiding spots around the city, but he won't be able to stay hidden. I'll find him."

"He wasn't there?" I ask, remembering that I didn't see him in the massacre, though I didn't really get a close-up look at any of their faces.

"No." He sighs. "He was gone before I could get there."

"So where else can we look?" I ask, eating more broth and eagerly awaiting hearing how I will be included in his plans.

"I—" He's cut off by the sound of knocking on the door. I wait where I am as Liam grabs his gun and checks it before walking to the door. He looks through the peephole and lets out a breath of frustration before he grasps the handle, and he must deem it safe because he opens it without bothering to raise his weapon. I stare in shock as Agent Dimples walks through the door.

"Hello, Margaret."

17

LIAM

MARGARET LOOKS SHOCKED to see Ford walk through the door. Her assumption was probably that he died in the blaze, and we haven't gotten around to discussing that part of the story since I got her out of the place where Anton was keeping her.

I'm still trying to figure out how she hasn't gone hysterical from everything that's happened. It would be the normal reaction, something like how she acted at first when she thought I was going to get her murdered, which I've almost done twice now.

It baffles me, but at the same time I find relief in knowing she hasn't run scared from what I've shared with her. Whether I like it or not, she's become important to me, and a small sliver of me hopes when I end this mission, when this is all over, she'll let me try again. I hope she'll give me a second chance so I can try to have a normal—or somewhat normal—relationship with her.

Relationship…fuck.

I never thought I'd say those words; I was determined to be the perpetual bachelor my entire life, but then Mo walked into it and changed everything I'd ever thought was important. Now the only thing I can think about is how to fix this mess I've made and get us both to a place where that can become real.

When I left her in exchange for Mike's family, I was sure I was never going to see her again, but when I got the call from Anton, I knew I couldn't let her be killed by that asshole. The fucking dick was so cocky, and by the time he'd sent me the location of where she was being held, I was already on my way, following the tracker I'd put in the phone.

When I asked my contacts about his whereabouts, several people knew where he was because it was where the heavy dealers picked up their 'quota' for the week, as they told me. They also told me it changed every week and I should hurry if I wanted to find them.

I didn't waste time. It'd already been two days since he'd blown up the safe house and taken her, and when I heard her yelling through the phone, when I heard the punch that hit flesh, I saw red. I was going to do to him whatever he did to her and worse.

I knew she was strong and wouldn't let him get to her, but I was worried that her mouth was going to get her into some serious trouble before I could find her.

Fucking Mo and her stubbornness—it's as hot as it is irritating.

Having Margaret in my life has changed a lot of things for me. In the short amount of time I've known her, I've let her get under my skin in a way no one has before. I'd never even been concerned with my own family because no one knows who I really am. That's been hidden deep, deep in the alcoves of the FBI's system, never to be released or used ever again.

"What—how—" Margaret stumbles over her words, staring in shock as he walks into the room. "You're alive!" she blurts out.

"Yes, I am, though not for lacking of trying on the Russians' part."

She shakes her head. "What about Agent James? Is she…?"

"She's okay, in the hospital resting. She took the brunt of the explosion, unfortunately, but she's tough and will probably try to attempt to escape out from under the doctors' noses."

"Oh, thank goodness she's all right." Margaret holds a hand to her chest and looks to me as she blinks and smiles shyly. "Oh, Liam…this is…uh…" She looks to Ford, but I speak first.

"I know who he is," I say, not liking that he was so efficient in getting here. I was expecting more time with Margaret before he arrived. Now, I know she's going to be pissed at me. "This is Ford. He'll be taking you somewhere safe." I don't have to wait long before her protest comes.

"'Take me'? What do you me he's taking me somewhere?" Margaret turns all her attention on me, folding her arms under her boobs, which pushes them up. I catch a glimpse of her cleavage and can't help but look. She's trying to intimidate me and it's cute, but I barely have to try to make my stance more intimidating before she glances back at Ford, breaking eye contact with me.

"Until I can figure out what's going on, I have to get you somewhere safe," I say, reaching for one of her hands.

Her eyes become big and her concern blantant. "No," she argues, shaking her head. "I go with you."

I sigh because I knew she'd fight me, and it's harder to be strict with her when all I want is her to be with me, all the time. I look to Ford and he takes the hint, going out into the hall to give us a minute alone.

"Margaret, I know you want to come, and I admire your strength with everything you've been through. It's absolutely frightening how strong you've been." I take her other hand and draw her closer; it's a strange yet comforting feeling. "But this isn't safe." I hold my finger over her mouth when she tries to interrupt. "I've almost lost you twice—I can't do it again."

"Don't be such a condescending asshole, Liam," she says, practically spitting the words. For someone who's had little to no nutrients, she sure is feisty. "I'm with you through the end here, and I have to get back at Anton. I am the one he messed with, so I want to be the one who takes him out."

This—this right here is why I don't get attached to women. They're fucking crazy. I love that Margaret is tough, but putting her life on the line—again—it not going to happen. "Mo, I cannot let you come with me. It's not safe." I cup my hands on the sides of her jaw and pull her closer. "When this is over, I'll come get you, and maybe we can have a do-over of that first date."

The fight seems to drain from her body at my words, and I feel her lean into me. Taking advantage of the situation, I keep hold of her jaw with one hand and pull her hips to mine with the other. I lean in, take her mouth with my own, and taste her.

God. It's as amazing as it was the first time, and I can't imagine depriving myself of this for the rest of my life. We battle for dominance and eventually she relents, letting me control the kiss and tipping her head just right to get a better angle.

After a minute, I pull my lips from hers, but I stay close. I open my eyes and laugh lightly at her still-closed eyes then give her another peck on the lips, prompting her to open her eyes again.

"I don't want to leave you." Her whispered admission rocks my heart. I've never had someone say that to me, have never had someone care before.

"I know, babe." I see her sigh. "But I've got to keep you safe, and I can't have you there as a distraction. Anton knows who you are, and if he has another chance, he'll use you against me."

"I understand. I hate every minute of it, but…" She sighs

again. "I do understand."

I look at her. Her green eyes are filled with a deep curious longing. Her look of complete devotion is enough to bring me to my knees, and I want to do everything I can to get her into my arms again as soon as possible.

"I promise, as soon as this is over, I'll come get you, and you and I...we'll start off on a better foot."

She chuckles. "Oh really?"

"Yes." I laugh along with her. I give her another kiss, this one as intimate and intense as the first one. It leads us down a dangerous path just as another knock sounds on the door. I groan this time, hating being interrupted. "I hate that door," I say, earning a cheeky smile from her.

Opening it, I see a disgruntled Ford holding a bag. "Delivery."

I grab it from him and let him follow me in then hand Margaret the bag and tell her to get dressed.

When she's in the bathroom, I look at Ford and see him giving me a know-it-all grin. "What?" I grunt out.

"Oh nothing, just a bit surprised is all."

"Surprised at what, exactly?"

I've known Ford for years, since we both joined the FBI around the same time. He's often a pain in my ass, but he's also generally a happy-go-lucky kind of guy. It chaps my ass.

"You and Margaret—it's very unexpected," he says, gesturing to where she's locked behind the bathroom door.

"Well, I like the unexpected," I say, surprising him again if the lift of his brow is any indication.

"Apparently."

I look at him seriously and point his way. "You keep her safe, you hear me?"

He frowns at me, seemingly hurt by my words. "Of course I will, Stokes. I feel like I let you down already with her."

I sigh. "You couldn't have known they were out there. They likely followed a random lead."

He looks at me seriously and steps forward, whispering like someone has the place bugged. "You think someone inside did this?"

"Well, how else did they find that place? They sure as hell weren't following me," I say with certainty.

"Who then?" he asks. He knows how serious this is. Everyone was thinking I was the bad guy, thought I was the one feeding the bad guys the information they needed to keep their drug operation under wraps, but I've had a feeling all along that someone else was in on this whole deal. I just didn't know who.

"I don't know." I look at Ford. I trust him; he's one of the few I do in this messed-up game we play. The FBI often feels like a life outside of the real world. We're the people hiding in the shadows, and depending on who you are, we're either there to hurt you or protect you.

"Well, we need to find that out."

I shake my head. "Your only priority is to protect Margaret. Everything else, you leave to me."

He takes my words in stride as Margaret walks out of the bathroom, fully dressed and ready to leave again.

"You ready?" she asks him, but she's staring at me. "You find that asshole, okay?" She tells me more than she asks, and I gather her into my arms and hold her snugly.

"You can count on it, Mo."

With a final kiss, I say goodbye and hope to all hope it's not long before I can keep those promises I made to her. I'd do anything I could to change this for her, for us, so we can live a safe and happy life together. I just have to deal with a few pressing issues first.

Priority number one: put Anton in a cell and throw away the fucking key.

18

MARGARET

AGENT DIMPLES—EVEN knowing his name, I can't bring myself to call him by it yet—leads me out of the hotel, both of us donning hats to hide our identities. My nose is still swollen to twice its normal size, so I'm grateful for the extra coverage in the broad daylight where everyone can see me.

I leave the hotel in much better shape than when I got there, with a clean body and at least a somewhat less dizzy head. I follow Agent Dimples over to the nearest convenient store—for what, I don't know, but I know now how these guys operate. They always need their essentials, and since I didn't get my cheeseburger and fries, I use this opportunity to grab some snacks for wherever it is he's taking me.

When I grab the package of donuts, I grin to myself, remembering the first time I was with Liam, when he gave me shit for stuffing my body with junk. Man, that feels like it was ages ago.

"You okay?" Ford asks, and I nod. It's hard to say what he thinks of me, but I'm guessing he's a bit concerned judging by the crease between his eyebrows. I am standing here smiling at a pack of donuts, and I mean, I have hit my head a lot. Maybe I'm not at one hundred percent... When we reach the checkout, the lady starts absentmindedly scanning items. When she looks up and makes eye contact with me, her eyes widen. Ford is getting into his wallet for money, and I try to give her a smile. I don't understand why she's looking at me like she is.

When we're about to leave, Ford starts away from the checkout and she reaches out, grabbing my hand. "You can stay here—he doesn't need to do that to you."

I give her a confused look and then it dawns on me what she's talking about. My face must look worse than I thought. "I was...in a car accident." I pat her hand with my free one. "I'm okay. Really."

Ford stops, his eyes observing the exchange. She looks between us again and lets go of my hand, releasing me.

"Everything okay?" he asks me when I reach his side again.

"Oh yeah, she thought you beat me up."

Ford's expression twists and his brows draw together when

he looks over to me. We've exited the store into the busy street, and he grabs my hand. "What did you tell her?"

"I said I was in a car accident."

He nods and looks at me again. "Just so you know…" He pauses and appears hesitant. "I would never do that to you—or anyone!" He rushes on, and I let him get it out. He's way more worried about it than I am. "I know we don't know each other, but I just…wanted you to know." He seems way less the confident guy he was when we met, and I pat his arm in much the same way the cashier patted my hand.

"I trust you. Don't worry." Ford nods and leads me to a black SUV that's sitting on the curb. We hop in, and I turn to him. "Is this stolen?" I ask.

He gives me a weird look. "No?" He replies like it's a crazy question, and I shrug. I guess Liam has conditioned me to stealing cars. That can't be a good thing.

We start our drive, but getting out of the Strip takes some doing. It's so clustered, and I can't even imagine being a taxi driver on these streets. How many people get hit in Vegas between the crowds, the drunkenness, and the excessive number of cars driving down the Strip? I make a mental note to google it later.

"So, where exactly are we going?" I ask as I bite into the chocolate frosting of the processed delicacy. I moan when it melts on my tongue, savoring the sweetness. Chicken broth can only do so much for your body.

"Well, I can't exactly tell you that," Ford says, turning on his blinker.

"Why not?" I scoff. "It's not like I'll tweet it."

"Tweet it?" he asks, perplexed.

"Yeah, you know, Twitter?" I reply. Unless you've been living under a rock, you know what Twitter is.

"Oh, right. Yeah, don't do that."

"No problem," I answer sarcastically. "But seriously, where are we going?"

"A safe house." I scoff again. Why I'm giving an FBI agent shit and not flinching, I'll never know. "What?" Ford demands.

"Oh nothing," I taunt. "That just went so well the last time."

Ford smirks. "Well, this time I'm prepared."

I decide to let it be. Surely, he knows what he's doing…I hope. "So, how long have you known Liam?" I ask, changing topics. I really do want to know everything I can about the man I can't stop thinking about, especially after our latest conversation. I try not to let myself become too hopeful. After everything that has happened in the last couple of weeks, I can't even comprehend having a normal life again, especially one that includes Liam.

"A long time," he answers. I don't think he's going to give me anything else, but then he says, "We basically leaned on each other when we started this whole thing. He's one of the few people I trust in this world."

This tidbit of information makes me turn fully toward him,

readjusting my seat belt to see him better. "Really? What's he like?" I already know enough about him to know I have some seriously intense feelings there, and now that I know they're reciprocated, it changes everything.

Ford sighs. "He's…shy. He doesn't really like letting other people into his life, which is understandable given our profession, but even I have my limits."

"Do you have a girlfriend?" I ask, my curiosity knowing zero bounds.

"No, I don't." He sighs again, like not having a girlfriend actually makes him really sad. "No one can keep up with this life."

"Even me?" The question comes out without me thinking about it. I know Liam wants to try, but who knows how this mission will turn out, or the next one, or where they'll send him after this is over.

"I don't know yet." He looks over at me. "You're different, that much is obvious."

I don't know how to reply so I sit in contemplative silence and eat my food, all the while wondering how Liam and I can make this work.

I don't know how much time has passed when I wake. It's dark outside, so it's impossible to tell where we are. I look over at Ford and see he doesn't look the least bit tired, but he's probably been driving for a while now.

"Evening," he says. "You were out for an hour or two."

"I'm sorry. I'm a bad co-pilot."

"That's all right. You've been through a lot."

We're in the middle of nowhere, the sun is long gone, and the road that stretches in front of us is endless and dark. We must be hidden somewhere good, and I feel a mixture of relief and anguish thinking about how I'm going to be safe, finally. However, Liam is still out there, still in danger and trying to take down that bastard who thinks it's okay to kidnap and hit women.

"Hey." I get Ford's attention, a curiosity about something that should have hit me long ago clawing into my thoughts. "How did they know where we were the first time?"

A sigh escapes the body next to me, and I can tell this is something Ford has been trying to sort through. "I don't know, and it's not something that's taken lightly. The FBI is already working on tracking down how he found us."

I nod, even though I know he isn't looking at me. "They couldn't have placed a tracker somewhere, right?"

"What do you mean?"

"I mean, when they took me, they couldn't have, like…put something in me?" I don't know why my brain goes to this place. Maybe it's one too many action movies; maybe it's the overactive imagination again.

Ford doesn't answer, which makes me believe it could be a possibility. I know escaping that place wasn't easy and it took a lot of Liam's humanity to get me out, but how come Anton wasn't there? To get his answers? To kill Liam himself? What happened that made it…not easy, but well, easier?

These thoughts plague me the rest of our drive, and thankfully it isn't much longer before we pull up a long driveway to a craftsman farmhouse. It's dark and old, but a clean space that looks to be well maintained, at least on the outside.

When we walk inside, Ford flips on a light, and we see dust covers every surface. It makes me cough, and I cover my nose when a sneeze threatens me as Ford says, "Uh, yeah, sorry. I guess this one hasn't been in use in a while."

I shake my head and wave him off, heading to an oversized chair in the living room and plopping down onto it.

"Hungry?"

"Yeah," I answer, a yawn cutting me off, and I let my eyes fall shut for a brief time, not wanting to sleep but not able to stop my body from doing what it has to do. It's not long before I'm passed out, and I only wake when the fire alarm blares and smoke fills the small house.

19

LIAM

I RUB AT the twisty feeling in my chest.

Being worried about another person is normal for most people—healthy, even—but not for me. I've only ever allowed myself to worry about specific people, and that includes my sister and her family, my parents, and my close friends. There aren't many due to how isolated I am.

This is new. This is me pacing a hotel room, her smell still permeating the air after her shower, her discarded clothes left behind, her smile etched into my memory. I can't pinpoint exactly what has me so wound up.

She's safe.

I trust Ford.

I force myself to focus on the mission. The truth is, I don't even want to finish this job now. All I want to do is find Margaret and run away with her. I scoff at my own thoughts and tell myself to knock it off. I'm not that guy, the one who abandons something just for a selfish need. I have to finish this mission. This is more than three years of my life we're talking about.

If I can finish out this mission and find Anton, I can act out the fantasies I have of being with her for real. The FBI will want to debrief me about everything that's happened in the last couple of years, but that doesn't have to stop us. Margaret can wait for me, if she is willing.

I walk over to the laptop set up on the table. The leftover breakfast has been removed, and my task is at the forefront of my mind now. Anton is too smart, unfortunately, and has many hiding places here in Sin City. He could be anywhere.

The FBI has surveillance that would be helpful, but I'm not permitted to access that kind of tech anymore. The only reason Ford was willing to help me was because he's known me for years, and he cares about innocents getting hurt. Nearly to a fault, he will always protect innocent people before he worries about catching the bad guys.

I'm still not sure who in the organization is working for Anton, but the more I think about it, the more I'm positive that's how they found out about the safe house and got to Margaret. I was worried about Ford taking her somewhere they could find so, despite my own needs, I didn't let him tell me where he was taking her. While that breaks me, I had to know that no matter what, she'd be safe.

I grit my teeth when I think of Anton touching her. If nothing else, he'll die for that alone.

The only way to find him will have to be the old-fashioned way: contacts. Vegas isn't exactly one of my stomping grounds, so finding someone who will willingly give up his location could prove almost impossible, but my options are limited with the kind of time I have.

He could escape from right under my nose, so I gotta find someone who will talk.

The club is dark, perfect for hiding from unwanted eyes. I've been following a trail that led me to a man named Sylvester Crum. Not exactly a very good alias if you're choosing one, but it does make you really easy to find.

He's surrounded by people, mostly scantily dressed women, no doubt hired to be here with him tonight, and two bulky guys are standing nearby as his security.

They're not enough to deter me from finding a chance to talk to Crum. He's a scrawny guy with expensive clothes, and I'm guessing if I checked his pockets, I'd find a few thousands of dollars' worth of cocaine, the kind only G3 produces.

Rumors about this guy being the biggest drug dealer in Vegas are what made me seek him out. Anton wouldn't want anyone but the best, and I'm sure he wouldn't want Crum to be selling anything but his supply.

There's a guy standing behind one of the security guards, half sloshed and nearly falling on his ass. I walk over, and he is completely oblivious to his surroundings. The guards aren't paying any attention to him, and I take my time walking around. It's crowded, packed over capacity, which makes this both easier and harder.

I stand out of view from the guards and lightly shove the drunk dude into one of them. He immediately turns all of his attention to the belligerent idiot, and when his buddy turns to see what's going on, it gives me my opening.

The drunk guy starts ranting, and everyone at the table turns their attention to the altercation, Crum included, which makes grabbing him a piece of cake.

"I swear to God I don't know anything! Please!" The man's wails turned muffled when I stuff the rag in his mouth, and his hands flex and pull against the ties restraining him to the motel chair. We're far away from the limelight and all of his coke-head buddies. No doubt his security guys are panicking that they let their paycheck out of their sight.

They probably wouldn't recognize him if they saw him now, I think as I wipe blood off of my hands. His face is slowly swelling from the impacts he's endured.

Dude's got some serious willpower. He hasn't let anything slip about Anton—yet—but I'm determined.

"Let me tell you a story," I start, watching his eyes go wide and worried. Good. "I've been hunting Anton down and slowly breaking apart his organization for about—oh, three years now. It's been hell, ya know? Living on the road, undercover, all alone." I pause, wondering where exactly I'm going with this, but then I think, Fuck it. They already know too much, and Crum here isn't ever going to see the light of day again if I have it my way. "But then, something happens. I find myself getting a girlfriend." Crum's brows wrinkle in confusion. "I know, right? I wasn't expecting it either, but I just couldn't help myself, man. She's amazing, and I couldn't let her go.

"Now, the problem is, Anton, your friend"—I don't acknowledge his shaking head as he tries to convince me how close the two of them actually aren't—"he took an interest in her, an I-want-to-use-her-against-you kind of interest, and that's bad, isn't it, Crum?"

He nods slowly. Tears stream down his swollen face, and he looks damn near ready to piss himself—if he hasn't already, that is.

"Yes, good. I'm glad you agree. So, I'm going to give you one more chance to tell me everything you know, or, for every time he's hurt my girl, I'm going to hurt you triple. You understand?" I ask, bending down to get in his face. I've kept my voice even and calm, inserting an authority into it that makes him take the situation seriously. If he's more terrified of me than he is of Anton, my goal is achieved.

I take his gag out and give him a couple of seconds to compose himself. I'm not a damn monster.

"I don't know where he is, man, I don't." I straighten up, getting ready to give him a little preview of what he's going to be receiving. "But wait—wait! I know he has some places he goes!" I lift an eyebrow, gesturing for him to continue. "There's a club called Vino—he owns it, but it's not a public place. It's for his close friends, and only people he knows get in. I've never been invited, but I know he hides out there when shit's going down."

"See, was that so damn hard?" I ask, just as my cell rings. I hold up a finger to my lips and he nods, agreeing to stay silent. He'd probably give me anything at this point. "Yeah?" I'm still using a burner phone, and only select people have the number. Ford is one of those people.

"It's James, Stokes."

I lift my head in surprise. "James? I thought you were laid up?"

"I was, just got out, but listen, I got word." She releases a breath, and I tense, waiting for whatever bomb she's going to drop.

"What?" I snap. It's never good when the FBI willingly contacts me and it's not for my immediate arrest.

"Ford—he's not answering. We also don't know where he took Margaret."

I know this. I knew Ford wasn't going to give it away to anyone and would only come out of hiding when he got word from me that Anton was done for. "I know. You're not supposed to know where he is."

A sigh comes through the phone. James has always been a bit of a control freak, someone who doesn't like to be left out of the loop. "Stokes, you don't understand. He activated a warning signal."

My chest constricts at the uneasy feeling that courses through me. "What do you mean? That's for emergencies. It has to be a mistake." Even I can hear the panic in my voice.

"I know. I'm afraid he's in trouble."

Fear, anger, and confusion all fight for dominance inside me. I want to scream, I want to hurt, I want to find her and never let her go.

20

MARGARET

MY BRAIN IS foggy as I look around the room. The smoke is overpowering, and I wonder if this is just some messed-up dream my subconscious came up with. Then I inhale a lungful of smoke and immediately start choking. I drop to the floor, trying to get away from it, moving quickly on my hands and knees, searching for Ford, wherever he is.

He has to be here.

"Fo—" I start to call out but my voice is hoarse, the smoke already tainting it and making it burn. I search the kitchen but can't see a thing, so I head to the back of the house and search for him there. I can't seem to find anything or anyone.

I look through as much of the house as I can before I find a back door and can't stand it anymore. I burst through it and cough, my lungs burning with a ferocity I've never felt before. I'm still on my hands and knees when I feel the sure pressure of a gun's barrel pressing against the back of my skull.

"Get up." The voice is deep and somewhat familiar, and chilly fear racks through my bones. I slowly get to my feet and face away from the man behind me. The barrel presses harder against my head and I move forward, walking around to the front of the house, where I see the man who's the new star of my nightmares standing over a body.

I recognize the clothes as Ford's, but his head is covered with a black sack—not that it matters because he's completely passed out. The sight is one I won't ever forget.

"Margaret." Anton looks at me, cocking his head to the side, his mouth spread into a thin-lipped smile. "You seem to love for me to track you down."

"I could do without it, actually. I'm kind of tired." I can't help the sarcastic quip that slips through, and at this point, I just don't care.

"Well, you seem to be an easy target, because here I am, getting to you a second time."

"That or you have some spineless coward who's decided to turn his back on his own country." The barrel of the gun presses hard against my head then. I'm guessing the coward I mentioned just so happens to be the one standing behind me with a gun to my head.

Good job, Margaret. Make him angry—great idea.

"My organization pays better," Anton replies, ignoring the grimace that fills my face. I hate this guy. "Let's go." He turns to walk away but then stops, lifting a finger and telling the man behind me, "Let's make sure she doesn't see anything, huh?" Not waiting for a reply, he stalks over to one of the dark SUVs behind him and gets in.

I start toward Ford but don't make it a step before something hits me hard in the back of the head. Everything goes dark, like someone flipped off a light switch.

I'm restrained again, but this time, my hands are above my head and chained. I also don't have the luxury of a chair like I once did. Ford is in the same position but still unconscious. He's on another wall where I can see him, but we're too far away to touch.

I want to cry, but I don't want to let myself give in to despair yet in case I can somehow get out of this like I did last time. I'm in a basement this time, which I can tell by the tiny hopper window. It's too small for me to squeeze through even if I could get out of these chains, which feel like they weigh a million pounds.

Squinting, I try to make out anything I could use to get out of this, but the basement is empty. There's nothing down here but Ford and me and our chains. That could be a song.

Okay, I tell myself, you're losing your damn mind. Calm down.

I stay quiet and try to think of good things. Liam. Liam is a good thing. Despite my current situation, I'm still happy I met the guy.

I've never met someone like him, so focused, so determined and strong. He's ruthless, but at the same time, he's compassionate. He's calculated and sure of himself, and despite what he wants to think about himself, he does care about people—several people by my estimation.

I wonder if he knows Ford and I were found at the safe house. I wonder if they called him like last time and tried to bait him with me, but in the amount of time I've been awake—I don't know how long that is—I haven't heard a peep from upstairs.

For some reason, that makes me more nervous than if someone had come down here and threatened me. Does that make me crazy? Probably, but I'll worry about that later.

I stare at Ford, worried he might not wake up from this. I think he's still breathing, but I can't tell from this angle. His body is limp against the wall, hanging from the chains and cuffs that dig into his wrists.

I wince at the sight. "Ford," I say, my voice a rasp, too quiet for him to hear, but I don't want to draw any attention. "Ford," I say again, this time a little louder, but he doesn't stir. A tear escapes my eye, and I sniff. The hope I had before quickly dissipates and my vision becomes blurred, both by tears and lightheadedness.

At this point, I know when I'm going to pass out, so I picture Liam's face and let the darkness pull me under.

Eyelids heavy, I blink them until the basement comes into view again. It's dark but there's a small bulb lit up now, and I wonder who was down here while I was out of it. I lift my head, my movements stalled by how stiff everything is from being in this position.

I remember Ford and look over to where he was before; he's awake, and I let tears fall, thankful he's alive. He looks just as relieved to see me awake.

"Are you okay?" I ask before clearing my throat. It's scratchy and in desperate need of water.

"Yeah. You?" he asks, looking my body up and down. I'm sure it's not the first time he's checked for physical harm done to me. He was out for a long time, and anything could have happened.

"I'm fine." I swallow, my sore throat the least of my concerns. My wrists are aching from how they've been hanging, and I try moving them a little. My legs don't want to stand anymore, but I force them to keep going, giving my arms a small reprieve. "Has anyone come?"

"Not since I've been awake." He looks around the room, much like I did the first time. There's still nothing.

"Someone came down here," I say, nodding at the light. "That wasn't on before."

"You were awake before?"

"Yeah, we've been here a while. It's a bit darker."

"Dammit," he says, more to himself than anything else. "Liam is going to kill me."

I chuckle despite the situation. "Nah, we might be dead before he can get even here." I don't think about the words before I say them, and I silently scold myself then apologize to Ford.

"It's okay." He laughs lightly. "I'm glad I'm stuck with you down here. Most people who aren't used to this world would be freaking out by now."

"Oh, I am, but this isn't my first kidnapping," I say in a light voice. I don't know how I'm joking about this situation, but my default sarcasm seems to soothe the worry building in my chest.

He doesn't answer, just looks at me with sadness. I can't quite pinpoint why my words bother him, but I think about how the first time I was kidnapped, I was taken from him that time too. "Ford, this isn't your fault," I say. My voice sounds unsure, like I'm not sure if that's what is upsetting him or not.

"It is my fault. I can't seem to keep you safe, Margaret," he argues, his tone harsh.

"Anton is absolutely insane—you can't control that no matter how much you want to. He would've have done this to anyone trying to protect me."

And just like that, the epiphany hits me. Everyone protecting me is getting hurt. Liam, Ford, Mike, Jenny, Agent James—even little Benny got caught up in this, and so did my neighbor!

I lose myself in the torturous thoughts for a long time.

We don't say anything for a while, both probably wondering what we're going to do to get out of here. There is no easy answer, no simple solution to this. I wish so badly I had some skill with fighting or wielding a weapon. Aside from shooting Ford one time, my knowledge is rather limited.

A squeaking sound comes from my right and I jump a little, looking down at my feet. A flash of something scurries in front of me and, without thought, my booted foot slams into it, blood and squishing coming from underneath.

I don't realize what I've done until a half a minute later, and as I stare at the stomped-on rat, its blood all over my shoe, I let out a bloodcurdling scream.

"Holy fuck," Ford says, grimacing at the sight then pulling his head back and looking away.

I breathe rapidly, air not getting into my lungs properly, my mind frantic. "Oh God, oh God, oh God," I chant over and over, the air still not cooperating and the world fading again.

"Margaret," Ford's voice cuts in. "Margaret, breathe!"

But I can't. I can't breathe and I can't compute anything that just fucking happened. What the hell is going on? I killed a rat and I'm having a panic attack. A rat. It was just a rat.

"Margaret," Ford tries again. I look up at him, his eyes focused intently on mine, and I breathe another deep breath. I stop my chanting and focus on my breath. In, out, in, out.

"You're all right. It was an accident." His voice tries to break in once again, and I listen this time.

"An accident," I repeat, continuing to inhale and exhale.

"Right. It's okay."

"It's okay." It's okay. It's got to be okay.

21

LIAM

I SEARCH EVERYWHERE for him, for them, for her—databases, flight lists, border patrol—but they are in the wind. If I didn't know about Vino, I would say he was gone, but according to Crum, that's where he hides, and that is my very next stop. I don't know how I know, but Anton has something to do with Ford triggering his warning signal. There's no other reason he'd have to use it, no reason he would ever resort to that kind of protocol unless there was something serious going on.

The FBI is temporarily letting me in, only to figure out how to stop Anton. Ford is one of ours, and we don't let ours get taken without a little payback. Margaret is my focus, however, and James knows that, which is why I was surprised when she convinced the director to let me access the databases.

They insisted I search through the correct resources before I went storming into his private club, even though that is where I wanted to go immediately after I got the call. I don't give two shits about protocol, not anymore, not with Margaret in danger, somewhere lost out there with no protection.

My fists clench at the thought, and I kept getting this aching spot in my chest whenever I think about it.

I am a man unleashed and I have to take action. I have to go to Vino, have to get Anton, have to get to Margaret and end this whole fucking thing.

Regardless of what the director of the FBI wants, that is my very next stop, and I couldn't care less if I end up with jail time for defying direct orders. I will get Margaret back if it lands me in hell.

The club is dark, the music so loud it shakes the floor I'm walking on. If my adrenaline wasn't high already, this would increase it tenfold. I don't see Anton right away, but I see plenty of his thugs lingering in the hallways, some with girls wrapped around them, others watching the people, the exits, the stages—me.

They know who I am. They know why I'm here, and they

don't seem to care much for it.

I'm immediately flanked by two of them, my senses on high alert as I march myself through the club. If Anton is as self-righteous as I think he is, he'll be in a private booth.

There's a flight of stairs that looks less than inviting and I hear right for it, knowing in my gut that it will lead me where I need to go. I climb, aware of the two men behind me and counting exits for a getaway.

If things go south, I may need a quick route. However, this place seems to be built like some kind of fortress, and the exits aren't marked, making my escape not so cut and dry.

As I suspected, Anton is on this level because of its privacy, and he's surrounded by half-clothed women of all kinds; it seems he's not the picky type. Most look like they're high out of their minds, and I wonder if they're even aware of where they are right now, if they even know they're with one of the most dangerous men in Vegas.

My guess is no.

"So, Danny boy, you've found me." His Russian accent is thick and his tone is mocking. He wanted me to find him; my question is why. "I wonder who gave me up."

"Someone who's not as afraid of you as you'd like, I'm guessing."

Anton laughs, finding humor even though I know it kills him to admit this. "I suppose I'll have to tighten my ranks." He stares at me, wonder in his eyes. "We finally meet face to face. Come, have a drink."

He snaps his fingers and a server I saw when I first came up here jumps to attention, pouring me straight vodka, the same drink Anton grips in his overly adorned hand. I accept it but don't drink. I don't have time to play tea party, and Anton knows it.

"So, I'm here—what is it you want?" I ask, trying to keep my tone indifferent. I don't want him to think he has any influence over me.

"I think the question isn't what I want—it's what you want." His eyes glimmer. He knows what I want and he knows he has it. It's pissing me off that he has any leverage in this situation, but I hold still, calculating the decisions I can make to get her out safely and not let Anton win.

"I want to kill you, get rid of your entire operation, and move on with my life," I say, deciding I might as well lay it all out there. Wanting to kill him is fine; that actually being an option is out of the question, but he doesn't need to know that.

"Ha!" He laughs, hitting a nerve that makes me want to chuck the glass in my hand at his head. "Well, I suppose you cannot be more honest than that," he says, still chuckling. Looking at me, his eyes assess me for a moment before he speaks again. "Unfortunately for you, I have something you want."

I cock my head to the side, let my mouth fall into a sarcastic smirk, and ask, "And what is that?"

Anton smiles, and it's menacing. He's trying to intimidate

me. "I have your girl."

I feel my chest tighten but don't let him see that he's affected me. Of course, we both already knew he has her; there is no other person who knows her connection to me, and she's been a big part of his game, something to hold over my head this entire time.

And this is why I've never had a girlfriend.

He speaks again when I don't answer. "Now, I know you are in the FBI, I know your real name, and I know the name of every relative you have. Tell me, do you think Layla would like to get to know Margaret? I could put them together, let them get acquainted. They can bond over your untimely death."

My veins go cold and I toss my drink to the floor, the glass shattering. "You don't go near my family." I practically snarl the words at him as I take a step forward, and his men step in on all sides, surrounding me, but he just laughs. "Where the fuck is she?"

I wasn't planning on talking about Margaret, wasn't planning on letting him take control of this meeting, but with Margaret in the wind and him knowing way too much, I don't have much choice at this point.

"I'll tell you," he starts. "But I'm going to need something from you first."

"What do you want?"

"Safety." He shrugs, trying to seem nonchalant. I see it, though, the slight twitch in his eye, the fear he's holding back.

It's brief, but I see it. "I want passports for me to return to Russia without interruption. I want a guarantee that I don't go to prison."

I scoff. "There's no way that's happening." Even if I can get the FBI to agree, I can't let him get away now, not after everything I've done to stop him.

"Show him." He snaps his fingers at someone and they come forward. They hand me a phone and I keep my eyes on Anton before looking at the screen. It's brief, but I see it, and it's enough to haunt me for the rest of my life.

Margaret hangs from chains. It's dark, but I can tell it's her, her new hair is hung forward shielding her face. She looks dead, but why would he show me this if that were the case? I ask him just that.

"She's not dead. In need of medical attention, surely, but not dead…yet."

I look him in the eyes and glare. I've never felt an urge to beat a man to death like I do right now.

"Fine," I snap, unable to handle thinking of her in such a state. "I'll get you your freedom. Now where is she?" I growl at him.

"No, no. That's not how this works. You get me my passports first, then I give you the girl. That's the deal."

I hesitate, because there's no way I trust him. I don't have much of a choice right now, though. There's nothing I can do; I'm backed into a corner.

"Fine," I repeat. We make plans to meet and I leave, being followed until I'm out the door. I head back to HQ, where James is no doubt pacing and wondering where I disappeared to.

I have to convince them to honor this deal. Margaret's life depends on it, and so does mine.

22

MARGARET

I DON'T KNOW what time it is. It could be two AM, or it could be noon; the basement is so dark it's impossible to tell. I've been in and out for hours. My body keeps giving in to the sleep, the only way it knows how to handle the abuse. With no nourishment, no sunlight, and no water, it's going into a state of shock.

I can't believe it, but as the thought hits, another round of nausea arrives, and I puke up whatever fluid is in my stomach. It's not much, and the result is mostly gagging.

"It's okay, Margaret. I'm almost there, I swear," Ford says, his voice ragged. He's been trying to escape from his chains for hours. I don't think he's slept, and I wonder how his body is putting up with this. He hasn't puked once. It's not fair.

"You're going to hurt yourself," I say, my voice barely a whisper. It's fading as fast as my body. Everything is fading.

"Hurting myself is worth us getting out of here. No one knows where we are, so no one is coming." He says the words that have been circling my head the whole time. I haven't been able to speak them out loud for fear of them being out in the world and thus becoming true.

I don't reply; I don't have the energy. With Ford's grunting in the background, I tell myself to think of happy things. I recall my first date with Liam, and a smile crosses my face. I think it does, anyway—it's hard to tell what's working anymore.

Whether or not my face can express it, Liam is a good, happy thought, Liam and the future we briefly discussed. After the mission, after this is over, we can be happy and normal. We can stay in one city or we can travel.

We can do whatever we want. We just have to survive this first.

I wonder where he is. Does he know I'm trapped yet again? Is he sad? Is he still tracking Anton? Does he care that I'm gone?

God, my thoughts are on repeat.

This is getting so old, and I almost wish for someone to come down here and acknowledge us. It feels as if we've been left for dead.

Maybe we have.

Maybe that's their game, and the longer we wait, the longer we suffer. It's a good strategy, making your prisoners suffer from anticipation.

I fully believe Ford thinks he's getting us out of here. I know he thinks that, but I'm not so sure. I barely escaped with my life last time, and that was because Liam showed up like the hero he is and pretty much saved me.

I have no feeling left in my arms. Tears leak from my eyes, but I don't make a sound. I can't feel anymore.

Everything is numb.

Everything is black.

23

LIAM

"WE'VE GOT THEM!" is shouted out into the large room. My heartrate skyrockets, and hope erupts in my chest for the first time in days.

I'm in the middle of negotiations with the director about getting Anton his freedom, something neither of us wants him to have, but we'll do it to save two of our own. As we discuss the situation, the words are called out by someone staring at the screen in front of her.

I rush over and ask what she means, and she explains, "Ford initiated a tracker. I don't know how he got to it, but it just was picked up. He must have just now been able to access it."

I squeeze the woman's shoulders as a thank you. I don't know who she is, but she's my damn hero right now. Without waiting for more than an address, I haul ass out of the building then realize I don't have a car.

Just as I'm contemplating stealing another one, James is yelling for me to jump in as she runs out of the building behind me. We both get into a black SUV, standard issue, and follow the GPS to a house in the middle of nowhere hours outside of Vegas. It must be one of Anton's hiding places.

"The fact that Ford initiated a tracker is a good sign," James says, her voice tight. I assume she is close with him. They were partners before she was laid up and he disappeared, and that's a bond you can't explain when you experience some of the things you do when you join the agency. She tells me to grab the vests that are in the back seat, and I help her strap hers on before getting my own on.

"It also means they could have been moved. Someone could have found that tracker and trashed it," I say, my tone clipped as my mind flashes to Margaret in that picture Anton showed me.

Motherfucker is definitely going to die.

"Ford hides his tracker pretty well. I don't think they'd find it."

I don't reply and look toward the side mirror. There's another SUV behind us, more agents following as backup since we don't have a clue how many people are guarding this location. Anton seems to think using Margaret is the best way to get me, and so far, he hasn't been wrong.

She came into my world and flipped it upside down. I've felt things with her that I never have before. She's gotten under my skin in a way only someone who wasn't even trying to could do. She didn't mean for any of this to happen, just like I didn't. There was no way to know when we went on that date that we would end up here.

I lean forward in my seat as we get closer and closer. I see a shadow of a house in the distance and keep my eyes open for anyone around. The area is deserted, and it doesn't seem like there's anyone out here at all. We pull off to the side and grab our favored weapons. We're far enough away that no one will have seen us coming unless they're keeping watch, and based on how still the house is, I'm guessing no one is.

We creep close to the shadows, guns at the ready and anticipating a surprise. There's no way this place doesn't have at least someone watching over it.

Unless Ford and Margaret are gone.

Dismissing the thought, I refocus. I doubt Ford would have let anyone stay alive after kidnapping him. As carefree as he seems, he's still an FBI agent, ready to take out any fucker who messes with him.

We check windows, James and I taking the front while the other agents who came take the back. I kick the front door in and search the immediate area—there's no one here. "Clear!" I yell. I hear the other agents yell it back, and we make our way around the house.

Two agents make their way up the stairs, and I head for a door at the back of the house. Wrenching it open and pointing my gun down, I don't see anything. It's pitch black down there, putting my senses on high alert.

James is on my six and we head down, creeping slowly and aiming at the shadows. I feel along the wall for any kind of switch and flip one on when I find it. Directly in front of me is a concrete wall, and Margaret is straight ahead, head lolling and body limp. I swallow a lump that forms in my throat and search the entire basement before making my way to her.

"Thank fuck," I hear Ford mumble. He looks just as bad, and James works on getting him released.

I put my gun away and grab Margaret around the waist. I feel for her pulse under her jawline, a pool of dread circling my stomach. My eyes fill unexpectedly, and I let out a shuddering sigh when I feel a pulse beating beneath my hand.

"Thank you, Jesus," I whisper then work on getting her cuffs off. I sneak a glance at Ford and see he's already loose. He falls to the ground, his legs not working properly after being restrained for so long.

When I get her cuffs off, I cradle her bridal style and turn toward the other two. "Are you okay?" I ask Ford. He looks rough, and these last few days clearly have not been easy on them.

"I'm fine." He grits his teeth and grudgingly lets James help him stand. "I'm so sorry, man. I failed you badly."

I shake my head, not wanting to bother with that right now. My only concern is getting out of here before Anton realizes I didn't show up for our scheduled meeting and figures out I have his only playing card.

"Let's just get out of here." No one argues with me, and we make our way out of the house. The other agents, having cleared the dwelling, bring the cars closer. James takes Ford to one, and I get in the other, laying Margaret on my lap.

I move her hair off of her face and breathe another sigh, allowing myself to be relieved for a brief moment before I squeeze her to me and thank whatever higher power there is that she's safe.

It's a few hours later and the FBI has put us up in a hotel room near their Vegas HQ. It's nice, something Margaret would enjoy if she'd wake up. They sent a private physician to see to her and Ford's wounds. He wasn't as bad, but the doctor hooked Margaret up to an IV. She is suffering from a bad concussion and dehydration, and if it gets worse, we'll have to take her to the hospital. That's what I said from the start, but they want to keep her here for now.

Ford comes over and sits on the bed opposite the one Margaret lies on. I'm not leaving her side until she wakes up.

"What happened?" I ask him. I try to keep accusation out of my voice, but it's difficult considering how angry I was when I found out what happened.

"I should have seen it coming." Ford shakes his head, and I can see he's having a hard time with this. I know he blames himself, as anyone would, but I keep staring at him, waiting for him to tell me. "One minute I was making us food while she slept only ten feet from me, and the next the room was filling with smoke. Then I was chained up in that basement."

"And who came to see you? Anton?"

He crinkles his brow in confusion. "No, no one came. That was the weirdest part. Margaret had woken up before me, but she was out of it. She didn't say much except that no one had come to see us. I never saw Anton or anyone else."

It didn't make sense, just tying them up and leaving, but it did show that he really did not care if they lived or died.

"How was she?" I ask, knowing how hard this has been on her, how much she's been through with this whole endeavor.

"She was okay…" he hedges.

"Tell me," I demand, leaving no room for argument. He sighs and rubs his head, the situation obviously weighing on him heavily. This kind of thing is unfortunately nothing new for us.

"It was hard. She was in and out and anxious. Hyperventilated once, but other than that, she slept. Her body couldn't take the abuse."

Abuse—that is what it was. Every part of this is abuse, and

I'm responsible for it.

I stare at her, so damn grateful she's okay and feeling fucking guilty as hell that she almost wasn't.

24

MARGARET

THERE'S DARKNESS EVERYWHERE. I feel it in my head, in my limbs, a dark weight pushing and holding me down, keeping me hostage. I don't know where I am or how I got here. My eyes won't open no matter how hard I ask them to. The fleeting thought that I'm dead crosses my mind, but I shove it away, praying it's not true.

I beg my eyes, Please, open. Tell me where I am.

But nothing is listening to me. My body won't respond to my pleas. A fear I've never felt pulls at my conscious, and I pray I can make it out of this basement, pray I can plead with God to make a deal. I can't take this anymore. I can't. Please, put me out

o
of my misery.

It takes hours—maybe days, but it's impossible to tell—before I feel a weight on my left hand, someone squeezing it? Someone pulling me?

I don't know, and the panic starts seizing me. The urge to kick and scream pulses through my body, and I push against the darkness to see something, anything. My eyes finally give in and peel open slowly. There's a harsh light, and they reflexively slam shut again. A groan rumbles out of my throat, and I hear someone mumbling beside me.

Liam.

I know it by the low grumble of his voice. He found me.

Or we're in a place I've never desired to be in.

I feel the shadows cover my eyes and I open them again. I take in my surroundings in a way Liam has conditioned me to do. Search for windows, exits, and threats. We're in a hotel room, like the one I was in with him before. I'm lying on one of the beds, and Liam is suddenly right in my line of sight.

He looks horrible, and for him to look bad, it had to have been a rough few days. He looks like he hasn't slept or showered in days. "Mo," he whispers, being sensitive to my aching head. He must sense that it's killing me.

"Liam," I whisper back, reaching my hand toward him. He grasps it gently, being mindful of the tube sticking out of my arm. I follow it to an IV above my head and squint in confusion. What happened to me?

Liam takes in my expression and starts to explain. "You were severely dehydrated when we found you. The doctor hooked you up right away and has been monitoring you." He stops and I stare at him, my eyes glassing over. He looks distraught as he says, "I thought you were dead." His eyes look wet, and I feel mine fill with tears when I get a sudden sense of relief upon realizing I'm not chained up, knowing I'm alive and with him now. "I thought I'd lost you."

He comes closer at my insistence and leans down, burying his head in my neck and letting me hold him. I finally take my first real breath in days. Inhaling slowly, Liam pulls back to take in my face, his eyes roaming over every part as if to make sure it's real, to make sure we're here. I don't have to think about it much when I pull him close and press my lips to his.

I groan at the contact; everything feels so raw right now. I lost any sense of hope in that basement, and the last however many days have destroyed the security I had around myself when I was ignorant to this world. I thought I was going to die. Kissing Liam is grounding me to the present in a way I didn't know I needed.

He pulls away before I want him to and when I protest, he smiles a small smile. "I can't let myself get carried away with you."

"Please get carried away," I say, unashamed at the contact I feel I need. His smile only grows. I try to pull him back down, but just then the door opens and a tall, thin man walks into the room. His face is kind, and he gives me a grin when he makes eye contact.

"I'm glad to see you awake," he says, and he shakes Liam's hand. This must be the doctor he mentioned. I'm proven right when Liam introduces him as Dr. Carter. He goes through the motions of a normal checkup and inspects a bandage on my head, one I didn't realize was there, and he then takes the IV out of my arm. "Well, your veins are looking better. You need to get some food in you, nothing too heavy, and get plenty of rest."

Liam's on the phone with room service before the doctor can finish his sentence, and I smirk at him.

The doctor leaves after that then something hits me. "Oh God, how is Ford?" I ask Liam as he hangs up. Walking over, he sits on the bed next to me, immediately grabbing my hand. There's a smirk on his face, so my guess is Ford is somewhere recovering as well.

"He's all right, a little banged up, but he's up and around now."

"Oh good."

"He felt bad about everything," Liam says.

"Please tell me you didn't make him feel worse," I say sternly, somehow sensing that is exactly how he would have handled the situation.

He squints his eyes at the wall above my head and feigns innocence.

"Liam, what did you do?"

"Nothing bad." I see him look at me seriously and decide to let it go. "Come on, time to get you feeling better." His fingers grasp my arm with a gentle authority, and I let him lead me toward the bathroom. Respecting my privacy, he helps me undress until I'm only in underwear then leaves the room. I almost call him back in, but I let my self-consciousness get the best of me and allow my dizzy head to take the lead.

I feel an extra sense of need with him that hasn't been there until now. The chemistry, the tension has always been there, but this is a new feeling, a sensation of wanting to be safe, to be held and comforted. It's something only he can give me.

LIAM

Margaret went into the bathroom over an hour ago to take her first shower in days. I sympathize because I haven't showered in as long as she's been gone, but as long as I'm around, her care will always come first.

The second her eyes opened up, it was like a weight was lifted off of my chest. Everything I'd been worried about exited my brain. She was okay.

It was the only thought that kept repeating itself over and over again. She's okay, she's okay, she is okay.

It was enough that she was awake—at least it meant we

could move forward—but she has exceeded all expectations. She is up, walking around, showering. I've never met someone as resilient as her since I left the military.

I sit on the edge of the bed closest to the bathroom and wait for her, listening to make sure she doesn't fall and hurt herself. I tell myself it's not creepy. It's for safety.

A soft knock on the door has my head shooting up, and I grab my gun off a nightstand. I walk to the door, peeping through the hole quickly, and I see Ford standing on the other side, hands already in the air. Smartass.

"Hey." I open the door and he closes it behind himself, stalking in after me. His injuries were pretty rough, but he's had much worse than that and bounced back fast. It also helped that he hadn't fallen into any sort of coma.

"Hey." He looks around the room and sees the empty bed. "She's awake?"

"Yeah." I gesture toward the bathroom door. "Cleanin' up."

He nods his head, a soft exhalation leaving his lungs. "Good, good." He mumbles the words and looks away from me, not making eye contact and giving me reason to believe he needs to get something off of his chest.

"What's on your mind?" I prod.

"I just…I want to make sure she's okay." He finally looks up at me. "I have to make sure, for myself." Ford looks toward the door again and leans against the wall. I've seen that look; it's the same one he had on a mission we were on a few years ago, before

I went dark. We had to rescue a hostage who was being held by some thugs who thought they were something.

It wasn't easy, but it was one of those missions that sticks with you. Unfortunately, it didn't go as planned, and before we could complete a safe rescue, one of the men we'd been tailing detonated a bomb. The woman was in the explosion and didn't make it out of the rubble alive.

That one haunts us, and anything that resembles that situation always brings those feelings up. Ford took it harder than anyone. I've known him a long time, and I can see the war he's fighting with himself right now.

"Ford," I say, my voice hard.

"What?"

"Are you feeling guilty?"

He doesn't answer right away. They were in a place that many people will thankfully never have to experience, and it was one that brought on a bond you can't compare to anything else. They were alone in that basement for a long time.

Being alone with someone that long can lead to a sort of camaraderie; my time in the Army taught me that. Those guys do become like brothers, some more than others, but you would lay down your life for any one of them.

"No," Ford says after some thought. "Yes," he corrects. Heaving a deep sigh, he looks at me, and worry seeps into his face. "I don't know. It just brought up some stuff for me."

Before I can press, the door to the bathroom finally opens

and Margaret walks out, freshly dressed in the clothes I got her. James was the one to actually pick them out, but she did so at my insistence. Margaret looks fresh and clean with no makeup on her face, as beautiful as the first time I saw her, but what really catches me is how relieved she looks to see Ford standing outside the door.

He's pushed off the wall and heads for her, pulling her into a hug with no resistance on her end. They embrace tightly like they don't want to let go, and I see the immense compassion Margaret has for others. She had it for Mike and Jenny, she has it for Ford, and she has it for me. Anyone who's around her feels immediately comfortable in her presence.

When they pull away, they take a minute to take the other in, and Margaret says, "I'm so glad you're okay." There's a happiness in her voice that nearly matches the tone that was there when she saw me sitting on the bed beside her.

I stand, knowing Ford needs a moment. He's one of my closest friends, a guy who would do anything for you and never ask for a favor in return. "I'll be outside."

I don't wait for them to say anything; Margaret looks hurt by it, but I just briefly squeeze her shoulder when I walk around them. Ford doesn't know what to say; it's clear in his expression, so I give him a nod and let him sort through what he needs to in order to assure himself everything is okay.

25

MARGARET

I WATCH LIAM leave the hotel room and worry my bottom lip. I know I flung myself onto Ford, but I was just surprised to see him there and relieved to know he's all right. I know how it looked, and now Liam is gone; I feel unease that I've messed up.

"I'm so glad you're okay." Ford's voice brings me back, and he places his hands on my shoulders. He doesn't move them, and I think it's to ground himself more than anything. I feel the same way he does right now; it felt like he'd be the last person I would see before I died.

"Me too—I mean, that you're all right." I fumble my words and chuckle a little.

"I honestly didn't think we were going to make it out of there. Thank God I got to the tracker."

"Tracker?"

He shakes his head. "I forgot you were unconscious for that part. I had a tracker in my shoe, and I was finally able to reach it after a ton of struggling. Once I enabled it, the FBI could see our location."

"Oh." I assumed Liam had gotten it out of Anton. I never once thought Ford was doing anything other than trying to break free of the chains. "I guess I was pretty out of it, huh?" I chuckle.

"Not so out of it that you didn't stomp the life out of a rat." He laughs at my expression when I remember that moment.

"Oh God." I grimace and place a hand over my stomach. "I really did that, didn't I?"

"You did." He's still smirking in amusement. "It was nasty as hell, too."

I groan and look at him. "Well, just add that to the crazy shit I've done then. First on that list: shooting you."

At that he throws his head back and laughs at me. When he composes himself, he takes a step back and his face softens. I wait for him to get whatever he needs to release off of his chest. "I can't tell you how worried I was about us getting out alive." He pauses and rubs his jaw. "I was on a mission years ago and…it was far too similar to what you've been through." His eyes lock on mine, and I interlace my fingers in front of me, giving him time to sort through his thoughts. "I am just so glad you're okay, and..." He reaches into his pocket for a slip of paper. "I wanted you to have this. It's my personal cell." Ford waits until he has my eyes again and says, "If you ever need anything, you can call. Day or night, next week or in ten years—any time."

"Wow." I'm truly surprised that he would give me this. Ford is definitely one of the good guys. "Thanks, Ford." He turns to leave, but I stop him with a hand on his arm. "Wait, I'm still gonna see you, right?" I ask, more worried than I should be about losing my new friend. There's an element here that I'm unsure how to interpret. It feels like I went from not knowing his name to being best friends.

"Of course." His dimples greet me, and he steps forward to give me a reassuring hug.

He doesn't linger long, and when he's gone, I go sit on the bed by the door. I get a whiff of Liam, his cologne wafting through the air and reminding me that he left too and I don't know when he's coming back.

The ache I've felt since I woke up hasn't left me, and I wish more than anything he were here so we could have some time, even if it's only an hour, to be together. I want to reassure myself and him that we're both real, that we're both in this thing—whatever it is we want to call it—until the end.

The door opens suddenly, and it's like my fantasy has brought him to me. I take a look at him, his eyes holding unspoken questions.

Of course, he left Ford in here alone with me so we could

talk, but they had time before I came out of the bathroom. Does he know Ford is struggling with what happened the last few days?

Deciding to wait on asking any of those questions, I take a shaky breath and take action on something I've been dreaming about since he left me at my apartment several weeks ago, since our first night together, since that spark of hope I had when I met him bloomed into something more.

Standing slowly, I cross the room. My hands go straight for his neck and his quickly wrap around my waist, his arms engulfing my body like he could crush me. I give in to the kiss, letting him take control quickly.

I touch his wet hair and pull away. "Did you take a shower?"

He squints. "Yes." He doesn't give me more, and my body can't wait a second longer. A sense of urgency drives me, and Liam is quick to reciprocate. He backs me to the first bed and lays me down. He takes a minute to look me over seductively and tries to bite back a grin when he sees how heavily I'm breathing.

Just his feral gaze makes my body heat. He bends over me, and his hand starts a slow trail from the column of my throat down between my breasts, the cleavage ample in this shirt. I lean up for him to take it off over my head.

My heart pounds in my chest, and I throw off my bra, letting it fall to the bed. He never takes his eyes off me, his gaze molten and perusing every inch of my exposed skin. I feel like he's worshiping me with his eyes, and a new sense of self-appreciation washes over me. His gaze alone makes me feel like a queen.

He slowly unbuttons my jeans and pushes them off my hips, taking care to take my panties down with them. I'm completely exposed to him, my curves wide but soft, and his touch makes my skin heat, makes my face flush just from having him watch my response.

His nose trails up my shin, over the juncture between my legs, and I jump at the contact. Up over my belly button he goes, stopping when he's at my left breast. His hand covers my right one and his lips clasp over my left nipple, making me take in a sharp breath.

Liam tortures me there, but my pleas go unheard, and he continues for a moment before making his way back to my face, kissing me like a man starved. His manner is soothing, and I take every little bit he gives to me.

He pulls away enough to look into my eyes, but his words are what make me melt. "You're so beautiful, Margaret."

I don't have the words to reply, which is probably a good thing because I probably would have told him I love him.

I'm not ready for that.

Neither is he.

My thoughts are cut off when I feel him trail back down my body in a slow perusal. His nose breathes me in and he sticks his tongue in my most sensitive spot, opening my folds with ferocity. I immediately shoot my hips up, and his hands press me back down.

Liam takes his time licking, sucking, moving from my entrance to my clit and back again. His hands grasp my hips so hard I'm sure he's going to leave bruises, but I don't care. I'd take those bruises any time if it meant this was how I got them. My right hand is clenching his hair tightly when I feel myself on the verge and my left arm shoots out, grabbing the bedding, trying to anchor myself there. "Liam." A deep moan wrecks me, and I scream when the orgasm shoots through me, so intense.

"You're…" I gasp. I can't seem to catch my breath and Liam looks at me, half cocky and the other half genuinely curious. "Amazing. That…that was amazing," I say on a laugh. His smile turns into a grin and I reach up, not done with him yet. I yank his shirt off over his head, nearly ripping it and getting it caught on his ear. "Sorry," I mumble, embarrassed but not enough to stop. I go for his jeans, but he stops me.

"I got it…don't want it to get caught…" He goes for his pants, and I noticed he's straining against the material, a laugh bubbling in my throat at his insinuation. My laugh quickly fades when he loses his boxers and his cock springs forward.

I swallow and look up at him.

It feels like it's been so long, so I try my best to appear unaffected by him though he's definitely the biggest I've ever had. I already know how skilled he is, and I know it's going to be just as amazing as it was then.

"I can't wait much longer." His voice is rough, and I nod my head. He grabs a condom out of the pocket of his jeans, and I raise a brow. "I've carried one ever since I met you," he says. I don't know how to respond to that, so I choose not to comment at all.

Liam leans over me again, moves us up onto the bed more securely, and presses his lips to mine. It's soft and slow, sweeter than before. He stokes a fire inside of me, bringing my untried senses to life.

When he's ready, he looks deeply into my eyes, and I soften my expression when I see how he's looking at me—like I make him feel loved, like he's just as unsure and yet so passionately ready for everything we could do together. When he pushes into me, he doesn't break eye contact, and I can see everything he's feeling, something I've never been able to do before. He lets me adjust to him, and I reach up to kiss him. He takes it as encouragement and moves deeper inside until he's buried completely. I can't get over the sensation of how it feels. It's quite possibly the best feeling I've ever felt in my life, and I'm more than grateful that I get to experience this with him.

Liam puts his forearms underneath my shoulders and holds me to him, pushing deeper with every thrust, and I let myself fall into this with him. He takes charge, and I follow him every step of the way. His eyes peer into mine, and I see something I've never seen before. Love is the only word I can use to describe it.

Wait, no—love, awe, understanding.

This isn't something he's experienced either; I can tell, and that makes it that much more powerful.

I feel myself edging to the brink of my second orgasm, and I close my eyes again.

"No," Liam says, his voice strained. "Open them." I blink my eyes open and watch his face, mine contorting as my orgasm slams into me. Our eyes stay locked as our breathing syncs, and Liam continues moving until his body tenses above me. I hold him close and let us catch our breaths, my mind going a million miles an hour.

Words I haven't and can't let myself speak come to the tip of my tongue. It makes my heart race with a deep urgency but I hold them in, fear keeping me from fully acknowledging the truth.

I truly hope I don't regret not telling him.

For now, I just hold on to the man who's changed everything for me.

26

LIAM

"HOW DO WE know we can trust him?" I hear the words spill out of a naïve newbie to the agency. He's been eyeballing me for twenty minutes as I sit across from Director Hayes and fill him in on my activities.

I've known Hayes for years. He was an agent before they promoted him to director, and he was my mentor, helping me hone my craft. I look up to him, and I'm hoping he gives me a chance to right what went wrong.

"Parker," he snaps, silencing the idiot in the corner. His petulance was really starting to piss me off, so I'm glad Hayes said something before I did.

"Sir." I speak up then, needing to lay out what I intend to do before I get interrupted by the adolescent in the corner. "I need to get to work on finding Anton. He hasn't gone far—I know he hasn't. I just need to figure out where he's hiding."

Anton didn't bother calling me this time when he found out I got his leverage out from under him without giving him the resources to flee the country. The first thing I did was make sure there was a team of agents guarding my sister and her family. She doesn't know she's being watched, but that doesn't matter as long as she is safe.

Now, Anton is in hiding, and I am going to track him down.

I just need Hayes to allow it or I'll be in bigger trouble with the FBI than I was before.

"Sir." Agent James enters the room and hands him a stack of papers. I can't read what they say. "Everything checks out."

Hayes looks over them, squinting in places and hiding a smirk in others. "So it does," he says, setting the papers aside. "All right, I'll give you one more chance, Stokes. You fuck up again"—he pauses, pointing a finger in my direction—"you answer to me, and I guarantee you won't like how I handle it. James, where is Agent Perk? Have we made contact with him?"

"No, sir. We're still working on that."

He sends us out of the room with a flick of his wrist and I stand, following James. "Thanks," I tell her. We don't know each other very well, but I know she and Ford have become closer since I've been gone, and if he trusts her then I do too.

"No problem." She shoots me a wink. "Now let's go get this bastard."

Laughter spills from the hotel room when I open the door, and I walk in to see Ford clutching his nuts and Margaret laughing uncontrollably. She looks like she's about to fall over, and when she finally notices me, she tries to pull herself together.

"Do I want to know?" I ask, walking over and placing a kiss on her cheek. It's nice to finally be able to do that without wondering if it's okay.

Last night, we made love again, although this time it was different than the last. It was more passionate, more meaningful, and let me tell you, it was also fucking amazing. I can't get over it. It's like a constant loop in my head, over and over again. I had to drag myself out of the room this morning to meet with the director because I didn't want to leave the nest we seemed to have buried ourselves in.

I also didn't want to leave her there alone, but she assured me she was fine. When Ford showed up unannounced, I let him take over the watch while I handled business.

I didn't ask what they discussed yesterday, and I didn't see Ford again until this morning, but I know it couldn't have been too hard for him to take if he was here laughing with her now.

Plopping in a chair, I uncover one of the silver dishes on the table, eagerly reaching for the food. While I wait for them to calm down, I think about how I am going to get Anton. He isn't about to go back to Vino; I know that. He is smarter than that. He will go somewhere new, somewhere no one will know to look.

His problem, really, is me. I am the reason he isn't free to do as he pleases, so I have no doubt he wants to find a way to get rid of me. He could do that and maybe have a small chance of getting somewhere safe. He isn't crossing any borders, though, unless he knows someone who can get him through undetected. I'm not about to say he couldn't pull it off; the guy has contacts he could use.

"How did it go this morning? I assume Hayes gave you a slap on the wrist since you're here and not detained."

"I'm free." As an afterthought, I add, "For now." I have no doubt once my mission is done they are going to have me completely debriefed, which is going to be an absolute nightmare, but I'll worry about that later.

"For now?" Margaret questions, sitting in the chair next to me. I think for a second before I drag it closer to me. I breathe easier when she's closer.

Fuck, I'm so fucked with this girl.

"I'm not worried about it right now," I say, not answering her question. "Right now, I have to focus on Anton, on where he is."

"Any ideas?" Ford asks. His brows furrow, and I see him slip into agent mode. He's a good guy to have as backup, despite his kidnapping, which wasn't his fault. He's helped me out of more situations than I care to admit, which is why I was grateful that Hayes assigned him to help me with this one.

"None," I say. "He has one hideout, a place called Vino, but that was the last place I met up with him. Now he knows I know he likes to go there, so I doubt he'll go there again."

"Why do you think there weren't any guards at that house?" Margaret asks.

I look at her and think about it for a moment before I shrug. "No idea. Best guess is he didn't think we'd ever find you, so there was no reason to post anyone there. Dummy move, but the more anxious he gets to flee the country, the sloppier he gets."

"Maybe we could use that to our advantage?" I raise a brow in question, and she continues. "Maybe we could use something to draw him out of hiding. What does he need more than anything to get out of this mess? Can we use it against him?"

I think about her question, of the things Anton needs, and really, he needs freedom. He needs people to get him his freedom because otherwise, he's fucked. "He needs safe passage. He needs help."

"So maybe we can use me to get to him?"

"What do you mean?"

"I mean, if we go out in public, maybe we can get his attention and entice him to walk into some sort of trap?"

I think about it for a second before shaking my head. "No, I'm not putting you in his path again."

Margaret's eyes hold a gleam of interest backed by a

determination I'm sure is supposed to make me back down, but I can't risk putting her in danger. She's had enough trauma to last a lifetime; she doesn't need one bit more. "Margaret." My voice holds a warning, but she doesn't look away.

"Let me help," she says adamantly. "I want to help."

"It's not safe." My voice hardens, and I see her eyes flicker, a brief sign of doubt crossing her face.

"I know it's not, but none of this has been and I've managed to survive this long. I'm fine. Let me help you finish this." She grabs my hand and squeezes. "So we can get to that normal you talked about."

She's using our conversation against me and I sigh, closing my eyes and thinking about how I can make all of this work.

"I have the perfect idea," Ford says, his eyes shining with mischief. I know I'm going to hate whatever he's about to say. "You guys get married."

"Uh, I'm sorry, Agent Dimples, say what?" Margaret sputters.

"Agent Dimples?" Ford asks. I can tell he likes that Margaret called him that, but I have more important questions to ask.

"What do you mean, we get married?" I ask, wondering what elaborate scheme Ford has circling in his mind. I'm surprisingly not against his plan so far.

"It's perfect. We get the agency to rent a church, one of the cheesy Elvis ones. You guys go there and pretend you're getting married then Anton will get word of it and will try to use it against you."

I think about his asinine idea. "I love it," I say. It's not a bad plan. Anton wouldn't be expecting it to be a trap. He knows—somehow realizing it before I did—that Margaret is important to me, and he has been using that against me this entire time.

"You do?" Margaret's eyes flick to mine, dubious astonishment lacing her voice.

A smirk forms on my lips. "I do."

She busts out laughing.

27

MARGARET

ROWS UPON ROWS of dresses line the store I'm standing in. Agent James is my company on this trip, part protection and part bridesmaid. We're out in the open, hoping word may get back to Anton that I'm here, in Vegas, searching for a wedding dress.

I can't settle the butterflies that take flight in my stomach at the thought of marrying Liam, fake or not.

I was most surprised that he was so into the idea of everything, of faking a wedding to pull Anton out of his cowardly hiding spot. Who knew a man so twisted would be scared of the government? I suppose once you know you're backed into a corner, you'll do whatever is necessary to stay away from them.

"What about this?" I ask and then stop, holding it up, looking at her in question. "Wait, what's your name?"

"Agent James," she replies stiffly, looking at our surroundings with a bit of disgust on her face.

"I know that one, but what about your real name?" I clarify.

"It's not important."

I let my arms drop from where I was holding a dress up to my body and give her a look. "Look, this might be fake, but it also might be my only chance to be a bride. I'd like to at least know my only bridesmaid's name."

She sighs and looks at me. Her face gives away her annoyance, but I don't let up on the stare I'm holding. "Fine. It's Gemma."

"Gemma James?" I say.

"I didn't pick it," she replies, raising her hands in the air. "Did you find one or not?" She gestures toward the dress in my arms.

"I don't know…this one is just not my style."

"What is your style?" she asks, quirking a brow.

I hesitate before replying, knowing my answer isn't what we're looking for, but it is the truth. "Pants," I say, chuckling lightly. I take a minute to watch her; she's a rigid woman, but she's beautiful. It's amazing that she's an FBI agent when she could easily be a model.

"How'd you get into being an FBI agent?" I ask her. I don't expect her to give me a real answer—she doesn't seem like a very personable person—but I want to know the people who have helped me out these last few weeks. She helped Ford and me escape our own personal hell.

"I didn't really plan for it." She fingers one of the gowns that surrounds us and sighs, her shoulders dropping and her gaze softening. "I was in school, finishing a pre-law degree." Now, a lawyer—that I can picture. "One night I was working late, and I didn't think about anything but getting home and getting to sleep. It was finals week and I was pulling twenty-hour days, sometimes more. It was dark, the campus only dotted with a few stragglers who were just as tired as I was. It wasn't supposed to be dangerous."

A touch of vulnerability reaches her voice and I wait patiently, knowing I won't like the ending but needing to hear it anyway.

"A guy I was classmates with came up to me really suddenly, and I didn't think anything of it. We were friends, kind of. I was always so busy in class that I didn't really make a ton of them, but we'd talked before and he was nice enough. He offered to walk me back to my dorm that night, and I said yes. We talked about the class we shared and how the professor was a dick." She scoffs, rolling her eyes at the memory and seemingly forgetting I'm there. She hasn't once looked up at me. "We were almost there when it happened. He asked me out and I—as politely as I could—turned him down. It wasn't even a bad excuse—I just said I was too busy with school, too tired to go out or start anything when finals were stacking up, but he couldn't take no for an answer. He easily outweighed me by about eighty pounds, and it took nothing for him to attack me."

Gemma clears her throat and blinks her eyes, the mist from them fading. When she looks up at me, she almost seems surprised I'm still there.

"Anyway, he got off on a fine, and that was when I decided I needed to change some things. I joined the police academy, then Quantico, became an FBI agent and never looked back."

She goes back to looking at the dresses in front of her, but I can tell she's not used to telling that story and it's made her vulnerable. "Wow." My mind is reeling after what she just told me, at the idea that one decision, one incident changed her whole life. "That's incredible."

Gemma doesn't respond, giving me a tight smile. "You said pants, right?" She walks over to a rack we passed a ways back. "I saw just the thing." She pulls out the hanger and my eyes widen, taking in the piece she's holding out—or should I say, the pieces.

"That's gorgeous," I say, fingering the sleeve of the top. "But I don't think I can pull it off. It's very…form-fitting."

Gemma scoffs. "Are you kidding? You have just the right amount of curves. Try it on." She thrusts it into my hands and pushes me toward the dressing room. "We do have a few other things to do before we take down the biggest drug lord in America, ya know?"

Her sarcasm catches me off guard, but I obey and go into the first open room. I pull the curtain closed and carefully hang the outfit on the hook. As I'm putting it on, I hear Gemma get a call, and I eavesdrop through the curtain. I mean, surely if it was that private, she wouldn't be standing right by the room.

"He got a tux? Like a real one?" Gemma asks, and my brows rise in amazement, a small smile touching my lips. Liam in a tux? Damn. I don't know if my ovaries can handle that. "Well, I think this one is her outfit, so we shouldn't be much longer," she replies to the caller; I'm guessing it's Ford.

She's confident this is the outfit when she hasn't even seen me in it yet. I finish up the last button and move around in it—I have to be able to move to do what we have planned. It's surprisingly comfortable.

I step out, and Gemma's only reaction is a raised eyebrow while I walk past her and onto the small platform so I can look in all the mirrors arranged there. I look up and scrunch my eyebrows. The garments don't make me look like me.

"Hold on, put these on." She puts heels in front of me, and I place a hand on her shoulder for balance as I nudge my feet into them.

"Huh, these are actually comfortable."

"Good. Heels make this outfit work, and you still need comfort."

The top is a fitted blazer with a deep plunge that makes my cleavage pop without being trashy. It's pristine white and all clean lines, the pants high-waisted and tapered at the bottom. The heels are an accessory I'm not used to, but they fit the outfit perfectly. With the soft waves I put my hair in earlier and the heavier-than-normal makeup I've applied, I look like I'm walking a red carpet more than having a fake wedding.

"Wow," I say, looking over at Gemma and raising a brow in appreciation. "You've got excellent taste."

"I know," she says and then walks over, grabs a hanger, and goes into the dressing room.

In a flash, she's out wearing a nearly identical outfit, except hers is sleeveless, and the brilliant red makes the white I'm wearing pop. Her blonde hair is in a low but expertly placed bun, and she could easily rock a runway somewhere.

"Dude." I give her a friendly hip bump. "Quit trying to upstage me on my wedding day." She smiles, and my mouth gapes open. "I got you to smile!"

"Whatever," she grumbles. "Come on, I need to find a place for a weapon in that outfit of yours."

We pay for our clothes and make our way back to the hotel room where Gemma finds a way to hide a gun on my body for emergency purposes. If all goes well, I shouldn't have to worry about firing it, but since we're referencing the last few weeks… well, let's just say this firearm really completes my look.

And here we are, my wedding day.

It wasn't what I expected, although I did dream of my

wedding day like most young girls do, dressing up dolls to get married and making Barbie kiss Ken, secretly dreaming it was me marrying the too-perfect Ken doll. I highly doubt little Margaret ever dreamed her wedding day would end up like this.

I walk slowly down the aisle, an organ playing out Pachelbel's "Canon", and my eyes shyly look up at the man waiting for me at the end of the aisle. A nervous giggle escapes my lips, and he lets loose a wide grin. I let myself, just for a moment, believe this is real.

The amused look suddenly leaves his eyes and is replaced by a tenderness as he watches me slowly approach. He has his hands clasped in front of him and his tux is sharp and clean, fitting him so perfectly I wonder exactly where he went to get something so right so quickly. His expression looks real, genuine, and I savor the moment. The man I've come to respect, the man I've come to love is marrying me today.

When I reach him, he grasps my hands in his and pulls me to stand across from him, Elvis on my left and Gemma behind me.

Liam's grin stays on mine as the officiant recites something out of a book. It's generic, and his impersonation is terrible. When I see Mike here, standing up for Liam at our fake marriage, I give Liam a questioning glance, which he answers with a shrug.

Elvis finishes and I hear Liam recite words after him, slipping a ring on my finger—Where'd he get a ring? Gemma hands me a matching band as I recite the same words to him, following the motions of putting a ring on his finger.

Oh God. My heartrate skyrockets as things progress, and I hear Liam say the infamous words 'I do.' When it's my turn, I say them back, giving him a questioning gaze. He tells me to stick with the plan by nodding his head, and I do, mostly because there's no turning back now.

"I now pronounce ya, husband and a-wife." Elvis makes the proclamation, terrible accent and all, and I'm about to break character when Liam leans in for a kiss to seal the deal. Just as he's about to cover my lips with his, I hear slow, mocking clapping coming from the entrance.

He's here.

"Well, isn't this a wonderful turn of events," Anton says, looking at us with hatred blazing in his eyes.

"Anton," Liam replies. He's looking at him head-on, and the members of our 'wedding party' act stunned. "What do you want?"

"I want my passports," he says, his anger visible in his clenched fists. "I want my fucking deal to go through!" His temper gets the best of him and he spits out his words.

"Deal's off," Liam says with cool confidence. "Now, if you'll excuse me." He turns to me and cups my jaw, leaning in for a kiss. We slowly release each other, our heads still close, and he stares at me with a stony resolve. He's bracing himself—I can feel it in his hold—and when he nods, I know the shit is about to hit the fan.

I open my mouth to speak, but then, as if in slow motion, my eye catches something in my periphery. Several men file into the room, Mike and Gemma moving fast. Elvis follows suit, as does the man I just married.

Forcing myself into the moment, I reach into my jacket, grasping what I need, and throw myself behind one of the pews as shots ring out over my head. I steady myself, catch my new husband's eye, and nod, ready for the fight.

Bullets start flying without warning, and the pews splinter above my head. Liam's firing back along with everyone else, and I cast a glance over the pew, not aiming before shooting back at Anton and his men.

I hear a groan as Elvis goes down and I gasp, hoping whatever injury it is can be fixed, praying this shooting will stop before anyone else takes a hit. I'm so busy staring at Elvis that I don't even notice when Liam clutches my arm in his, dragging me farther down.

The room is still loud with the gunfight. Where is the FBI? They were already supposed to be here.

As if my thoughts are heard, men filter in from behind Anton and his men. I breathe a sigh of relief as the notorious man is handcuffed, screaming and cursing the entire time, and Liam walks over there, leaving me on my knees, half-hidden from view, watching Liam as he reads Anton his rights himself, finally putting an end to this mission.

I remember Elvis and make my way over there; Gemma is

already there assessing the damage. I reach out and take his giant glasses off his face.

"Shit. Are you okay?" I look for any more wounds, and when I don't see any, I look back into his face. I'm greeted with dimples shining back at me.

"Aw, don't worry about me. I've had much worse." As he says the words, his eyes slowly close, and he doesn't respond when I call out his name, nor when I shake his shoulders. I feel tears suddenly start falling down my face, and Gemma's voice yells for paramedics over the continued chaos around us.

Liam hears the commotion and joins us beside Ford. "Ah, dude. Don't do this to me," he says, moving me aside so he can put pressure on the wound.

I stare at him and will him to just open his eyes, hoping I didn't just watch my friend die. Paramedics rush in and take over from there, hurriedly loading him onto a stretcher and putting him into the back of an ambulance. Liam and I follow everyone out of the church, and I take a deep breath of fresh air. The adrenaline starts to leave my system, and I feel like I could sleep for a week.

"He'll go to a private wing. They won't let us in," Liam says, grabbing my hand and pulling me to a curb to sit down.

"Will he be okay?" I ask, watching the ambulance pull away.

"He'll be fine. Ford won't let a bullet take his life."

As we sit in silence and watch the FBI agents mill around us, I relish in the feel of Liam's hand in mine and let my mind go over everything that happened. My finger brushes over his ring, and I wonder where we go from here. I'm hoping a hotel room, but I don't want to be insensitive to what we just went through.

An older man waves Liam over, and he tenses beneath my hand. "What is it?" I ask.

"Margaret, ah, I have to let you know what happens now." He doesn't look at me, keeping his gaze on our hands.

"What do you mean?" I look over to the man standing there. "I was thinking we could get a room, whenever you're done with him, I mean."

But Liam's expression isn't relieved. He's still got creases by his eyes and his mouth is tight. He's holding something back from me, and I brace myself for whatever it is. He finally looks at me then, and I hate what his gaze says.

Goodbye isn't what I was expecting.

"How long?"

"I don't know," he says quietly. "But listen, when I'm done, I'll come find you, and everything I said will happen. I swear to you." I believe he thinks that, but it's hard to see it actually happening.

"And I'm supposed to...what? Return to normal?" I ask, thinking the idea is preposterous.

"Just for now."

I scoff and pull my hand out of his, standing and putting my hands on my head, not able to comprehend what is happening. Of course, I should have seen this coming, shouldn't I have? How many times has he left me hanging, left me behind?

"Mo, hold on."

"Stokes." The man in the expensive-looking suit snaps his fingers, and Liam tenses. I look to him, wondering what he'll do, but when he looks me in the eyes, I know exactly what he's going to do.

"It's all right," I say with a shrug of my shoulders, even though it absolutely is not all right at all. "I get it." Lies. Lies. Lies.

"Mo, this is just temporary, I swear. I'll come find you as soon as I can."

I nod as he comes close and wraps his hand around the back of my neck. I look into his dark eyes, and they tell me what I want to hear, but it's not enough, not after everything. He presses his lips to mine and I realize this could be the last time. With that in mind, I grab the lapels of his tux and pull him tight to me, kissing him with everything I have, telling him with the kiss what I can't let myself say out loud.

We break apart and stare at each other for a moment before he backs away, the man behind him waiting impatiently. I let go of his hand only when I can't hold it anymore, and I watch him walk away.

He's put in the back of a black SUV, and it quickly pulls away from the scene. I can't see through the dark tint of the windows, but I doubt he looked back. Liam doesn't look back.

It's then I realize I'm stuck in Vegas with no idea how to get myself home.

"Hey." I turn and see Mike walk up to me. How did I forget

he's here? He hands me an envelope, and when I open it, I see a plane ticket to Denver along with the ID I thought I'd lost, a wad of cash, and a phone I've never seen before. "You get to go home now." His smile is forced. Somehow, a guy who's basically a stranger knows Liam hurt me more than Liam himself knows it.

"Yay," I reply with false enthusiasm.

"It'll all turn out well."

"How? I mean, what am I supposed to do now?" I think about returning to my life as a sales clerk and immediately want to puke. I can't go back to that. I just can't do it. It's not what my life is for. I'm not meant to deal with crabby people who can't follow simple rules, who get pissed at me when I don't make their menial lives easier.

I need more. I deserve more.

"Go home," Mike says. "Figure out what it is you want."

"What I want just left in an SUV without looking back." I swing my arm out in the direction they went. I've already lost sight of it.

"I get it." Mike nods. "But he'll be back."

"When?" I ask, a slight whine in my voice that I hate.

"That isn't something I can answer, unfortunately." Mike leans in and gives me a hug, saying goodbye, probably for the last time, and I look to the busy street for a cab.

On the ride to the airport, I look down at my outfit; it's now smudged and wrinkled. The ring I forgot I was wearing sparkles when the lights from the Strip flash into the cab. I feel tears gather in my eyes, and I hold them back.

The phone Mike gave me vibrates, and my breath catches at the words on the screen.

I'll find you as soon as possible. I promise.

I don't reply, because I know the only thing I want to say isn't something I'm brave enough to put out there, especially with how we left things.

I tuck it away, thinking over the last few weeks, thinking about how much has changed, how much I've changed. I can't go back to the life I had before. I have to find something more. I have to change my life to fit who I've become.

28

LIAM

THE ROOM IS dark, and the light hanging above me gives me a killer headache. I can't tell how long I've been in here, but the air has become stale and the coffee in the cup that rests beside my hand has long since grown cold.

They told me it wouldn't be long before the director would be in to talk to me, but it's been hours, and at this point I don't even know what day it is.

I'm still wearing the tux I wore to our wedding—our fake wedding—and Ford's blood is still splattered across it. They told me he would be okay, but I couldn't see him as he's being held in the hospital and my free will is no longer an option, at least not for the time being.

The light catches on the gold band that wraps around my left ring finger. I stare at it and then feel a slow smile spread across my lips. I close my eyes and picture the moment when she walked down the aisle. I'd never admit it out loud, but my heart was beating so hard I was worried everyone in the room could hear it.

When she stepped up next to me and placed her hands in mine, it felt so real. Everything about it was so natural, and for the first time in my life, I knew I could see myself with her for real, long term. All those words I'd said before about being with her, having a normal life and normal jobs and real, normal dates—they all suddenly become a clear vision in my head.

I pictured us moving in together and walking along the streets in whatever city we ended up in. I saw us arguing over what meals to eat, what food to buy, what kind of furniture we should put in our house, even though I couldn't care less about all that as long as I am with her. As long as I can wake up to her in the morning and see her face, I don't care what I do any other time. I don't care where we live or what we do; I just need us to be doing it together.

When she said I do, my heart about burst from the joy I felt. I knew when I said it to her, I meant it. When I slipped that ring on her finger, I was really committing myself as her husband.

It was real for me.

The fact that she is God knows where right now, spending

our wedding night alone, makes my chest ache. She deserves better than that, better than the FBI saying, Have a nice life.

She deserves better than me, but I am going to do everything I can to make sure I give her the life she's always dreamed of.

The door finally opens and Hayes walks in. He looks as worn out as I probably do, and it's not a good sign that the stack of paperwork he's carrying is a mile high.

"You've gotten yourself into quite the situation, Stokes."

"Yes sir." I learned a long time ago that treating him with respect goes much further than being a cocky son of a bitch.

"We've reviewed everything you've tracked for the last few years, and…" I know everything I've given them will show the truth, but my breathing still pauses, waiting for him to sentence me. "It checks out." He finally looks at me and gives a smirk.

"Any idea how they kept finding Margaret?"

"Yeah, actually, turns out your little theory that someone in the FBI was in on it was actually true."

My eyes widen slightly, and I try to quiet the rage inside me. "Who?" My voice is hard, and I wait for him to tell me one of my worst nightmares has come true.

"I don't know if you know him. His name was Thomas Perk, and he was working directly under Agent James. She's pretty pissed about it—punched him in the face when we brought him in."

"So he's in custody."

"Dumbass was at the chapel with his new buddies."

Fucking idiot. I grit my teeth before I lose my shit. I hate that it's so believable that one of our own was behind helping the Russians run their business, that he was feeding them everything they needed in order to operate quietly and not let me get the jump on them.

"Where's Margaret?"

Hayes looks at me as he contemplates his answer. "She's on her way home."

I deflate slightly and look back down at the table. It's not like I thought they'd have her outside the door waiting for me, but sending her home sucks. I won't be able to see her for a long time.

"What about her record, everything that's happened?"

"You think she'll tell people?" His brows crease with worry, and I shake my head.

"Nah, but I do think this shit on her record would make her life harder than it needs to be."

"Her record is clean."

I blow out a sigh and relax. At least I didn't screw that up for her. "So, we're good then? I'm clear?" I stupidly allow the blossom of hope to open in my chest, and I'm already planning what I'll say to Margaret when I show up on her doorstep this time.

"You're clear, but you're not done yet."

"What does that mean?"

"As it turns out, Anton wasn't our head honcho." Hayes slides a folder across the table and I take it, flipping it open to see the file of a completely different guy. "This is the guy we need to take out."

I nod. "Where?"

Hayes lets a small smirk curve his lips and says, "Russia."

Fucking shit.

29

MARGARET

Seven months later

MY STARE GETS lost in the bright sky, not a cloud in sight for one of my many days on patrol. It's become a habit of mine to lose myself in my surroundings whenever I get breaks, the open air and bright sunshine a reminder that being free isn't something I should ever take lightly.

We're taking a lunch break, one I have no doubt will be interrupted just as I'm about to eat, as tends to happen often, but that's just one of the many aspects of this job.

After leaving Vegas, I went straight to my old job and quit. I thought it was going to be some amazing, empowering moment for me, but the only thing they said was, "You should check your voicemails." It turns out after spending a few weeks away without contacting them at all, I was fired anyway. It was anticlimactic at best.

It took a little time to figure out what I wanted. I knew after spending time with Liam and Ford and Gemma that I wanted to be of service to people. I wanted to make a difference, even if it was a tiny one. I thought about a lot of options using my degree, but nothing interested me enough to hook me. As I sat in an apartment I couldn't pay for, eating food I shouldn't have been eating, I saw a commercial for respecting the those in blue, and something in me clicked.

I spent six months in the police academy, and it was the hardest thing I'd ever done. Studying for it was absolutely insane, but I graduated second in the class and immediately got assigned to the Denver Precinct, working with Officer Gray, who has been on the force ten years. He isn't much older than me, a good-looking guy and a total asshole.

I think that's why we get along okay. He would never be my friend, as he's made clear since I was assigned as his boot, but I am determined, as I am with everyone I meet, to be his friend.

Whether he likes it or not.

"So, what'd you do last night?" I ask, taking the first bite of my taco. The local food truck that sits outside the precinct is awesome, and I go here as much as possible. Who can say no to tacos?

"That's none of your concern," Gray says, taking in his surroundings. Dude's a paranoid bastard, not that it isn't warranted. Crime is everywhere, but it makes it difficult to enjoy my food when I watch his neck twist from side to side like an owl.

I'm one of the few people who truly knows how much bad is really out there, though no one knows what happened to me all those months ago. After my name went into the system when I joined the academy, I had a visit from the director of the FBI, Liam's boss, or at least he was Liam's boss. I wasn't expecting it and he was an intimidating bastard, but he had to make sure I was going to keep my mouth shut.

There's nothing on my record about what happened with the FBI because I was an innocent civilian, but he wanted to make sure I wasn't spreading around the fact that I was a part of one of the biggest drug stings in history.

Even if I wanted to gloat about it, I wouldn't, because Anton's actions still haunt my dreams.

Before I could ask any more questions, Hayes—the director— was gone.

"Come on, Gray, just give me a little something." I flash him my cheekiest grin, knowing it seems to work on men and encourage them to give in to me. How handy.

"Fine." He grunts, and I pause my movements, waiting for him to tell all. "I went on a date."

I sit up, eagerly anticipating details like he's one of my

girlfriends. "And…" I draw out.

His mouth opens to answer me, but he's cut off by our radios. "Units be advised, 10-31, robbery in progress, 1920 Chesnut Place."

Gray picks up his radio first. "Copy, unit 23 in route."

We jump up from our seats, quickly dump out half-eaten food, and make our way to our patrol car. Rookies almost always drive, and Gray has made me painstakingly memorize every route over the last few months.

I turn on the lights and pull out into traffic. I've always been an okay driver, despite the fact that I didn't have a car for the last five years. Thankfully, I was never afraid of driving. Being an officer means my driving has to be amazing, and being in Denver means I have to have incredibly fast reflexes. Drivers downtown are the absolute worst, and sixty percent of my job is writing tickets for reckless driving.

When we pull up to the bank, there are already several officers in place, surrounding the building and standing behind the wall of parked patrol cars. The street is blocked off, and Gray walks over to the officer who arrived first. Officer O'Reilly is a complete badass, and personally she's my hero, but I'd never tell Gray that. I think he wants to believe he holds fills coveted role.

"What's the situation?" he asks her, looking toward the building.

"Robbery in progress. They're armed and have hostages. We don't know the count, though."

"So, basically worst-case scenario," he replies.

It's a big building for a bank, meaning they have some serious dough in there, but I can't figure out what kind of idiot thought it would be a good idea to rob a bank of this size with the Denver PD around.

"Negotiator?" Grays asks, looking around at all the officers.

"Still waiting on him," O'Reilly answers, looking pissed off.

"We can't wait forever," Gray says, going to the trunk of our patrol car, and I'm right beside him. Where he goes, I go.

We strap on our vests and O'Reilly comes over to us. "What are you thinking, Gray?" She looks like she wants to protest, but she already knows Gray doesn't take orders as well as he probably should.

"There's a back door here, and I checked the security with the manager because this is my bank. We can go through it, and it's hidden so the robbers likely don't even know it's there."

His reply is calm, and I smirk a little while looking down at my vest and strapping it on tight, trying not to show that I'm impressed.

"And if they do?" she asks him smartly.

"Then we handle it," Gray says. He nods at me and I try hard to keep my face straight, but the adrenaline starts coursing through my body in anticipation of what we're about to do.

"Hernandez!" O'Reilly snaps, and I see Hernandez is already strapped in a vest as he hands one to his superior. He and I were in academy together and both got positions with the DPD. I was ecstatic when we were both assigned to the same precinct. Even though I've been through a lot of scary situations already, this is another ball game altogether. It's hard to have all of this experience under my belt and not be able to talk to anyone about it, to not be able to say, This is scary, but I've been through worse.

I can't talk to anyone about it.

Shaking my thoughts away, I follow Gray's lead as he edges around the side of the building. There aren't many windows, which makes it much easier for us to hide from the watchful eyes inside. I swallow and take a deep breath. I can't let my nerves and added adrenaline make me screw up. There are innocent lives that need to be protected.

This is why I joined the force. This is why I wanted to be a cop: to protect innocent people from the dangers of the world, the ones that pop up when you least expect it. When bad things come at me, I want to be prepared for any scenario.

"Davis," Gray snaps, tilting his head toward the door. It opens out so I stand beside it and aim at the lock. I hit it, and Gray pulls it open with a hard yank. He enters first, and I'm at his back. I feel O'Reilly and Hernandez come behind me, and all four of us enter the building as silently as possible.

This part of the bank has offices for the managers, but it seems abandoned. The criminals obviously put everyone into one part of the building to keep them together.

A whimper sounds somewhere and I pause, signaling to the others with my left hand to let them know I hear something.

They stop and scan their surroundings; I see something out of the corner of my eye and gesture to indicate to Gray where I'm going.

I round an office door, gun drawn and ready to take down whomever is hiding behind it. When I turn to take them out, I stop immediately and put my gun away. A young girl is sitting behind the door, her cheeks stained with tears and her face full of fear.

"Hey," I say softly, hands raised as I kneel to the ground. "It's all right, you're safe."

I take her hand, and O'Reilly instructs Hernandez to take her outside. I'm surprised she wants me to stay, but I don't disobey, nodding at Hernandez when he grabs the girl and takes her outside.

I breathe a sigh of relief. One life down, several to go.

I resume my position, this time behind both Gray and O'Reilly, and keep my gun drawn toward the door that's already open. We hear shouting from the front of the bank and pause, listening for any sounds indicating them coming our way. If they see us in here, it's game over.

"This is the Denver Police Department. We have you surrounded. Please let the hostages go and come out." We hear the boom over the bullhorn outside and I cringe, hoping it doesn't antagonize whoever is inside.

"No way! You'll kill me!" The voice sounds low and loud, but there's fear in his tone, undermining his false confidence.

"We have no reason to hurt you. Just come out and we'll decide how to precede." This negotiator is horrible. This isn't how you talk someone down.

"No, you need to let me go. If you don't, I'll kill one of the hostages." A cry sounds from somewhere in the main lobby, and the sound of flesh hitting flesh makes my vision turn red. "Shut up, bitch!"

I look to Gray and O'Reilly, waiting impatiently for an order. Gray signals for us to spread out to get the best vantage and we nod, following his directions. I find a spot where I can see the man standing there. He's sweating horribly, and I can tell things are not going the way he wanted them to. That can make a person reckless.

With how we fan out, I'm the closest one to him, and his back is turned toward me. I could take him from here, but I don't want to kill him.

I look over to see Gray signaling what he wants me to do, and I take a deep breath, nodding as I place my gun back in my holster and ready myself for what's about to happen.

A shot rings out and I take a running leap, tackling the man to the ground. I use my momentum to take him down, which isn't easy with him clutching his leg where Gray hit him, and I straddle his back. He struggles, his resistance making it impossible to grab his arms, so I lift a fist and throw it into his jaw. The force knocks his face into the ground, and I take the chance to cuff his hands behind his back while he's distracted.

"You're under arrest," I say calmly, and I don't notice right away that the hostages are standing. Some are crying, and all of them are clapping. I bite my lip and will the blush to go away as I haul the perpetrator off the floor and through the doors.

I read the man his Miranda rights as he's placed in the back of our patrol car.

Gray approaches me, and I stare in shock at his raised hand, which is apparently waiting for a high five. I've never seen Gray high-five anyone. "You did good, boot." It's high praise coming from him.

Damn, that feels good.

We take the man to the station and book him. The only part about this that sucks is the paperwork, but it's worth it to see a man like him behind bars.

No one should have to deal with that kind of person.

My smile slips from my face when I think about the one person I would share this with, the same way it does whenever I want to tell him something or share a piece of my life. It feels like he was just a dream, and I was the fool who fell for him.

It's been seven months since the night I essentially married him, and the only contact I've received is one letter, one letter (presumably) from Liam saying he was trying his best to get to me but had unfinished business to take care of so would be a little longer. I don't know what it meant, and there was no return address on the envelope, no way of contacting him back.

The letter was marked with an L, and that was it. No I miss

you, no I'm thinking of you. Nothing.

I sit by my locker and stare at my phone, scrolling through the contacts. Finding one I forgot about, I hit call without thinking too much about it. I bring it to my ear and hear an automatic voice say, "We're sorry, the number you have dialed is no longer in service."

Sighing, I end the call and hang my head. I guess Ford is gone too.

I think about moving on, and I'm trying to. My life is good right now, and my job is excellent. I feel like I'm finally doing something rewarding with my life, and despite the fact that the man I love is out of reach, despite not knowing when or if he'll ever pop up again, life could be worse.

30

MARGARET

A year and a half later

A SIGH ESCAPES me as I shake my head, the rookie in front of me shuffling nervously as he stares down at the guy I had to take out because this boot was too scared to take action.

Sometimes I hate this job.

It's been two years since I decided this was where I wanted to be in life. It's been a long road to become who I am, but I don't regret a single second of my time as an officer. I've taken on a lot of bad people in this city, putting away some serious assholes. It's a dream job, one I'm sure I never would have pursued if not for the unique experiences I had.

That said, as I look at Nervous Nelly in front of me, I wonder if I made the right choice.

"What are they, Johnson?" I ask again, my impatience showing through in my tone. Only a true idiot can't remember the Miranda rights, but I'll wait, even though I don't want to, until this guy gets it.

"Y-You have a right…" He takes a deep breath as I tilt my head to the heavens, hoping and praying for some damn patience. Probably shouldn't say damn, but I can't help it when idiots are present, which is far too often for me. "To remain…uh, silent."

"Oh, Jesus." I'm talking to the Big Man right now. I'd pray out loud if I were a complete bitch, but I at least still have some heart. Something about this job has hardened me a bit over time. It's amazing how I've fallen into my role so well here. I have a duty, a real purpose, friends, and even though Johnson is maybe the worst rookie anyone's ever seen, I have a lot to be thankful for.

"You have the right to remain silent." I step in, picking the guy up off the street, ready to get a move on. "Anything you say can and will be held against you in a court of law." I pause briefly and glare at him. "You listening, Johnson?" He nods. "You have the right to an attorney. If you cannot afford an attorney, one will be provided for you. Do you understand the rights I have just read to you? With these rights in mind, do you wish to speak to me?"

"Fuck off." Good enough for me. I shove the man in the back

of the patrol car and move around to the driver's seat. Johnson isn't to be trusted to drive my car, and I won't even try it today. My mind isn't in the right place for that.

"If you can't remember the Miranda rights, why are you here?" I ask him before he has a chance to even get his belt on. Gray wore off on me with the gruffness, and it seems necessary to carry on a tradition of giving a rookie the go-around to make sure he's cut out for the job.

"I can, I just froze. Sorry, ma'am."

I shake my head, not sure what to say to that.

"Even I know them, man," says the junkie in the back, fresh off of being caught shoplifting.

"Shut up," I snap. My patience for men is running real thin today.

I think about how Gray left me behind after being promoted to detective. I'm happy for him, really, but I'm damn pissed I had to get someone else as a partner. I worked with Gray for a year before he left to move on. He still works here in Denver, but it's not the same as having him at my six day in and day out.

We get back to the station and I sarcastically ask Johnson if he can book our guy. When he says he can, I ask, "You sure?"

He straightens his spine like I'm a drill sergeant, and I look at him funny. "Yes ma'am." I roll my eyes at his back.

"Looks like you've taken my role pretty easily."

I turn to the familiar voice and a smirk curves my lips. "Gray," I say as he leans down to give me a hug. "What are you doing over here?" Detectives have their own special offices in another part of the building, one I don't get over to very often, if at all.

"Have a new case I'm working on, looking for a PI I was supposed to work with but can't seem to find him."

"You mean Greg?" I ask, referring to the only PI the PD seems to work with, at least from what I've seen.

"Nah, someone new," he says, looking at his phone. "Stokes."

My breath stalls at the name. It can't be what I'm thinking… it's not an uncommon name. But it really is, my inner voice says.

"You know him?" Gray asks when he sees my reaction.

I shrug. "No, probably just a coincidence."

"All right." Gray gives me a look like he knows I'm lying, but he drops it and gestures to where Johnson just went. "How's the boot?"

"Don't ask," I say with a smirk.

"Ah come on, even you were difficult."

"What!" I exclaim with a smile still on my face. "I was a damn angel."

He smirks right back. "Yeah, an angel dressed in black."

I scoff and slap his shoulder. He was a great officer to learn from, and I picked things up faster than I'd thought I would. He started treating me like an officer around eight months after I was assigned, and we really clicked. I knew where he was at mentally at all times, and he read me like a book. We were seamless when we worked together, and that's why I took it pretty rough when he left.

"Well, I'd better go find this guy. They say he's the best." We hug, and when he leaves, I turn back to my desk, groaning internally at the mountain of paperwork sitting on top of it. The one downside to this job—endless amounts of paperwork.

Soon enough, I'm walking up the stairs to my apartment, the weight of the day lifting from my shoulders as I walk, ready to relax in a bubble bath and drink a glass—no, a bottle of wine and forget my cares.

I moved to this apartment a year ago. It's a huge step up from the one I was in before, and I don't have to avoid the old man downstairs anymore, the one who still remembered the throat punch Liam gave him. It took a lot of cookies to get him off my case, but he finally forgave me after the third batch.

This one has two bedrooms and a real kitchen. It's still on the smaller side, being that rent in Denver is astronomical, but I love it and won't ever move. It's got a great view from the small balcony that overlooks most of the city, and it's my escape after a long day of work. No one bothers me when they see the officer is home—another perk of the job.

I set down my bag, still in uniform because I was too tired to change, and immediately I sense something is off. I grab my gun, heading for the hallway. I see nothing unusual in the main living area, but I can feel a presence. No, I'm not the ghost whisperer, but the atmosphere is definitely different.

Gun raised, I say, "Hernandez, if that's you, you're going to regret it." Hernandez has a bad habit of trying to pull pranks on me. I don't get mad, I get even, and if this is another attempt, I'm seriously going to kill him.

I march down the hallway, checking my office. I see nothing, so I make my way to the bedroom and feel my breath rush out of my lungs when I see a figure sitting on my bed. It's not Hernandez.

"Liam?" My voice is filled with disbelief.

"Hey, Mo."

31

LIAM

SHE'S SO GODDAMN beautiful.

I can't believe I went this long without seeing her.

"What are you doing here?" Her voice doesn't crack like I expected it to, and it isn't soft like it used to be. Instead, it's hard, confused, and not so nice.

"I told you I'd come back," I say, standing up from the bed. I put the framed picture I was studying back on her nightstand and take a step toward her. I don't get far due to the gun that is still pointed at me.

"Two years…" Her tone is exasperated, her head shaking with disbelief. "Two years ago, you made me that promise."

"And I'm here to keep it." I never intended to take this long, or to be here for more than one reason.

She scoffs and raises the gun again, like I'm an enemy. Maybe I am in her eyes. "You don't get to come into my life like this. I've made something of myself. I have a real career, a real life."

I nod at her, eyeing her uniform. I knew she worked for the police department, but I didn't realize she was an officer. It isn't exactly a safe job, and not something I ever thought I'd see Margaret doing, but I guess I didn't know her like I thought I did.

"I realize things have changed…"

"Yeah, ya think?" I try not to smirk at her snarky tone. The spice that attracted me in the first place is still firmly intact. "This is pathetic—truly, really pathetic, Liam. I don't know what you want but—"

"You." I walk forward until the gun is pressed into my chest. "You gonna shoot me, Mo?" I ask, my voice low, an attempt to draw out the girl I once knew. This isn't that girl anymore, though; she is all woman. The Mo I once knew isn't the only one there now. There is a maturity to her, an air of authority that surrounds her, one I find appealing.

"I don't know," she replies, lifting her chin and cocking her head to the side. "Do I have a reason to?"

I don't answer. Does she have a reason to? Probably. There are things I've done that shouldn't be forgiven just because of my job, but have I ever purposefully hurt Mo? Never. I don't intend to either.

"Where have you been?" she asks, taking a step back.

"Russia." I watch her head snap back in surprise.

"Russia," she murmurs. It's not a question, and her brain—the one that has been trained to put the pieces together—starts churning. I see it when she gets it. "You had to finish the mission."

"I did." I leave off a bit of information on purpose, given that her gun is still aimed at me.

"I thought after we got Anton, that was it."

"That's what I thought, too, but as it turned out, he was a very small part of the bigger picture." I reach up and push the gun down. She doesn't release it, but she does lower it to her side. I take a minute to take in her features. She's even more gorgeous than I remember, and her face was a permanent fixture in my mind for the last two years. Her hair is back to its rich chocolate color and almost as long as it was when we met. It makes me want to throw her down on the bed and get back to where we were, but it's her eyes that stop me. There's a wariness there, something holding her back, and I know it would be foolish of me to rush this too much.

She's not ready.

"So, did you finish it then?" she asks, walking around me, putting space between us.

I keep my hands at my sides, turning to follow her movements and resisting the urge to pull her back. "I did, for the most part." I'm not technically lying.

"So…" She pauses, licking her lips. "What now?"

"Now, we make love, we live that life I promised, we work normal jobs, and we love the fuck out of each other." I don't actually say any of that, of course, but I want to. "Now…it's up to you," I say instead, letting her take us in the direction she needs to go.

I would do anything for her, even keep a lid on my feelings.

"I don't know what you want me to say."

"Are you seeing anyone?" I didn't think so. I kept tabs on her through the FBI and there was no indication that she was, but that doesn't mean I didn't miss something.

"Not really."

I don't like that answer. "No, or not really? Those are two different things," I reply, my voice a little harder than I want it to be. Calm the fuck down, man.

"No," she says, lifting her chin again. I realize she's doing that to try to make sure I don't see through the shield she's keeping in place. "I've been focusing my attention on my career."

I nod, taking her in. God, it's been way too long. Once I had her, no one else would do. No one else would ever compare to her. Getting back to her was my ultimate goal, and it was a hardship to finish out what was expected of me.

"I see that. Took me by surprise when I saw you in the uniform."

"You didn't seem surprised." She bites her lip and sets her gun on her dresser. "I've worked hard to get where I am. I was…

lost when you left me in Vegas."

I shake my head and remember the look on her face. "That was the last thing I wanted to do, I swear to you. I didn't have a choice."

"I know." Margaret pushes her hair out of her face, resting her hands on the top of her head. "I know you didn't have a choice, but…" She blows out a breath. "I didn't think that was how it would end."

"That's not how it ends." I take a step in her direction, but she tenses, so I pause my footsteps. I hate that she doesn't want me near her.

"God, you didn't talk to me for two years!" Her voice reaches a hysteria I've only ever heard once before.

"You didn't get my letters?" It was the best I could do under the circumstances.

"Oh, you mean these?" Her sarcastic question distracts me for a moment as she rushes to the dresser against the wall and grabs some crumpled pieces of paper. They look as if they've been rolled into balls and flattened a hundred times. "Dear Mo." She starts reading, and I rest my hands on my hips and sigh. "This isn't much, but I'm okay. L." Her eyes glow with a savage inner fire, and she flips to the next page. "Dear Mo, I hope you are doing okay. I know this isn't how we wanted everything to go, but I'm doing my best. L."

I grimace at the lack of communication I was able to get to her, but I couldn't put specifics in the letters. If I had, someone could have easily gotten hold of it.

"Dear Mo." Her voice catches and I look up at her, seeing her face lose the carefully placed mask, showing a hint of vulnerability, showing me she still cares far more than she wants me to know. "I can't wait for our life. L." Finally, her head comes up, and she looks at me like I'm the worst person she's ever laid eyes on. It breaks my damn heart. "Three letters in two years… that's all I got."

"I'm here now," I say, a slight tremor in my voice. I hate that I couldn't do more. I hate myself for hurting her.

"Well, I don't know if that's enough." Her soft, hoarse voice breaks something in me, and I steel my spine, ready for her to tell me to get lost, ready for the blow I know is coming, the one I know I deserve.

"I'll do anything to make you trust me." I harden my voice and look into her eyes, searching for a small bit of hope, anything to hold on to.

"I don't know how to do that."

Nodding, I rest my hands in the loops on my jeans and think about how to approach it. An idea hits me and I ask, "You hungry?"

Hesitating, she glances down at the wrinkled papers in her hands and smooths the edge of one. When I catch her eyes again, they're clear and her wall is back up, but she just says, "Gotta change first."

I bite my tongue at the remark about loving a woman in

uniform and nod before wandering out into the living room, taking in the space that is all Margaret: bright colors, books on every surface, and clean. I imagine her in this room, relaxing on the couch and watching TV after a long day, and I want to join that fantasy. I want to be the man she comes home to, the one she can tell everything.

Margaret is the game changer, and I plan on winning.

32

MARGARET

MY HEART IS still lodged somewhere between the back of my tongue and the top of my collarbone. It's been there since the second I saw Liam in my room, in my domain, sitting there like he had every right to be sitting on my plush yellow comforter.

My mind couldn't fully comprehend what was happening, but I didn't know how else to act, so I kept my gun trained on him until I could make myself understand what was occurring, until I could decide if I could trust him. As much as I love—loved—him, I've seen what he's done. I've seen what the FBI has made him do, and him showing up out of the blue raises some red flags for me.

He leads us down the sidewalk, cars passing us in a rush to get home, and we're not far from my old apartment now. The area is familiar, and a memory hits me: the last time I walked down this road with him.

Liam tries to get us into a conversation, tries to ask questions and get some sort of answers, but I can't give them. I don't know what he wants me to say, but falling into the trap of our easy banter is something I can't let myself do.

It's been two years since I last saw his face, and as sad as it is, I felt my heart tick a beat with just a glance. I know deep down I'm not over him. I thought I'd never be over him, but I didn't actually think he'd ever come back to me, and I was resolved to think that way, accepting that I was on my own from here on out.

I put every ounce of anger, aggression, and any shadow of depressing thoughts into my career. It's why I was only considered a rookie for six months or so before I started to get respect. When I wasn't in our patrol car, scouring the streets for assholes to lock up, I was reading the handbook, absorbing details and codes and making sure I knew the big book backward and forward.

Yes, I thought of Liam in my dark moments, sipping a beer and looking over the city from my balcony at my new apartment, wondering where in the world he was and why he didn't bother coming back for me. I thought of him shot in the head, or in a ditch, or locked up in prison for going against the FBI.

I had not a clue where he went, because after Vegas, I didn't hear from him. Letters that barely gave me anything, not even his name, didn't count. It's also been months since his last one, and anything could have happened between then and now. I wasn't feeling inclined to ask the director where he was because I didn't think he'd answer me anyway, and also I didn't want it to look like I cared.

I didn't hear from Mike or Jen, and I didn't get a call from Ford or Gemma, though I wasn't surprised about that last one. That was just who Gemma was. No matter if I thought we could be friends, that wasn't her MO, and even though I'd had Ford's number, that was just a last-ditch attempt. I didn't really need him; I just wanted to know what had happened. Had they all just picked up where they left off and continued with their lives as normal after Vegas, or were they just as out of the loop as I was? I doubted it seriously.

So, Liam's fruitless attempts at conversation are not reciprocated, and I know he is worried that I'm not going to engage with him. I can see it on his face, and that gives me pause because Liam never lets anyone in, never lets anyone see what he is really thinking or worrying about. I see it, though.

He is terrified. It makes me scrunch my eyebrows together when I see how stressed he is about it, but I don't comment on it—I can't. Letting him think I care or am worried is the quickest way for me to lose my heart—and my head—all over again.

We turn another corner and are surrounded by people going to and from restaurants. This is a heavily populated area for dinner and drinks after work, and it's packed, as is usual at this time of night. I stare down at my spiked, heeled, black leather boots over tight skinny jeans. My leather jacket hugs my curves in all the right places, and I am glad I spent the money on it, because Liam about choked on his tongue when he saw me out of uniform.

The uniform is unflattering. I know that—everyone knows that—but I do like that it gives me authority over other people. They may make lewd comments toward a female cop, but they are usually not stupid enough to act on anything that would get them into trouble with me.

Liam slows to a stop and I look up, swallowing my surprise when I read the sign. I should have known this was where we were going, but I was too lost in thought to pay attention.

O'Callahan's Pub…the location of our first date.

I walk in after he holds the door for me, and I make my way to the bar. There are plenty of tables open, but for some reason being at the bar gives me some sort of comfort, like a safety net for dates. This isn't a date.

"Hey, Margaret," the bartender says. His name is Jimmy, and nearly every time I come in after a shift to get a drink with fellow officers, he is working. At first, I resisted coming here, but then the thought that I was going to have to get over it eventually pushed me to frequent the bar often, which is why he has a pint of Guinness in front of me before I even sit down.

Liam raises a surprised eyebrow at me and comments,

"That's not your drink."

I shrug my shoulders but don't answer, taking a fortifying swallow. When he orders the same thing, I try not to blush and wonder if he knows I started drinking it because it was what he drank on our first date.

It was stupid to do that, but I couldn't help myself.

"You guys eating?" Jimmy asks, directing the question at me.

"No," I say at the same time Liam says, "Yes."

We look at each other, and Jimmy says he'll give us a minute. We sit silently and sip our beers; the bar is loud, and Dropkick Murphy's "Hang 'Em High" plays in the background of the chatter that comes at us from all sides, people grateful to be off work and enjoying time out with friends.

I have finally had a bit of that with some of the other officers recently, and it's a nice change to go from every friend being married or having babies to being around people who have the same goals and ambitions as you.

"Are you gonna look at me at all?" The question comes out hoarse, and I look over to Liam's worried gaze.

"What do you want to talk about?" I ask, grabbing a cocktail napkin and bending and folding it between my fingers, my eyes trained on it because I know if I hold his stare too long, I'll give in to whatever it is he wants from me.

I feel him looking at me, and after a sigh and a rub of his head—an old habit of his—he asks, "How about how you're doing?"

I nod. "I'm great," I say, not giving him much. A part of me wants to gush about how amazing I am, wants to say that despite him breaking every promise he made, I did something with my life and actually enjoy living it again.

"I'm glad. I didn't really see you as a police officer," he comments, grabbing his Guinness.

"Well…" I pause, thinking back on when I decided on to become one. I didn't think the FBI would hire someone like me, but at least the police academy would. I desperately wanted a job that would get justice for innocent people like myself who got caught up in stuff they shouldn't, and the academy offered that option to me. I finally settle on saying, "I couldn't go back to what I was doing."

He nods his head and continues to look at me. "I'm sure you're great at it," he replies. When I don't say anything, he goes on. "I've got a new job too." His eyes shift away from me.

"You do?" I ask before I can stop myself.

"Yeah, a PI. I'm helping a detective at your precinct, actually."

I stare at him, absorbing the words and the trying to hide the panic. He can't come into my world. That's not fair, not after all I've done to push him away. "Gray."

"Yeah, he was telling me about how he was your partner." He smirks at me and says, "I barely held back that you were my partner first."

I scoff at his audacity. "I was never your partner." I practically growl out the words, and the shine in his eyes dulls slightly. "A partner doesn't abandon you. Partners don't push each other away, and they sure as hell don't make promises they can't keep." My voice is much louder by the end of my rant.

"Mo."

"Don't," I warn, not wanting to hear his fucking excuses. "Where the hell were you anyway?"

He sighs. "I had to be debriefed. It was pure hell, and it took for-fucking-ever."

"Two years?" I ask, my doubt clear in my voice.

"Not exactly," he hedges, and I tilt my head, waiting for the right answer. Unfortunately, there is no answer he can give me that will forgive him leaving me. "I had to go into Russia."

"So you've said." I scoff again and take another gulp of Guinness, but the intrigued part of me is too curious to not hear what he has to say now. "Why?"

Another sigh. "There was more to the mission than even I thought. Apparently Anton had his hands in more than one pot, and there were a lot of fires to put out once he was behind bars. There was a leak in the FBI." He looks at me and I finally settle into the seat, my back having been ramrod straight since we walked into the bar.

"Hmph. Figured there was. Who was it?" I ask, not sure I want to hear the answer. What if it was Gemma, or Ford?

"Perk."

"Perk?"

"Yeah, you met him once, at the cabin where Jenny was."

Fuck, that's right. Perk—he was the dirty agent who helped Anton at the safe house, the one who dragged me and hit me in the back of the head. No wonder I didn't remember—he must have hit me pretty good. "I met him twice." Finally, it's Liam's turn to look confused, so I fill him in. "He was at the safe house. He dragged me around to Anton and whacked me in the back of the head when they took me to that basement." I repeat what I was just thinking, and when I look at Liam's face, I see a fire burning in his eyes.

"He hit you?" The anger is evident in his voice, his hands fisted on his thighs.

"Yeah. It wasn't the worst thing that happened. Did you get him?"

"Life in prison," is his short reply.

I take him in. Even though I hate him slightly, I know him at the same time. "The job wasn't done, and you had to get your guy."

He nods. "Yes. You of all people know how important this is to me."

I relent a bit. "I do." It's a fucking excuse, but damn if it isn't a pretty good one. "That doesn't explain why you couldn't have called or sent me something more than excuses and pathetic reassurances. It's not like I was going to guilt you into staying."

Okay, that might be a lie. Us women don't always know we're doing it when it's happening.

"I didn't want to get your hopes up."

"That what? You wouldn't die?" I ask, a chuckle in my throat.

"Yes."

"No, uh-uh, that still doesn't excuse it. You broke a promise."

"I know, Mo, and I can't even begin to tell you how sorry I am about that." He takes a breath and steadies himself. "I want to make it up to you. Please tell me you'll let me."

I stand, unable to take another second, and dig into my pocket to grab a ten to leave for Jimmy. I don't want Liam to give me one more thing.

"Mo, wait," he says, rushing behind me and throwing his own cash on the bar. I barely make it out the door before his hand wraps around my wrist. "Please." His voice makes me whip around and yank my arm from his hold.

"You broke my fucking heart!" I mean to yell it, but my voice catches and tears starts to prick at my eyes. I gather myself again and look at him, trying for the no-bullshit face I use when I'm working. "I can't take another chance on you." Steel lines my voice, and the façade I often have to use in my line of work falls into place.

"What can I do to change your mind?" His gaze desperately searches mine, and I shrug. As much as I want to take him back and give him a million chances, I'm a new person, and I need him to not be in my life.

"Not a thing."

Liam crumbles. I see it in his eyes, but then a determination falls over his face and I turn away, walking quickly so he can't say whatever it is he wants to say.

I keep going, moving quickly on the heeled boots, and I don't look back. He's not following me, that much I know, and a part of me—the stupid one—feels sad at that fact. Still, I know better than to let him in.

I hope I won't regret it someday, but there's no going back now. Liam is not in my life anymore.

I ignore the ping that hits my heart.

33

LIAM

THE DENVER POLICE Department is like most other departments I've seen and been to in my career, except this one is definitely the cleanest. I'm a private investigator now, to everyone here at least, and hopefully to anyone watching.

In the last three months since I started, I've already helped close five cases. It's what I was meant to do, and I am damn good at my job. Even if it is a front for now, I can easily see myself doing this for the long term.

I've worked with many different districts within Denver, and this is the first time I've been needed at Margaret's. I may have omitted the fact that I've been here for some time, but I didn't want to give her more reason to be mad. I thought once I explained what had happened, she would fall into my arms and thank God we were back together again. It must have slipped my mind how stubborn she is, and I know after that night, I'll have to work a hell of a lot harder to win her over.

After the pub, I don't bother her again. Even if it kills me a little, I need a plan to win back her trust, and that is going to start with two things.

One, the package of processed donuts, the really-bad-for-you ones, that I left in her locker this morning, and two, questioning Detective Gray while working with him.

I haven't told him I know Margaret. I haven't told him I have a history with her that goes back long before she joined the academy. No matter how brief it was, it's one that isn't going away, one I won't ever forget. I have ways to get guys like him to spill all about their careers, and this guy, no matter how tough, is no different than all the other men who are overcompensating with their badges.

I am meeting with Gray to go over any details he has on his missing person case. It's a fifteen-year-old girl, a good girl, according to her parents. They say she never gets into any trouble, and for her to go missing is out of the ordinary.

"Friends?" I ask Gray, staring at the mass of photos and notes on the board he and his partner Hanson put together.

"Questioned them all," Hanson says. "According to them, she missed cheerleading practice Tuesday afternoon and she had acted normal all day, no indication that she was in trouble or upset about anything." He doesn't like that I was called in on his case, but he doesn't get a fucking choice when someone's been missing for three days without any progress in the case.

"I'd like to talk to the parents," I tell him, and I get their information. Hanson leaves soon after, and I stick around, pretending to study their notes even though I already have all of the details memorized. Gray hangs back, looking over his files, trying to find anything he could be missing.

"This detective stuff more fun than being an officer?" I ask him, leading into a conversation and knowing he'll follow.

He scoffs and shakes his head, stands tall, and crosses his arms over his chest. Gray is a fit guy. He's not old, either, and I'm sure lots of ladies around this precinct think he's charming, Margaret probably included. "Sometimes, but others I wish I was still in a cruiser with my old partner. Parts of it were way easier."

"Your old partner, Officer Davis, right?" I ask, the name feeling weird rolling off my tongue. Didn't think that I'd ever call her that.

"Yeah." He eyes me. This is the second time I've brought her up, and I can see right away that I didn't give him enough credit. "You know her?"

I shrug my shoulders and keep my eyes on him. "I may have a while ago."

"You may have, or you did?" His eyes drill mine and a look falls over his face. I imagine it's one he uses when questioning people.

"I did," I admit. I wanted to keep that information to myself, but seeing as how I am having to go behind her back to find out who she is now, I don't see too many options.

"Really? I didn't think Maggie ever dated," he declares, and I clench my teeth, hating that they are close enough that he has a nickname for her. "We were partners for quite some time, and she never told me she was with anyone."

"Yeah, well, it was before Officer Davis became Officer Davis."

His eyes widen and he says, "Oh shit. You're that Liam?"

I perk up hearing this. She talked about me? That's got to be a good sign. "Yeah, I'm that Liam." Even I cringe at the cocky sound of my voice.

"Huh. I mean, she mentioned you once but never explained who you were. It was about a year ago and something hit her weird. We'd just found some people who were being kept in a basement. It was brutal—they were all chained up and shit. Fucking assholes were using them for a ransom." He shrugs, not realizing what a big fucking deal that must have been for her. "It wasn't even our deal, but Maggie was insistent that we help, threatened to request a partner change if I didn't get on board." He chuckles, and even I let a smirk mark my lips—of course she threatened him. "But anyway, after we'd gotten those people out, when I asked why it was a big deal, she said, 'If Liam didn't give up then I don't want to give up for anyone.'"

My heart thuds in my chest, and I clench my eyes.

"I don't know what you did, and I didn't really get to ask—she's private about that shit—but whatever it was, she admires you for it. Anyway"—he looks at his watch and walks to the door, clapping me on the shoulder—"let me know what you find ASAP, yeah? We gotta get this girl." I give him a curt nod.

As I'm heading toward the parents' residence, I think over what he told me, about how Mo was insistent about helping people who didn't have a clue what they were being held for, ones she knew were innocent. It makes her reasons for becoming a cop crystal clear, and I wish I had told her how proud I was instead of acting shocked that she is an officer.

I was a dick, and she saw right through it. A sigh escapes me as I pull up to the house. I am going to get Mo back if it kills me, but first I am going to rescue an innocent girl.

It's what Mo would expect of me, and I'm not going to give her reason to doubt me ever again.

34

MARGARET

I SIT ON the bench by the lockers where we store our civilian clothes and bags, staring down at the bag of donuts in my hands. The memories are ones that are weird to be fond of, but I can't help but smile at the snack.

For some reason I'm surprised he remembered how much I loved these, even though nowadays I don't really eat things like this. I try to keep myself in shape now that my job is so tough on my body, but I allow myself the guilty pleasure and toss them into my bag before swinging it over my shoulder and walking out the door.

My apartment is only a few blocks from the precinct, and

because of that, I always walk to work. I'm always armed, of course, but I do walk. Before I can make it out the door, someone grabs my arms and whirls me toward them. On instinct, one of my arms twists out of the hold, and I grab the perp's hand, bending it painfully. My left knee comes up and makes contact with his groin, and a groan slips from his mouth.

My hand immediately releases and goes to my mouth to hold in a gasp, watching Liam breathe deeply for a minute before he can catch his breath.

"I'm sorry," I say through my hands, the words muffled. I walk over and pat his back, trying to be comforting after kicking him in the balls. People walk by, looking at him groaning and me with my sheepish smile, and I nod and wave my hand as if to say, No worries here, move along.

Liam finally stands up straight and breathes out a gust of air, looking at me like he has just been rejuvenated. "Damn, I should know not to sneak up on you, but I didn't think it'd result in that."

"I'm sorry," I say again, and despite still being pissed, I really do feel bad. Groin hits are low blows—no pun intended.

"It's okay." He gives me a smile, his eyes soft in a shyness I've only seen in Liam, and he gestures toward my bag, where he can see the donuts sticking out. "I just wanted to make sure you got my present."

I chuckle slightly, feeling bad and awkward and trying to keep a wall up against him. "Yeah, uh, I was surprised you remembered."

"I remember everything about you, Mo." His voice is low, respectful of the fact that there are ears around that might overhear something I wouldn't want them to.

I don't reply, just give a little nod, and we stand there, both taking the other in. There's no escaping how good he looks, and he's still got scruff on his face that looks like he just decided not to shave for a few days. His hair looks like he's been out in the sun, but it's still dark and cut short. He's gorgeous, and my inner whore wants to say, Screw self-respect—jump him! But I ignore the tension I'm suddenly feeling and shut her up with the promise of donuts later.

"You working a case?" I bite my tongue after I say it, because it's the only reason he'd be here.

"Yeah, missing person."

"Rebecca Myers?" I ask, thinking about the girl who disappeared a few days ago. As part of everyday patrol, there is always the rule to keep an eye out for anything suspicious in case we stumble upon somewhere people could be hiding.

"Yeah. We've maybe got a lead on her, but we have to nail it down before the police can go in and take her."

"You guys need help?" Just the thought of jumping in on the action makes my adrenaline spike, and I hope he'll say yes.

"They've got it covered. It could be really dangerous, Mo." His soft voice rubs me the wrong way, and our nice conversation takes a turn.

I steel my spine and look him in the eyes, my face blank. "I'm a cop, Liam, not just some innocent girl you only protected out of obligation." My voice is hard.

"That's not—dammit, I'm sorry," he says, holding his hands out, palms up, showing me he knows he's lost this conversation. "I didn't mean you couldn't handle it. I'm just not used to you being the one who goes in when shots are fired."

"Well, you don't have to get used to it," I snark then walk around him, back into the station where I find the chief and beg to be let in to help with this case. "I'm good, sir. I can help, and I know a female officer would be better at getting to a teenage girl than a man would."

I use that to my advantage. I don't think it will actually matter much, but it can't hurt. The chief looks at me for a moment, pursing his lips. He's always liked me, and I think it's because of my sass. I've never disrespected him, but I haven't let anyone walk all over me either. I've kept to myself and done a damn fine job since I was hired.

"You sure?" he asks.

I just finished a short shift, and I could go ten more. "Yes sir." I feel Liam behind me, keeping a respectable distance but listening all the same.

"Okay, Davis. Suit up and be ready to go. We have a house, and we're about to see if there's someone to take out."

I nod and don't waste another second, brushing past Liam and heading to get myself ready. I pass Johnson, and he gives me a look.

"Everything okay, ma'am?"

I hate that he calls me ma'am, but it's expected, and there's not a lot I can do about it. "I'm going in with the unit tonight," I reply, voice firm as I continue to the lockers.

"Should I go too?" he asks, his voice unsure.

"Do you think you should?" I'm testing him. He should, at the very least, volunteer, but he's too chickenshit, and I'm guaranteeing he won't last long here.

"Well, shift ended..." God, I swear I hate him, and I don't hate people often.

"Okay then." I keep my voice even and head to change, not wasting another second on him. I spent the whole damn day dealing with his whiny ass, and I'm not about to worry about him all night too.

Time to show Liam what he's trying to get himself into.

We're waiting a few blocks away, and somehow, Liam talked his way into riding in my patrol car. The lead detectives are suited up and ready to bust down the doors, and as soon as we get the go-ahead, Christianson and I get to follow them in.

I've always liked Christianson, and he's a huge flirt, so it's almost like poetic justice to let him flirt with me right in front of Liam. I mean, if he can't handle this, can he really handle dating me for real?

"Signs of three bodies," a voice says through the radio. "Two upstairs, one in basement."

Since we don't know who has her or if this is really them, we have to approach the situation carefully and have officers on each side of the house. We are a block down and idling, ready to take action and charge through the front door at any time.

"Shots fired!" That's all we have to hear before Christianson hauls ass to the front of the house. I keep my eyes ahead and see Gray and his new partner Hanson pinned under the windows as the pop, pop, pop keeps coming. The windows are shot out, but I can't tell who is shooting or where they are.

Adrenaline is pushing me forward, and as an afterthought I yell into the back seat, "Stay here!" The look on Liam's face says, Yeah, the fuck I will, but he doesn't have a weapon and I don't wait. He can handle himself as far as I'm concerned.

Shooting toward the house, I make sure Gray is good, and Christianson follows my lead, checking on Hanson before I take the initiative to bust through the front door—my favorite move.

"Davis!" I hear Gray yell at the same time I hear Liam's, "Mo!"

But I don't wait.

I think of Rebecca and charge inside, hands steady and ready, hoping Christianson will follow. I take out the first person I see who didn't pause to look where I was before shooting. He missed by a mile, and I get one shot in his shoulder before I feel people enter behind me. The radio is loud in my ear, someone shouting orders at anyone listening, and I heed them, but only because someone else got the second guy.

I direct the officers behind me to go down the hallway while I head through the sparse and nasty-looking kitchen. There's a door off to the side and I wait for Christianson to be on my six before I wrench it open, exposing blackness.

I click on the light on my gun and head down into the dark basement. Why the fuck is it always a fucking basement?

Breathing deep, I push away my own insecurities and think of the young girl who might be down there without any idea if help is coming. I don't see anyone until a slumped figure on the floor to my left catches my eye. "Christianson, go right," I direct as I head left.

After carefully checking my surroundings, I yank the blanket off and see Rebecca curled in a fetal position. I raise my gun off of her and touch her shoulder, praying she isn't already too far past saving. She jerks away as a whimper escapes her.

"Rebecca," I start. "You're safe, sweetie. We're here to help."

Her head turns toward me, and I take in her grimy hair as I give her a smile and reach out my hand. Reluctantly, she takes it, and I haul her up easily. Luckily, on a quick inventory, she doesn't look like she was physically harmed, and relief rushes through me.

It doesn't take away the fact that this sweet, innocent young girl was kidnapped, but at least the demons might be a bit easier for her to fight.

Christianson follows us up the stairs and out of the basement, and everyone upstairs lets out relieved sighs upon seeing that she's okay. A paramedic comes up to us on the lawn—a woman, thank God—and takes Rebecca's hand.

The girl looks at me, and I give her a kind smile. She thanks me, and a sob hits her. She shakes her head as she says, "I thought I was going to die."

I don't think before I wrap her in my arms and give her any kind of comfort I can, knowing exactly how she feels and hoping to convey that to her. "It's gonna be okay, Rebecca."

She nods then allows the paramedic to take her away. Before they even reach the ambulance, Gray is in my face. "You don't fucking think!"

I smirk and pat his arm. He's always like this after I take the lead on something. "Gray, calm down. Everything is fine."

"Maggie, you didn't know who was in there. If you died, I woulda killed you myself!" I laugh a little as he sighs, running his hands over his head. I wait for what I know is coming, and he gives me a smarmy smile. "Yeah, okay, you did good. Is that what you want to hear?"

"Yeah, actually." He shakes his head and walks away, and I check on Rebecca once more, seeing that she's good before heading over to the chief, who I know will want to talk to me. On the way, I'm intercepted by a very pissed-off and maybe proud-looking Liam.

"What the fuck was that?" he asks, speaking quietly. It's so calm that I'm not sure if he is doing it intentionally or is just in too much shock to yell.

"That…was awesome." I point to Rebecca. "And absolutely worth every second."

"Mo…you about gave me a heart attack."

I see the chief beckon to me over Liam's shoulder, and I give him a pat much like the one I gave Gray. "Gotta go. Good job on tracking her down." For maybe the third time since Liam reentered my life, I walk away without letting him talk. Being left behind again isn't something my heart can handle, and I can't trust that he's going to stick around.

35

LIAM

SINCE MY ASSIGNMENT with Gray and Hanson has ended, thankfully on a positive note, it isn't going to be as easy to get into Mo's space as it was for those two days I was needed. It was the first time I wanted a case to take a while to crack, which I know makes me a bad person, but I couldn't help that little sliver of hope.

She isn't picking up her phone. I talked Gray into giving me her number after he saw how she responded to me, but she isn't giving me anything.

Gray casually mentioned that they always frequent one of two bars after work on the weekdays. The first one, O'Callahan's, was empty of off-duty cops, so I went to the next spot, Mile High Brothers.

It is packed to the brim on a Thursday night, but that's how most of these bars are in the downtown area. Ever since meeting Margaret, I haven't been back to many bars. She was my very last date on that idiotic app, and I haven't had a chance to do anything about my urges. One, because I was too busy sorting out my shit with the FBI and Russians to worry about it, and two, because the only one I want to sink into is Margaret.

That girl rules every part of my life without even knowing it.

It's been two fucking years, and I would go even longer if it meant she was in my bed at the end of the night.

I spot her right away. She sits facing the door, her head thrown back in laughter, the smooth column of her neck exposed to me, her hair long again and falling around her shoulders and down her back. She is still fucking gorgeous.

She lifts a Guinness to her lips, and I watched them touch the edge with envy. It didn't escape my notice that she now prefers my drink of choice. The idea of that makes warmth spread into my chest, and I don't try to stop the grin that spreads across my lips.

"Stokes!" I take my eyes off of Margaret for a second to see who's sitting next to her: Hernandez, a guy who helped out Gray and Hanson on their case and who I've met a couple of times. He waves me over to their table and I head that way, knowing Margaret is glaring at me before I even take a step.

Unfortunately for her, I'm not giving her up like she wishes I would, and she's going to have to get the fuck over it.

I take a chair from another table, not asking if someone was using it, and spin it around to take a seat right smack dab next to Margaret—so close to her, in fact, that I can smell her perfume. A mix of vanilla and lavender, even her scent makes me want to rip her out of her chair and get the hell out of here.

"Hey, Mo." I give her a wink and a smirk. Her smile is forced, and I see through the wall she's put up, see that she's trying very hard not to give in to me.

"You guys know each other?" he asks, pointing between us.

"Oh yeah," I say when I see Margaret open her mouth, no doubt to deny any kind of connection. "We go way back."

Hernandez raises a brow at Margaret and laughs. "You told me you were single." I look at him then, wondering if there's a lingering crush there, but I see mirth in his eyes and decide he's just goading a friend.

"I am," she says quickly, more loudly than necessary. She realizes and lowers her voice. "Very, very single."

"Huh," Hernandez answers. Then he gestures to the silent man to his right and says, "Stokes, this is Rev." Rev gives me a slight nod and goes back to looking at his phone. "Don't mind him," Hernandez tells me. "He's not used to being out in public for this long. We got put on a twelve-hour shift today and he's still sore about it."

Rev starts arguing with him, and I take the time to look

over at Margaret, leaning close so I can whisper in her ear. "You look amazing tonight." She really does. She's in her civilian clothes again. Her uniform is no doubt hot as shit, but there's something about her new style that hits me in the gut. All dark and leather—it's hot as hell.

She tries not to blush, but she can't help the red that tinges her cheeks. "Thanks," she mumbles.

"I missed seeing you this week," I say honestly.

Looking up at me under her eyelashes, she replies, "I didn't notice." Her voice is soft, so soft I have to lean in to catch what she says, but I'm a little surprised by her admission.

"You didn't, huh?" I ask, trying for a teasing tone.

"Nope," she shoots back, popping the P. She certainly didn't lose her feistiness.

"Well, I may just have to change that." I risk throwing an arm over the back of her chair.

Margaret takes another sip of beer before she decides what she wants to say. "How are Mike and Jen?"

I'm genuinely happy she cares enough to ask about them. I know what we went through when she met them was out of the ordinary, but I also know she and Jen hit it off. Her getting along with some of my best friends was a good feeling. "They're good, actually. Expecting another little one any day now."

"Really?" Her eyes shine with happiness.

"Yeah, a little girl. They're really excited about it," I say. "I spent a couple weeks with them a few months ago, making sure they were good and everything."

"Wow. I'm glad they're good. I wanted to reach out but…" She licks her lips. "Well, I didn't have any way of contacting them."

Her pain is clear. After our little stunt in Vegas, she was basically cut off from everyone she'd met since I took her along on the dangerous journey. The twisting sensation in my chest is a clear sign of the guilt I'm feeling about hurting her. "I'm sorry," I repeat.

She shrugs. "What's done is done. I have a new life."

I can tell it's not what she wants to say, but she doesn't want me to think she's affected at all, even though that's far from the truth.

"How's Ford? And Gemma?" she asks, changing the subject.

I shake my head. "Ford is good, I think. He's on a mission where I can't get ahold of him, so I can't say for sure." I pause, wishing I could contact my friend because I hate not knowing what's happening, but I can't exactly give him a hard time about it either, given that I've done much worse. "James is good, too. She's still doing her job, quickly moving up the ranks. I bet she'll be director before we know it."

Margaret smiles a real smile at this, the first one since she saw me. "I bet. She's so smart. I liked her a lot."

"I could give you her number if you want."

"Really?" Another smile. I'd get her the fucking president's number if she'd smile at me like that again.

"Yeah, no problem."

"Well, it's been fun," Hernandez says, standing up. Rev follows his lead, and I wonder how I forgot they were here. "But I've got a five AM alarm and a lot of sleepin' to do."

We say our goodbyes, and when the waitress comes by, I'm surprised Margaret orders another beer. I do the same and relax slightly now that it's just us. It seems she's happy to sit here, even with me.

"So…" she starts, no doubt wondering how to move forward. "How's the PI business?"

I smile and indulge her. "It's good, actually. I'm enjoying the change of pace."

"I'm surprised." She nods. "I thought you would've stayed in the FBI as long as possible."

"I had more important things to do with life." My words are stated as simply as saying I like sugar. It's a fact, easy. I see her throat move as she swallows, and I move in closer. "How about you? How do you like being an officer?"

Margaret animates before my eyes, and she rambles in a familiar way. She tells me how much joy she gets from her job, how she loves being able to protect innocents while doing it with authority. She has a passion for this work that you rarely see in most law enforcement, and I can't help but fall in love with her damn hard as she speaks.

I knew I was in love with her years ago. I knew it, and I didn't do the right things to make sure she understood that. I wasn't allowed to do much about it when I was being debriefed, and I wasn't allowed to doing anything about it when I was in Russia.

I wish I could have made her understand it before we got pulled apart.

"Well…" She stands after three beers with me. Most of the bar has cleared out, though I didn't realize it was happening, too enraptured in her to give a shit. "I've got work tomorrow, and I already broke my rule about two drinks on a work night." She gives me a shy smile, and I stand with her.

"I'll walk you home."

"That's not necessary, Liam." She waves her hand around. "It's only a couple blocks."

"Still." I shrug, pretending it's only for me, and lead us out of the bar. I already know which way to go, and I wait for her to come out the door. When she does, I hold my hand out to hers. It's instinctive, and now that the gesture has been made, I can't take it back—not that I want to.

A buzz zaps into my hand when she takes it, and I tuck it close, walking her to her apartment.

We walk in silence, both taking in the night. There are busy people still on the streets, idiots coming out of venues and bars, drunk and stupid, but I don't care about them. I only care about the girl whose hand is wrapped in mine, the girl who's letting me in.

Even though it's small, it still fucking counts.

When we reach her door, I take a minute and wish I could go up with her, wish it was our normal. I wish me going home with her at night was something we did as a couple, wish it was a ritual: drinks after work, walk home together, go to bed together, ravish each other like the first time, and wake up together in the morning.

Instead, I turn toward her and open my mouth to take a chance, to ask her out. I want to do it as a normal person, not an undercover FBI agent, not as Dan Cliff, but as Liam Stokes.

"Go out with me." I don't add anything to it; I don't have to. I want to be with her. She already knows that, but the only way to get there is to take the first step.

"Liam…" Her eyes are guarded and she bites her bottom lip.

I reluctantly shift my gaze away. "Just one date. One date, whenever you say." I gently pull her closer and she's right underneath my chin now. I grip her hip with my free hand and hope she can see how serious I am. "Give me one more chance."

"I don't know." Her voice is low and husky. She's trying not to act affected by me, but she is.

"One more shot." I squeeze her hip. "Please."

She closes her eyes, and I can't tell if it's the alcohol affecting her or the close proximity of our bodies, but she drags in a deep breath and then refocuses her eyes on mine. "Just one."

36

MARGARET

IT'S BEEN A few weeks since Liam dropped himself back into my life, and I am still trying to navigate him being around again.

I couldn't figure out how I was feeling about Liam. After one too many drinks with him a couple weeks ago, I almost let my urges get the best of me. Between his hand in mine, the memory of us walking to my apartment the first time, and the comforting feeling I get around him, I let him lead me to my apartment, let him hold my hand and act like we were fine.

In my alcohol-induced state, I let him talk me into giving him a chance. Why did I do that?

Because you fucking love him, duh.

I roll my eyes at myself. I can't stop thinking of the date. He calls at nine o'clock every single night, and I stare at it ringing in my hand, my thumb hovering over the green button until it finally rolls over to voicemail and I let out the breath I'm holding in. I can't answer, can't tell him I'm ready for the date I told him we could have because I am terrified that it will be so easy to let him take over my heart once and for all.

While in the back of my head I am thinking about my insatiable yet confusing desire to see Liam, to be around him again and give in to whatever it is he wants, in reality I am suffering through another round of Johnson being my partner, even though I explicitly told the chief I was not interested in being on patrol with him anymore. Unfortunately, that isn't my call, and since I 'recklessly' ran into a dangerous situation to save Rebecca Myers, I'm not in a good place with him at the moment and my pull isn't as strong as it usually is.

"Johnson," I snap. I know I'm being bitchy, but his need to be on his phone pisses me off so badly. His head pops up like he's surprised he's in a cop car. I honestly don't have any clue how he got this far. "What are you doing?"

"Oh, I was just—uh, well, I was looking at—" I reach over and take his phone. As his superior, I shouldn't invade his privacy, but as a person, I am so sick of being ignored.

"A dating app? Are you serious right now?" I give him a look of disbelief. "You are working. Put it away."

"Yes ma'am." I shake my head, not understanding

incompetence.

We continue our patrol for three more hours before our shift ends and someone else takes over. I bite my tongue so many times I bet I could put a ring through it without even flinching. I know Johnson thinks he's going to make it here, but whether he believes it or not, I am going easy on him.

I make my way to my locker and change into my civilian clothes, not at all surprised to find another package of donuts waiting for me. Liam is definitely trying to fatten me up. I don't know how or when he sneaks in here, but it's a weirdly comforting thing to see every day. I can't ever admit it, but I look forward to it now.

I miss him; there's no doubt about that. I was mad about that man, was ready to change my entire life for him. I followed him anywhere he told me to go. I lured a bad guy out of hiding to help him finish something so we could be together.

So yeah, I love him. I can't even fool myself into thinking I don't, but the thing with Liam is that he came into my world like a slow-moving silent storm. You see it coming, but you don't know the damage it's going to do until after it's done.

He killed a little piece of me every day he didn't reach out (his pathetic excuses for letters not withstanding), and it hurt to think I'd never really know what happened, to think I was so insignificant that no one bothered to call, to write, to do anything.

The only contact I had was when the director of the FBI

paid me a little visit, and I was way too intimidated to ask him point blank where Liam was. At that point, I was thinking if he hadn't really contacted me yet, we were done with whatever we'd started.

It fucking hurt.

Much like whenever he sent me away each time we ran into trouble, but this time, it's permanent. I'm not with the FBI or one of his buddies. I'm alone.

God, just thinking about it gives me a headache. I am looking forward to soaking in a bath, bubbles filled to the top, maybe a pint of ice cream…I don't know, this could go anywhere.

I flick the lock open and enter my apartment. There's a nice autumn breeze coming from a window I leave cracked, and I breathe in the clean scent. I hang my bag on the hook by the door and kick off my shoes, immediately heading to the freezer to check my ice cream supplies. I like both brownie fudge and mint chocolate chip, but with the day I've had, it's a full-on brownie fudge night.

As I shut the freezer door, I jump back a foot, a startled scream ripping out of my throat at the sight of the six-foot blonde bombshell in front of me. "Shit, Gemma! Warn a girl!"

A small, tiny smirk forms on her face, showing her sick satisfaction in managing to scare the shit out of me. "What the hell are you doing sneaking into my apartment?"

"Your locks could use some work. It was almost too easy." She shrugs. Walking to my small dinette set, she pulls out a chair and plops down into it. Letting out a sigh, she asks, "Got any wine?"

I turn, still confused, and look in my pantry for the bottle I know I purchased recently. I haven't been in the mood to drink it much so there is still plenty in it. I pull it out along with two glasses and pour us each one. I eye her where she sits, wondering why she is all of a sudden showing up unannounced.

After I take a seat and let her sip the wine, I raise a brow at her and wait. "What?" she asks, her voice tinged with annoyance.

"Well, I mean, it's not like I'm not happy to see you, because I am, but it's a little unexpected that you're here."

She opens her mouth to reply just as a knock sounds at the door. I again raise a brow, wondering if she was expecting someone else to join us, but she just shrugs, sipping more wine. I get up and walk over, looking back over my shoulder at Gemma.

When I wrench the door open, a handsome Liam stands on the other side, and I take him in. His jeans fit snugly around his waist, a white t-shirt is topped by a leather jacket, and his smile is stretched into a lazy grin only guys who look like him can pull off.

"Hey." I scold myself when my voice leaves me sounding breathless. He does not literally take your breath away, Margaret.

"Hey," he replies, pulling an arm around from behind his back, bringing a dozen white roses into view.

"Wow," I whisper with a grin of my own as I take them from

him. He leans in like he wants to kiss me and hesitates; I don't know how to react, so I just stay still. Just as his lips are about to touch mine, a throat clears behind me.

Liam stands up straight and gives me a glare, jealousy flaring in his eyes as he takes a step around me.

I let him and follow as he sees Gemma at the table—I practically forgot about her when Liam showed up. He walks over and stands above her. "What the fuck are you doing here?"

"Liam!" I scold. "What the hell? Be nice!" I don't necessarily have a reason to defend Gemma, but I don't have a reason not to either…

"It's okay, Margaret. He wasn't expecting me," she snarks at him. Neither are looking at me, and if I didn't know better, I would think this was a lover's quarrel. A feeling of dread sits heavily in my gut, and I toss the roses on the counter.

"Well," I start, not sure where to start. Liam and I haven't actually talked in weeks, just some texts. I never asked if he dated anyone after we parted ways, but I guess my assumption was that he didn't. "What is going on?" I ask, my hands out in front of me, my confusion clear.

"So, you haven't told her then?" Gemma asks Liam, casually taking a sip of her wine and waiting on his reply.

"Shut up," he growls. "You shouldn't have come here."

I hate how that sounds, like he is hiding something from me, but do I even have claim? Dammit. I have no idea. "Liam," I say, crossing my arms, "what's going on?"

He closes his eyes and looks to me; his eyes are sad, and it seems like whatever he's about to say isn't going to be something I'll like. Walking until he's standing right in front of me, he grabs my elbows and says, "I didn't want you to find out like this."

I school my features. "Find out what?"

"Jesus, Liam, you should have fucking told her the second you saw her," Gemma snaps. I don't look at her, though; I look to Liam and wait.

"I haven't been totally honest with you about some things."

"Like?"

He closes his eyes and says, "Like…that I'm not in the FBI anymore."

"What?" I ask, not understanding what he's saying. "You're a PI now…right?"

"Technically, yes."

"Technically? So, what are you really?"

"I'm…undercover…kind of."

I shake my head and take a step back, effectively knocking his hands off my arms. "What the fuck, Liam?"

I don't really understand what is happening, or why Gemma is here, or what the fuck is going on.

"I didn't tell you because I didn't want you to be concerned yet. I didn't want to have you looking over your shoulder every second. I was hoping I could finish it then tell you."

"Finish what?" I ask, but Gemma cuts in.

"It's too late, Stokes."

He looks over at her and sighs. "What do you mean?"

"According to our sources, Margaret has already been made."

I stare at Liam's face as it crumples and he turns to look at me, his face pained. "I'm sorry, Mo."

"Sorry? Sorry for what?"

It's Gemma who answers. "Unfortunately, Margaret, you're in danger—again."

37

LIAM

MARGARET IS IN her room packing a bag of essentials to take with us. It's the second time she's had to leave her home in order to save her life and one of the many times she's had to hide because of me.

"You should have told her," James says, twirling her wine glass on the table.

"I fucking know, okay?" I snap back. I don't want to be a dick, but as my handler with the FBI, it's her job to deal with my mood swings, and right now, my mood is black.

"I didn't know she didn't know. You said you had her handled, so I showed up assuming you would already be here and she would

    be in the loop."

I sigh and run a hand over my head, looking toward the hallway Margaret went down. She stayed composed when she heard the gist of what was happening and asked what she needed to do, not once questioning us but just wondering how she could help.

I didn't ask her to do anything. I just wanted her to tell me she didn't hate my fucking guts.

"Things haven't been easy since I got here," I admit to James. She doesn't care much for empathy, a strict It's just a job type of person. She never gets attached to anyone or anything, and it's what makes her a shoo-in for the director position.

"What happened?"

"I just… Things got crazy after everything that went down, and I haven't really…" Fuck. I am going to have to tell her. "I haven't really been in contact with her since."

"Why the hell not?"

"Because…I thought I'd be done. I thought I could put it all behind me and move on, with Margaret, here."

"But since you got assigned here, you were forced to see her and could no longer keep her in the dark." I nod in affirmation, and she replies with, "You're an idiot."

"Thanks," I mutter sarcastically.

"What?" She laughs loudly, something I don't see often. "You left her in Vegas with nothing but a plane ticket and then didn't talk to her for what, two years? And you expect a 'Welcome back, honey'?" Her voice is annoyingly high in a poor imitation of Margaret.

I pause in my response because I know there's nothing I can do to make myself sound better. I know I screwed up by not talking to her, by not truly communicating with her, but after everything that already happened to her, all the things that were done to her because of me, I couldn't bring myself to drag her into it all over again.

Margaret chooses this moment to walk out wearing her leather jacket. It fits snugly around her breasts, and I suck in a slow breath to calm myself down. She looks like a badass, a black backpack over her shoulder and her hands in the pockets of her jacket. "So, where to?"

We go to a safe house the FBI sets up for us, and Gemma tags along for the time being to make sure Margaret is up for sticking with me. If I know anything about her, it's that she doesn't back down from a fight, and she sure as hell isn't going to hide out while I take care of things for us.

I'm checking my guns for the hundredth time while Gemma gives her a rundown. I would do it, but now she doesn't trust that I'll give her all the details.

"So basically, Anton was a tiny piece of this, and this

other guy, Alexander, is the one who started the whole thing?" Margaret asks. Her tone is formal, and I watch her slip into cop mode. I haven't been able to tell her how truly amazing I think it is that she turned herself around the way she did. Watching her in action in her new job, it's crystal clear that this is where Margaret was meant to be.

"Yes, and he's here, but we're not a hundred percent certain where."

"Which is where Stokes came in," Margaret finishes, and I sigh at her use of my last name. She hasn't talked to me since we left her apartment, and whenever she refers to me, she uses my last name. It's what all the officers and agents do, except she and I aren't just colleagues, and I'll be damned if she thinks she can build that wall back up between us.

"And the other agent, Perk? He was in on it from the beginning?"

"Yes." James sighs, and I can tell she hates admitting that because technically he was working under her at the time. "But we've got him now, which is why we know all about Alexander."

"Okay." Margaret bites her lip, her face in deep thought. "And my job?"

"I'll contact your precinct and let your chief know what's going on, to an extent, and once this is over, you can go back to work. For now, are you capable of being Stokes' partner in this?" It's not protocol, but I know why Gemma is helping me here, and I'll forever be in her debt. I don't work with partners, and

I wouldn't work with a partner on this if it were anyone other than Margaret.

Giving Margaret a job with me…well, it's a sure-fire way for me to get a hell of a lot closer to her.

Yeah, I owe Gemma a few bottles of wine for that.

"Of course," Margaret confirms. "Whatever I have to do."

Gemma nods at her and says, "You have my number. Use it for whatever you need. Otherwise"—she stands to leave and gives me a nod—"we'll see you two as soon as you know where Alexander is."

I walk her out the door, making sure to lock it behind her, and I watch her make her way out to the black car she drove us here in.

Tonight, we debrief.

I head back over to Margaret, and she's looking over the files Gemma gave her on an iPad, her face pinched in concentration. It's adorable to see her so focused on something. I know her job involves a lot of paperwork, like most jobs in law enforcement, and cases like this seem to intrigue her. It wouldn't surprise me if she wanted to be a detective someday.

"Mo," I start, wanting to come clean and apologize but also not wanting to start a fight.

"Don't worry about it," she mumbles, her head still tilted down.

"No, hold on," I snap, losing my head for a minute. I take a breath and she glances up at me, surprised I used a tone I haven't used in front of her before. "I know I fucked up, okay? I get it. I should have included you from the start." Her eyes are glued to mine and I know I have her; I just have to get through to her. "I should have called you the second they said I was going to Russia. I should have found you the minute I was moved here, but I didn't, because I care about you. I didn't want you mixed up in this shit all over again. I didn't want to come in and flip your new world upside down."

She doesn't say anything, so I continue, digging dip for the guts I need to say what I need to say.

"I'm so fucking proud of what you've done with your life. You're seriously the most badass woman I've ever met, and fuck me if I'm not completely in love with you." I drag air in, thinking over the words I said and feeling terrified that I may have done something I can't come back from.

I wait for her to say something, anything, and I blow out an amused laugh when she replies with, "You love me?"

I grin at her and bend in front of the chair she's sitting on. "Yeah, I do. I fucking love you. I have since I saw you fight your way out of that warehouse in Vegas. No way I couldn't." I take her hand in mine, running my thumb over her left ring finger. "I've never loved anyone the way I love you. Living apart…" I blow out a sigh and sober when I look into her eyes. "It's not an option."

Margaret bites her cheek and seems to think about what I've told her. Her eyes are shiny with tears, the wall she erected to keep me out starts to fall, and the tablet is abandoned on the table. She clears her throat, her brows furrowing. "I'm terrified you'll leave again." Her admission makes a lump form in my throat, guilt and worry seeping into my bravado.

"I swear to you, I will never leave again, and if I have to go, you're coming with me."

"I—" A shrill ring slices through the air, and I close my eyes, hating all that is technology. I can't ignore it, so I hold up a finger to tell her to wait for a minute.

"Stokes."

"Stokes, there was a camera hit on Alexander, a nightclub aptly named Church about six miles from your location. Get there now. Sending the information." Gemma hangs up, and the iPad beeps with an incoming alert.

Everything we need to know about where Alexander is stares at me on the screen, and I look over to Margaret. She nods and says, "Let's end this, and then we can figure out everything else."

Unable to resist, I wrap my hand around the back of her neck, catching her off guard. A surprised gasp leaves her and I bring our lips together, savoring her taste before we pull away, breathless. "Let's go."

38

MARGARET

THE NIGHT IS cool and quiet, the street we're on completely abandoned save for an old car that looks like it has seen better days and a group of raccoons that are sorting through a tipped-over trash can.

My breathing is erratic, not because what we are doing is unsafe or scary, and not because the man we are hunting is one of the most dangerous people I've ever encountered, his rap sheet one to be beat by some of the biggest thugs around.

No. It's because of the man beside me. It's because of the words he spoke earlier that seem to echo throughout my head like a disc skipping on a loop.

"...fuck me if I'm not completely in love with you."

This gorgeous, kind, brilliant man who sits not six inches from me is in love with me. Me, the girl who puked on him the second time we met, the girl who got us into so much shit just by existing, the one girl—ever, probably—who pushed him away.

And he sat there telling me he loves me.

It was an admission that rocked me to the core. I immediately started feeling like I was going to be sick and simultaneously wanted to cry. My resolve was to hate him, to push him away and not let him get through the wall I built just for him, but somehow, somewhere along the way, he's been knocking it down brick by brick until he could climb over the rubble.

All I want to do is give in, crawl across the tiny console between us, and show him how much I want all of that, how much I want him to stay and be with me, how I want it all to come true the way I've been hoping for all this time.

Even though it's what I want, I can't do that. Not yet. Right now, we have a job to do, and I have to focus on that. Until this part is over and the bad man is put away, I will wait to do more than a chaste kiss on the lips when I tell him I love him too, because that moment deserves more. It deserves a bed and endless hours to spend in it.

"No movement, James." Liam's voice pulls me out of my cloud of thought and back to this moment.

Alexander is no dummy. He chose one of the more popular

places to hang out in to conceal his identity. I've never been to the Church nightclub for pleasure, but I have been there for business on more than one occasion. As far as nightclubs go, it's one of the nicer ones, and it isn't at all surprising that there is a Russian mobster hanging out there.

I looked over the file the FBI has been compiling over the last two years, and it is extensive. I've never seen him in this nightclub before, or at least he's hidden himself very well within its walls, which is good and bad. It means there is a very good chance he is in there, but it also means getting to the part of the building where he is might be tricky without starting something we don't want innocent civilians to be a part of.

"We've IDed him through security cameras and know he entered the building at eleven. Nothing on him leaving." Gemma's voice comes through the comms we're wearing in our ears. It was pure luck that we caught him while she was still in town, and she and other officers are waiting in a black van two streets over.

With Liam and me in this car, we don't seem as obvious as a surveillance van would, and we are going to use that to our advantage tonight.

Because I didn't know what they would need from me when I was packing, I decided to throw in a little black dress I wore to a colleague's wedding some months ago. It was a guess, but after Vegas, I had reason to believe it might come in handy, and it did.

It's a bit on the short side, but it's perfect for the club. Liam is even luckier in his dark jeans and tight grey Henley. Guys have it so damn easy.

"All right, Mo and I are going in," Liam tells her, and he looks to me. "Ready?" His eyes tell me he's got me. Even though I know how to handle myself in these types of situations now, I still take a cue from him and give him a nod.

We walk hand in hand to the front door. There are a few people ahead of us to get in, but the line moves quickly, and before we know it, we're in. Our IDs are checked, and luckily there are zero body checks, though it's unlikely they would have found where I hid my gun.

The music is loud. I can feel the bass thump through the floor, and the people move in sync with one another. From a distance it looks like one massive group dancing together. It seems we've come on a night when a live DJ who looks mighty popular is playing, and everyone is jumping in unison when the beat asks for it.

Not a single soul pays us any mind.

I take in our surroundings; the nightclub is literally a church. The cathedral ceilings are in immaculate condition, and the stained glass windows reflect the strobe lights that shine brightly throughout the room.

There is a bar set up to the side, and Liam leads me there first, ordering us some drinks while I observe the scene. Liam doesn't stop touching me, his hand on mine, on my hip, or around my shoulders at all times, and I'm not complaining one bit.

I turn when Liam tells me to and smirk when I see he's gotten me a cosmo. "Memory lane, much?" I say into his ear. I have to lean into him and am not shy when my hips meet his, my right hand holding his shoulder for stability, his left arm wrapped around my hips.

"Best night of my life," he replies into my left ear.

I lean back and furrow my brow, a smirk still on my lips. "That was the best night of your life?" I ask, leaning closer again when his arm pulls me in tighter. "Why is that?"

He leans away only enough so he can meet my eyes with his own, and there's a smile on his lips when he says, "It was the night I met you."

I open my mouth to say something, anything as sweet as that, but come up empty. Instead an awkward giddy giggle stumbles out, and I shake my head. Thankfully, he just laughs at me.

I give in to an urge I've had since I opened the door to his grinning face earlier, and when I press my lips to his, he reciprocates easily, abandoning his drink so his right hand can cup the back of my neck. It's his signature move with me, and I love it.

His tongue meets mine, and I savor the bitter taste of Guinness on his tongue. I didn't think I'd ever like the taste of it as much as I do now.

"Guys, mission please." Gemma's voice startles me away, and I pull myself up. Liam grips me tighter and presses a last kiss to my closed lips. Our moment reminds me that we also have cameras on our bodies, giving Gemma a front row seat.

"Sorry," I say, mostly for her, even though I'm not the least bit sorry. I'm about to clarify that to Liam when I see a character who looks wildly out of place move behind a curtain. "Behind you," I say subtly, leaning into Liam like I've had too much to drink. "Follow my lead."

"Mo." His eyes give me the warning his mouth doesn't.

"Just trust me."

I see him want to argue, but then he thinks better of it and follows closely behind me. I turn my smile up to eleven and wave out into the crowd. There's no one there, but I want anyone watching to think we're just two people greeting a friend and looking for a place to hook up.

I walk through the curtain like I know what I'm doing, allowing the beat of the bass to propel me, an extra confidence in my step with a soundtrack for my movements. Behind the curtain are stairs that lead down into the basement. I know that because I've been in this part before; the only difference is, instead of a uniform and a stick-up-your-ass bun, I'm wearing a revealing dress and my hair flows in waves around me as I pull Liam down the stairs.

He keeps up, and I only pause slightly when I hear Gemma's voice again. "Remember, he might know who Liam is, guys. If he recognizes you, you need to get out." Her stern warning makes me shiver, but I take the opportunity to turn to Liam the moment we hit the bottom of the stairs, giving him another kiss. He's not expecting it, his face already stern, but I giggle like he's the funniest guy in the world and implore him with my eyes to follow along. His mouth immediately breaks out into a grin, following my lead, and I turn us so he's walking backward. I'm all over him, my hands in his hair, his lips on mine, and I look over his shoulder, noticing there are more than fifty people down here.

We find a place to sit, a foot of space on a bench Liam snatches up before pulling me onto his lap. We are both eyeing everyone around us, looking for anyone or anything that doesn't belong. We keep our heads bent together, talking low and whispering like two lovers who haven't left the honeymoon stage—which, when I think about it, is true for us.

"I got him," Liam says quietly, keeping his mouth on my neck while looking over my shoulder. I tell my libido to chill out and focus, but it's damn hard when his lips are caressing my skin.

"Liam," I start, but he's already standing.

"He saw me—he's bolting." One minute we're making out, and the next Liam is chasing someone out the back door and I'm left to catch up with him.

"Liam went after him!" I yell, letting Gemma know to get her ass here now. Hopefully she was already doing that, but I grab my gun from where it's secured on the inside of my thigh and chase after the man who just messed with my psyche.

Busting through a door into the back alley, I immediately

hear the gunshots, but I don't know who's shooting at what. It's dark as hell and there are plenty of drunkards going to and from the bar, but none are keen on noticing what's happening.

I finally catch a glimpse of Liam ahead of me, and just as I take a step toward him, a shot rings out and his silhouette goes down.

Tears spring to my eyes and my breath leaves my body in one word. "No!"

39

MARGARET

I RAISE MY arms and shoot what seems like endless rounds at the figure moving at the end of the alley. I see him jerk but I don't think, don't pause to wonder if he's dead or hurt. I run for Liam, forgetting the mission, my only concern figuring out what just happened to the man bleeding on the ground.

I hit the rough pavement beside him, and the asphalt slices into my bare knees, but I don't care. All I'm aware of is Liam, who seems to be passed out. God, please just be passed out.

I see the bullet wound and apply pressure immediately, trying to remember the procedures and scenarios I've been trained on, knowing I've done this before, but being faced with saving a stranger is easier to think through than trying to revive the man you love.

"Gemma! He's hit! We need an ambulance! He's not waking up." I scream the orders, knowing it's unnecessary and someone will hear me, but the hysteria is overwhelming me.

"We got him, Margaret!" I hear Gemma cheer through my ear, but I don't give a shit.

"Ambulance, now!" I growl out, holding the wound as blood pours over my fingers. I don't want to release a hand to feel for a pulse, too afraid loosening the pressure could be the tipping point for whether or not he wakes up again.

"Fuck," I whisper, tears blurring my vision as I look down at the man who has changed me in more ways than not. "I did it for you." My voice is hoarse, but I look at his pale face and hold back a sob, letting the words pour out. "I did all of it for you. I wanted you to be proud of me." A rushed breath leaves me and I suck in another, clinging to the tiny spark of hope in my chest. "I love you. Please, please don't leave me."

"Margaret!" Gemma comes up from behind me and kneels at my side, checking his pulse and eyeing where my hands are pressing against his wound. "Shit. He has a pulse, but it's faint."

I shake my head, wanting to clear the thoughts and visions that assault my brain. Please, God, don't take him yet. I'm not ready. I can't do this.

I hear an ambulance come up to the mouth of the alley and Gemma runs toward them, explaining the situation and rushing them to Liam. I lean over him, trying to keep the blood from escaping, and I can barely see his face through the rush of tears.

"Ma'am, let us in there, please. You did good." A man has to remove me, and Gemma immediately takes me into her arms. I look at her and see her determined expression, wishing, not for the first time, that I was as tough as her.

As I look back at the man I love and have loved for two years, I feel like I won't ever come anywhere close to having that kind of strength.

We got him.

Alexander—we got him. Everything Liam has been working toward for five years now has been accomplished. We have Alexander behind bars, and he gave us a list of people who have helped him and a list of places where he grows, makes, and distributes drugs in order to strike a plea deal. It won't do him much good, but he's willing to give up everything, so the FBI will play along until everything is done with.

I haven't moved an inch since I came into this hospital.

The waiting room is cold and grey, the décor perfectly matching the mood of those who sit within it. It's sad how well it fits. Gemma has been my strength since we arrived, and I've had to rely on her more than I care to admit. She's the only one who's coherent enough to actually be able to get information on Liam.

I'm technically not anything to him, but she somehow is getting updates on everything he's going through.

He's having surgery to get the bullet out, but they're not sure how well it will go, saying we won't know more until afterward. That was the last update we received, and it wasn't nearly enough to pacify me. Not even close.

I don't cry, though; I haven't since Gemma planted me in this chair. I stare blankly at my hands. They're soaked in blood—Liam's blood—and I wonder what the hell am I going to do without that man in my life.

Before when we parted ways, there was always something lingering, some other way for us to overcome being separated. That something, I've discovered, was hope.

I used to have hope. I should still have hope, but after everything the two of us have been through, hope is…hopeless.

"Hey." Gemma comes over and rubs a hand on my shoulder. She's been more affectionate than I've ever seen, and I'm sure it's making her more uncomfortable than it's making me. "We need to clean you up."

"No."

It's the first word I've said since we got here.

"Margaret." Her stern voice reminds me of my mother's, one I haven't heard in a couple weeks, and I finally look up at her. "Liam's family is coming. They'll be here in an hour. The last thing they need is to see his girlfriend covered in his blood. Do you understand?"

I blink at her, my brain slow to process her words.

Liam's family...I've never met them. They don't have a clue who I am or what Liam means to me. Oh God. The tears I thought were gone rise again, and I blink them away.

"Come." Gemma doesn't give me a choice, and she drags me to the restroom. I don't know what I'm doing. It's like I'm a stranger in my own body. My movements are sluggish, but I force myself to get a grip and try to help Gemma help me.

She strips my dress off without asking, and I don't question it when she shoves a set of scrubs at me. I just put them on after I've scoured Liam's blood off of my skin. I watch the red liquid swirl down the drain and cry silently. This trauma is too much for me to take, too much to process and understand, and for the first time in years, I pray. I pray that God will pull Liam through this. I pray that he won't take away the only man I've ever loved. I pray that he won't make me live in this world without Liam at my side.

I pray that Liam lives.

I let the silent prayer out and follow Gemma out of the bathroom. I feel a bit better without his blood all over me, but in a weird, sadistic way, a feeling of loss hits me when I stare at my clean, soap-scrubbed hands. We walk toward the waiting room and I hear Liam's name spoken; it's a small voice, and when I look up, I meet his eyes—except they're on the face of a tall brunette.

"Layla," Gemma calls out, walking toward her. She pats her

shoulder awkwardly in a way that only Gemma could make comforting and leads her to some seats by the wall.

I don't move from the spot her eyes froze me to. Layla is here because Liam is her only sibling, and now he's hurt, maybe hurt too badly to make it out alive, and it's all my fault. This entire thing is my fault.

If I'd been quicker, reacted faster, I would have been able to get there in time to give Liam backup.

I don't belong here.

Layla doesn't know who I am or what I've been through with her brother, and seeing me will only add to her confusion. Shit, Liam doesn't even know how much he means to me.

A tear threatens to escape, and after a quick glance at the two of them, I make my way toward the door, needing an exit, a place to get out of my head where they won't see me lose my shit and break down.

"Margaret," a voice says to my back, halting my movements. I turn and see Layla standing behind me, her eyes full of worry, but also determination.

I don't know what to say that will get through to her, that will make her understand what he means to me and how heartbroken I am to have possibly caused any pain for her. So, I settle for something generic. It's not much, but it's all I have. "I'm sorry." My voice is cracked, timid.

She stares at me and I want to look away, but I don't. My eyes fill with tears I don't want to spill over, but I'm not sure

I have the willpower to keep them back. Layla's fill too, and suddenly she's pulling me into her arms and sobbing. I don't embrace her back at first, shock restraining my movements, but then I think of a woman who has maybe lost her only brother and my arms grip her tightly.

We stand like that for a long time, both crying, her loud breaths erratic as she tries to hold in her sobs, and mine silent, mourning a man I never got to have a real life with.

Pulling back, she wipes at her face and looks at me. She gives me an embarrassed smile, and I take her hand, leading her to the chairs she and Gemma occupied before, her presence now missing as I let Layla lean on me for support.

"I can't believe this is happening," she whispers, her tears still tracking down her face, her expression riddled with grief. I don't say anything. I don't have any words to give her that could possibly make this situation better. "He told me about you."

My head whips toward hers and a soft gasp escapes me.

"He told me about his 'Mo'." She grins, and an ache in my chest beats harder when I see Liam's smile on her face. They look so much alike; it's scary and painful, but beautiful. "A while ago, he came home and visited." She smiles through her tears, no doubt thinking of the last time she saw Liam. "He told me a lot of what he'd done, which was unusual. He doesn't normally share that information with me, to keep me safe, but he did this time, and I couldn't figure out why…until he brought you up." She sighs and stares at our clasped hands. "He told me about Mo, the girl who'd changed everything for him. Liam said you were stubborn and bullheaded, the strongest woman he'd ever met, and he couldn't wait to get to you, to love you and finally be with you in a real way."

A sob escapes my chest and I use my other hand to cover my embarrassing cry. I should have told him. I should have told him I love him. I knew better than to wait, knew better than to think I could actually have a normal chance to do it right.

Doing it right isn't always what we think it should be. It's not about the perfect timing or the perfect setting; it's about letting your heart lead your words and actions. I shouldn't have held back. In that safe house, when he told me he loved me, I should have said it back.

Why didn't I say it back?

Another heart-wrenching sob leaves my chest, and I just allow myself to cry. Layla says nothing, doesn't move, just holds my hand in both of hers, giving me support simply by being there.

It's hours later when we get word from a doctor. Layla stands and tugs me up with her, and I don't struggle even though I want to. I want to stop her, want to stop myself from moving across the floor. I don't want to hear what the doctor has to say. I don't want to hear anything that could alter the rest of my life.

I just want him to be okay.

I need him to be okay.

We stare at the doctor's sullen expression and wait for the

bad news to come.

40

MARGARET

IT SMELLS LIKE roses.

That's the first thought that hits me when I wake the next day. I don't know why, as it's not exactly a smell I tend to surround myself with, but that's what comes to me.

I lift my neck to look around, and the crick in it makes me realize I must have passed out at some point in the middle of the night—or early morning, depending on what you want to call it. Layla lies on the small couch, still sleeping soundly.

The doctor informed us that Liam was still here with us after the surgery to remove the bullet from his left shoulder. He said it was lucky Liam didn't get hit in the heart and told us the wound wasn't anything they couldn't repair; however, there was trauma from the way he fell to the ground. He hit his head on the concrete, which was why he wasn't conscious when I got to him.

Liam had woken once when he'd gotten to the hospital, but shortly after that he'd passed out again and was rushed into surgery.

My feeling of disappointment in myself only hit me ten times harder when I walked into the room to see Liam hooked up to every tube imaginable. There was an IV in his arm and many others I didn't recognize. I didn't know what each one did, but I knew they were keeping him here with me.

He just needs to wake up, and no one is sure when—or if— that's going to happen.

I look to the door when it opens, revealing a nurse. She gives me a kind smile and checks the machines, writing things down on his chart. I already know what she would say to me if I were to ask questions; she's give me a placating look and say, Only time will tell. That's not what I need, though. That's not what I want to hear or want anyone saying. There's nothing they can ever say that will make this better unless it's, He's awake. He's alive. Those are the only things I want to hear.

Grasping his hand again, I send up another prayer. I couldn't tell you how many prayers I've sent up in the last twenty-four hours. Hell, it feels like it's been weeks since we got here, but it's barely past the one-day mark.

After the nurse leaves, I check to make sure Layla is still

asleep before scooting my chair even closer and staring at Liam's peaceful face. He still looks handsome, even in the state he's in now. I pull his hand gingerly between mine and lean in, resting my chest on his hand, and speak in a whisper. "I love you." Shaking my head, I continue. "I know it's too late for that, to say that to you, but it's my truth and I needed to say it. God, Liam." I close my eyes and take a shaky breath, trying not to cry yet again. "I messed up. I should have let you know what I was feeling, because it's the same. I love you so much I wasn't even sure what to do with myself when we parted ways. I threw myself into work, trying to forget you…but I never did, and I'm so, so sorry." I cough, trying to stop the breaking that's happening inside me. "Please, please don't leave me here alone. I need you." My tears spill over, and I rest my head on his hand and let them fall. I let myself feel everything I need to feel, because I deserve every bit of pain that comes with losing Liam.

And that's how this feels—like I'm losing him.

I'm still in the same position hours later when Layla coaxes me out of the chair. My hand doesn't want to leave his, and I tell her that. I tell her I can't leave him. She gives me a pitying grin and I look away, sick of seeing that look on everyone's face. Layla has been taking this better than I am, and I think it's because she still has the one thing I'm missing: hope.

I don't feel the familiar spark inside my chest that makes me look forward, that makes my brain conjure up images of the future. Even when Liam and I parted ways, I still had those pictures flashing in my head, the ones where we were together.

We were apart, but in the end, we were always together, and that's something I don't want to replace. I can't replace that with anything else.

If he goes, if he doesn't wake up, I might as well say goodbye to any kind of future.

Without Liam, a future is pointless.

"I love you," I whisper one more time, squeezing my eyes shut and, with everything in me, willing him to open his again.

41

LIAM

I HAVE NO idea what happened to me.

Everything is foggy. My brain is muddled with flashes of what I think could be happening, but nothing makes any sense, and I can't seem to get my eyes to open no matter how hard I try.

I concentrate on one of my hands, one that feels something covering it. I focus on moving one of my fingers, and I must do so because I hear a voice now and the pressure grows. I squeeze more, and I think I smile when it works.

I try again to open my eyes, but it's hard. The lights are bright, and I'm not sure where I am.

I think of the last thing I remember: the club, the lights, the music, Alexander, and Margaret. Margaret was there with me before all hell broke loose. I remember standing up and running, shoving a door open, maybe catching sight of someone in an alley, and reaching for my gun.

That's where it ends.

Fuck. Margaret—where is she? Is she okay?

I will my eyes to open and finally, finally, I see a sliver of light. I close them again, a headache pounding in the back of my head. I gotta open them. I gotta get to Margaret.

This time, I don't let the headache stop me, and I open my eyes, except everything is blurry. I panic for a moment, but then I blink and things start to slowly come into focus.

I'm in a hospital. I recognize the machines beside me, and I search the room for the person I'm looking for. I don't have to wait long, because when I turn my head to the right, she's right there in front of me.

A sob escapes from her chest and she pulls my hand close, clutching it with a strength I didn't know she had. I breathe a sigh of relief. She's okay.

"Mo," I say, or I try to, but my voice catches and I'm choking.

"Get some water," she says over her shoulder. I try to follow her line of sight, but I can't see who else is in the room, and I focus on trying to breathe. After a beat, Margaret sticks a straw into my mouth, and I take slow sips, trying to soothe my throat.

When I finally do, I try again. "Mo," I repeat, reaching

forward with my left arm and cupping her cheek.

"I love you." It's nearly incoherent when she says it, but I hear it, and it makes my chest expand to the point of pain. I close my eyes, the relief I felt at knowing she is all right even more palpable upon hearing those words.

"I love you too, Mo," I say, pulling her closer as best I can. Her lips press to mine before I can ask for it, and I kiss her back slowly, not strong enough to do what I'd like to but not complaining that I've been given a chance to even have this moment with Margaret again.

"I'm so glad you're awake." Her voice trembles as she pulls away. I don't want her to go but she reaches behind her, holding out a hand, and a woman whose features practically mirror my own comes into view.

I smile at my sister and open my arms for her. She approaches cautiously, and we embrace for several minutes. I know she's crying, but she's trying her best to hold herself together. She was always the tough sibling.

"When did you get here?" I ask her.

"The second I heard something went wrong, I hopped on a plane." She smiles at me when she pulls back. "You look good for a guy who was unconscious for two days."

My smile slides away. "Two days?"

She doesn't get to reply before the door is pushed open and a doctor walks in. He looks like he's been doing this for far too long, but I sit up and listen patiently as he explains the extent of my injuries. Turns out, Alexander was a good shot. Even running from me, he managed to hit me twice, once in the leg and once in the left shoulder. The one in the leg went all the way through, but the one in the shoulder lodged itself within me.

As I listen, my eyes keep tracking back and forth between the doctor and Margaret's face. She's got a hand in mine and is biting her right thumbnail, her eyes trained on my legs as she listens to something she's no doubt already heard.

As pale and exhausted she looks, she is still the most stunning woman I've ever met.

The doctor leaves, and before I can say a word, Margaret excuses herself and rushes out of the room. I frown at her retreat and am still staring at the door when Layla speaks up. "She's been tough."

I turn to her, really giving her a once-over for the first time. It's almost surreal that she and Margaret are in the same room.

"She's been trying to keep it together, and I'd bet she's finally allowing herself to give in to some well-earned tears at this point."

I grab Layla's hand and squeeze. "I'm glad you were here for her."

Layla scoffs. "Are you kidding? She was here for me, not the other way around." She pauses, giving me a look that tells me I'm about to get a sister lecture. "I like her."

I watch, waiting for her to say more, but she just shrugs her shoulders. "That's it?"

"Look, I know I'm tough on girlfriends, although I haven't had to worry about that for several years now." She smiles and looks to the door, making sure we're alone before she says more. "That woman out there, she loves you—like for real love. I saw her when I first got here. Gemma was walking her away, and she was in shock. She was drenched in your blood." She swallows, and I try to picture how horrible that must have been. "Her entire dress was ruined, and it was just…everywhere, but it was her expression that told me everything I needed to know. She was absolutely tortured. Heartbroken."

Absorbing her words, I lean back against the bed. I wish she hadn't had to deal with any of that. No one should ever think the one person they love most is going to die. I've been in that situation with her more than once, thinking I was going to lose her, thinking I was going to have to live a life without her in it.

It's my definition of hell.

"I'm one hundred percent Team Miam." My sister smirks, and I furrow my brows before I understand.

I smile at her and say, "Don't call us that."

It's been hours since I woke up. I'm exhausted, and I've been poked and moved and prodded and bothered ever since I woke up. All I want is for Margaret to crawl in this bed beside me and for me to get to sleep for two days.

She's been somewhat standoffish. I'm not sure why, but she's stayed off in the corner of the room in an uncomfortable-looking plastic chair, watching everyone around her. She's still in the scrubs Gemma told me she forced her into, which means Margaret hasn't left the hospital since I was admitted. I'm surprised no one forced her out.

Finally, the last person leaves us alone, and she stays where she is, watching me with curiosity.

"C'mere," I rasp at her. After talking to doctors and nurses and Gemma—fuck, she was relentless in her questioning—and everyone else who felt the need to visit, my voice is done for.

Margaret makes her way to my bedside, and I grab her before she can get away, pulling her down on me. She gasps and tries to catch herself before falling too hard, but I don't give a shit if she hurts me. She's all I need.

"I don't want to hurt you," she whispers, gently leaning her head on my shoulder.

"You leaving would hurt me."

She doesn't answer, but her arm tightens around my stomach and I just hold her. I hold her and I thank God we're here now, thank God we've been able to trudge our way through all this shit and get to this point right here.

I think, in the back of my mind, there was a little doubt. I never wanted to acknowledge it, because I never wanted to give up hope, but I wasn't positive I was going to get Margaret in my arms again, wasn't sure I would be able to openly love her.

But fuck, it's my only plan.

I don't care where I live, where I work—as long as I have her. I just need her.

I tighten my arms around her and close my eyes, breathing in her scent and kissing the top of her head. "I love you." My whisper drifts out of my mouth with no thought, just the conscious feeling of it needing to be expressed.

Thinking she's asleep, I lean my head back on the pillow and allow sleep to start pulling me under, but before it can, I hear her whisper back a promise I'll hold with me forever. "I love you, too."

42

MARGARET

About a year later

"YOU'RE DRIVING ME crazy!" My words shoot out, the exasperation in them clear as I stare at my boyfriend, who's casually sitting on the couch—the couch that's in the wrong spot, the couch that is starting to make me feel like we really should have gone with armchairs instead.

"Mo, you're being crazy." Liam holds a beer in his hand, one foot kicked up on the small ottoman I thought would be perfect in our new living room.

My eye twitches at his comment. "Crazy, huh?" I ask, a hint of false humor in my voice, and I stalk into the kitchen, looking for something that would hurt him just a little but maybe not make a mark.

This apartment is even nicer than the one I just moved out of. Liam and I finally took the plunge and got our own place, and it's heaven. The balcony is bigger than my last one, and this one I can even put some plants on. I was stoked about that part.

We're still in the heart of downtown, which was expensive on my budget, but when we decided to live together, we were able to upgrade. He's been trying to get me talked into moving in with him since a week after he was released from the hospital so many months ago. That was a long week for him, and I think he was just desperate to get out, so I didn't take him seriously. I told him to give it a year and then if he was still serious, I'd move in with him.

We're only five minutes from my precinct, which is amazing for me. I have a new partner, a woman this time, and we are getting along swimmingly. I can definitely count on her to have my back when I need it, and I can see us working together for a long time. I love my job. It is hard, challenging, and exactly where I am supposed to be.

Gray is still doing detective work and trying to talk me into moving in that direction. I think eventually I will, but for now, life is sweet. I am enjoying it fully for the first time in years, and I'm not ready to change it.

Liam's sister is even a part of our lives now. She isn't living in our state, but we FaceTime her every week, and we've been out to visit a couple of times since I was welcomed into the

Stokes family. His family is completely different than mine, and I honestly can't believe they allowed him to go off the grid for as long as he did.

His mother threatened his life if he did it again, and once he agreed, she moved on to her next important thing: babies. "I need more grandbabies." I think my face went pale at that comment, and she laughed joyfully then walked away like it was nothing. Liam gave me a wink and followed as I downed the beer his dad placed in my hand, and it wasn't brought up again, at least not to me.

But life is good—more than good, really. I'm not looking to change anything any time soon, including the location of the couch, which is currently in a different spot than I originally placed it.

"Liam." I sigh, walking out of the kitchen. "I really like it where—" I cut myself off when I see him again. This time, instead of sitting on the couch drinking a beer, he's on a knee in front of me. "Oh my God." My breath is stolen from my lungs by an unknown force.

"Mo." He grins his childish grin that I love. It's a more permanent feature of his since we've been living life outside of the FBI this last year. "I think it's time for another change."

I laugh outright. "Liam." I shake my head. "Everything's perfect."

"Not quite." His grin doesn't leave his face when he opens the box he's got in his hands. "I wanted to buy you something new, but…" When I see what's in the box, I let out another giggle and move toward him. "When I found the ring in your dresser, I knew it was fate. It's what we used at our first wedding, and frankly, that was one of the best days of my life."

He stands and looks at me with an expression I'll never tire of seeing, one that, about a year ago, I never would have thought I'd get to see again. It's unconditional love, unbreakable trust, and a willingness to do whatever it takes to prove he loves me. I know it's true, because he has.

"Will you take my hand, Mo?"

Without hesitation, I reach up and interlace my fingers with his. Holding them up, he slips the ring I wore for a short time back onto my finger. His eyes study mine, searching for the answer that spills easily from my lips.

"I will."

43

LIAM

IT'S ONE OF those days most men don't really think about too often. I mean, guys don't give a shit about weddings.

Nah, our goals are much simpler. We want to find a partner who will love us, flaws and all, and we want them to be willing to stick around for a long-ass time.

It's true that I never thought about that before. I didn't think I'd ever want to be tied down to one person for the rest of my life, but Mo changed all of that. She made me rethink everything I'd ever thought when it came to being with someone in that way. We never stood a chance against fate.

She's the one who saved me from a life I didn't realize I

hated.

She's the one who put purpose back into my life, who gave me a reason to get from one day to the next.

And as I stare at my future wife coming up the sand aisleway, I think about those reasons. I think about her laugh, her smile, her humor, her happiness, and I thank my lucky stars I'm the one who gets to have all of them.

They're mine now.

She and I, we're a force to be reckoned with. We're never going to let anything come between us, and it's one of the reasons we work, one of the reasons we'll always work.

The officiant starts the ceremony, and I don't let my eyes stray from her, not to the family who flew down to have this wedding with us or the ocean behind us. We don't have bridesmaids or groomsmen, no flower girl or ring bearer. All we need is each other—and the dress I want to rip off her body, but that's not really anything new.

"I do." I hear her say it, and the realization that we're already here hits me. When the officiant asks me if I take Margaret to be my wife, a thoughtful smile curves her lips. She has no idea how captivating she is when she smiles at me that way. I give her a grin and say, "Hell yeah I do."

She laughs, and I don't wait for any kind of announcement. I kiss her the way I do every day, with every ounce of love I've got.

I kiss my motherfucking wife.

"I love you, Mrs. Stokes," I mumble against her mouth, not

wanting to pull away, and she laughs against my lips.

"Oh boy, I love you too." She shakes her head, the excited light vivid in her eyes under the Caribbean sun. "So, so much."

Grinning, I take my wife's hand and lead her away from the ceremony, off to a honeymoon that will be just the beginning, the beginning of a love without an end, the beginning of endless laughs, the beginning of many fights that will end with her mouth on mine, the beginning of everything.

And I can't fucking wait.

THE END

EPILOGUE

MARGARET

THE WORDS ON the page start to blur in front of me. It's been weeks of me staring at the same pages on the screen, begging my brain to comprehend everything that's on it, trying to absorb as much as possible.

"Babe, you're still looking at that?" My husband's voice filters in behind me, and his hands come down on my shoulders. He massages them gently before closing the laptop in front of me. "You have it down, Mo. You'll pass."

I sigh and turn in the desk chair in our home office. "I know, I just want to be positive, ya know?" I ask the rhetorical question and look up at Liam's face. He's got a few days of scruff, and I let myself ogle him for a moment. It's my favorite look on him.

He doesn't answer, just pulls me out of the chair and switches positions on me, bringing me down onto his lap. He puts his hand behind my neck, urging me to come down to him. I do so without much resistance, and I let his lips fight against my own. It's a sweet kiss, but I urge it to move in another direction. "That's not what I was going for, hon," he says against my lips, a hint of humor in his voice.

"I don't care," I say back, working on opening his shirt, trying to get it off without popping more buttons off. I hate sewing them back on, mostly because I'm terrible at sewing, but also because…well, no, I just hate sewing.

He helps out by slipping my shirt off as well, and before I know it we're both down to our underwear as I lean precariously over the back of the chair to close the blinds; the old man across the way doesn't need to see anything.

Liam rocks into me and I let out a low moan as I take control of the situation. It's easy to do with him confined to the chair, and he doesn't really care who takes control, letting me experiment as I like.

Sometimes my experiments are fun, and other times… well, let's just say it's sometimes hard to explain things at the emergency room.

Slowly and seductively, his gaze slides downward and watches the connection. The heat in his eyes tell me he's close. There's a tingling in the pit of my stomach, and when I reach that peak, it triggers something in Liam. It doesn't take long before I feel him release, and his groan is so loud I wouldn't be surprised if the downstairs neighbors could hear him.

"Damn." He pants and gives me a hard, sensual kiss.

Resting my head on his shoulder, I murmur, "I love you." I give him a kiss on the cheek and then reluctantly hop off.

"Love you too, baby. I swear that gets better every time." He shoots me a wink, and I feel my cheeks redden. This long together and he can still make me blush.

After we're cleaned up, I start to head back into the office to keep studying for the NDIT, the exam officers have to take to become a detective, which Gray finally convinced me to take. There's a knock on the door, so I take a detour. I walk past the kitchen where Liam is looking in the fridge and ask, "You expecting a package or something?"

"Nope," he says, continuing his perusal.

I step up to the door and look through the peephole before answering, but I don't see anyone. I open the door, look down, and see nothing, and I'm about to shut the door when a figure appears. My breath catches in my throat, a fear I wasn't ready for sneaks in, and I stare in shock at the person standing in front of me.

"Uh, Liam, you might want to come here." The person at the door gives me a smirk, and I see his prominent feature.

"Ford?" Liam asks when he sees him there, and he looks as confused as I feel. We haven't seen Ford in years, and Liam hasn't even heard from him since before we got married.

"Hey guys." He shifts on his feet, his expression showing a worry line between his brows.

"What are you doing here?"

"I, uh…I need some help."

GOT YOUR SIX
COMING NOVEMBER 2019

ACKNOWLEDGMENTS

First and foremost, I have to thank my wonderful husband, without your support, none of this would be possible. I know I'm not the easiest to deal with when I'm in the middle of a book, but you're help was always appreciated. And to my daughter, you may not totally understand what I do yet, but when mommy needs to work you are so good about bugging your dad instead.

Second to the rest of my family, those dirty looks I shot you whenever the words "how's that book coming?" left your mouth, I realize looking back you weren't trying to hurt me; I apologize.

To all my AMAZING beta readers, you guys KILLED it. Thank you for the honest feedback, you all tried so hard not to hurt my feelings but also were so honest that it made this book the best it could be. So, I thank you, it wouldn't be what it is without you.

To my editor, Caitlin, I realize that my 'tenses' probably make you tense... but I appreciate you working through it anyway! You are seriously magic.

To E.J. Louise, you are so amazing! The daily messages and encouragement from you to keep going even when I was freaking out about changing the whole book; you settled my nerves every time. I know you're going to do amazing things!

To my newest author friends for the amazing encouragement: Autumn Archer, C.R. Ellis, Autumn Ruby, Clare

Lesbirel, Britney Bell; you guys are so much fun, and I love having y'all at my back!

To my readers, you may be few, but each and every one of you is SO important! I love you guys, thank you for taking chances on my books and loving these characters.

To all the authors who help me with books releases, you guys are amazing! I love this community so much and the fact that you help a little fish like me means the world!

And finally, but always first in my heart, to my Lord and Savior. You make everything possible.

thank you <3

J.S. Wood is from Denver, Colorado.
She's been writing short stories since her late teens but never was brave enough to put the words out in to the world. She's a wife, a mother to a sassy three-year-old daughter, two fur babies, two horses and a bunny. Her hobbies include reading and coffee—lots of coffee.

Made in the USA
Monee, IL
05 September 2023